PRIVATE LESSONS

PRIVATE LESSONS

Cynthia Salaysay

CANDLEWICK PRESS

Copyright © 2020 by Cynthia Salaysay
Epigraph quoted in *Britten* by David Matthews

First edition 2020

Library of Congress Catalog Card Number pending
ISBN 978-1-5362-0960-0

20 21 22 23 24 25 LBM 10 9 8 7 6 5 4 3 2 1

Printed in Melrose Park, IL, U.S.A.

This book was typeset in Dante MT.

Candlewick Press
99 Dover Street
Somerville, Massachusetts 02144

visit us at www.candlewick.com

To my mother

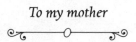

It is cruel, you know, that music should be so beautiful.

— *Benjamin Britten*

CHAPTER
— *One* —

I've done everything I could to make Paul Avon like me. I listened to every sonata and concerto and prelude and fugue and fantasy I could for a whole week before my audition. I packed a change of clothes and my toothbrush so I could freshen up right after school before I left for the train. Resprayed down my primary cowlick with hair spray. Checked my shoes for gunk. There isn't anything left to do but be myself, which honestly doesn't seem like enough.

"Paul's very good. One of the best in the area," my piano teacher said at our last and, I hope, final lesson. "But he's definitely not the teacher for everyone. He's picky. Hard to please."

I'm on the BART train to San Francisco, where he lives, Liszt and friends leaning against my thigh in my backpack. I didn't know what to bring, so I'm bringing what seems like the whole canon. The houses slide past the window, fading in color as the light fails. Then down, down underground, where the train starts a high-pitched scream as it descends under the bay. We're underwater. I know this is supposed to be normal—everyone in here looks calm—but I white-knuckle it. All I can think about is the tunnel collapsing and filling with water.

If it weren't for college applications, I would never have gotten up the nerve to come. My guidance counselor was the one who suggested I try piano competitions. It was at my first one—I went alone, in case I had a breakdown—that I heard Paul's name.

Everyone—guidance counselors and science teachers and basically every auntie who comes to the house—expects me to have a bright future.

"You need to shine," Tita Alta said at dinner after one of mom's prayer groups. "Grades aren't enough for the Ivies or good scholarships."

My mother said something in Tagalog, and Tita Alta nodded. Another family friend touched Tita Alta's shoulder to get her attention. "Didn't your daughter was homecoming queen?" she asks. Her English is very Filipino.

Tita Alta nodded. "Nag-aaral siya sa Princeton. Third year."

Awed looks, all around the table.

Princeton. The only thing I knew about Princeton is that F. Scott Fitzgerald went there. But I looked into it and it doesn't seem to be an artsy place. Not for me.

By the time I get off at Civic Center, it's four thirty. Rush hour. It smells different here, of mildew and ice. Preppies on bicycles act suicidal, weaving themselves into the car lanes. Women in heeled booties and skinny jeans stare hard in front of them, talking into the air, phones in hand. I check my own phone, read a map, and find my way uphill, toward Alamo Square. Homeless people on park benches. People wearing camping gear like it's high fashion. Even though San Francisco is considered diverse, there are still many more white people here than at home. But there are so many kinds of people here — glamorous and poor, tailored and casual — that I feel anonymous. No one seems to pay any attention to me.

Past the museums, past city hall. The store signs are smaller compared to at home, and not so garishly lit. Cakes, anointed with whipped-cream pompadours, fill a shop window. Another store sells seashells, coral. The houses become flouncy. The air is so wet, it feels like a cloud is seeping through my clothes, like it's going to rain, even though it's May already. San Francisco has its own weird seasons. I haven't been here much, but it's always colder than at home.

I turn a corner onto a postcardish street, with cheerful candy-colored houses of pastel and lace. I know which one is his before I read the address because I hear Chopin doing his bright best, gushing out the first-floor window of a cherry-ice-cream-pink house. Prelude no. 1. It instantly puts me at ease.

I should knock, but instead I look at my feet, listening.

My shell of a heart has creaked open. He plays like it's burbling out of him, all gushy and sudsy, like he has to restrain the notes from coming out all at once. It almost makes me forget how nervous I am. That I'm not supposed to be here. My mother, who has no idea where I've gone, feels miles away.

I feel a little bad I didn't tell her, but I know she just would've made me even more nervous if she'd come with me.

The prelude ebbs away, over before I wish it to be, and I knock.

"Hello!" Paul says through the open window, his face hidden. I'm surprised how normal he sounds. "Can you wait outside? Just finishing up here."

"Okay," I call, probably too loud.

I sit on the steps, listening, pulling my socks back up— the elastic has blown, and they've been sliding into my shoes the whole way over. The music starts again like a blaze. It sounds so ridiculously good, I want to laugh. He makes it seem easy. Not for the first time, I wonder if I should even have come.

I get absorbed in my phone, and soon the door opens. A girl with blond hair in a loose bun and a navy peacoat with the collar turned up waves at me, then takes the handful of steps in a jump. I'm stunned. That was *her* playing. She looks like a J.Crew model. And she looks my age.

"You must be Claire," says Paul, the words flowing out glycerin-smooth. He has an earnest, curious expression. Shots of gray in his thick sandy hair. Even though he has glasses on, I can see how startlingly blue his eyes are. They're curved like apostrophes, downward over sharp cheeks. I shake his offered hand. It's soft and warm, without calluses. "You need tea, I think. You look cold," he says.

I hide my hands in the pockets of my hoodie and follow him into the house. He isn't wearing any shoes, just black argyle socks. "It's warmer at home."

"Where did you come from?"

"Fremont."

"All the way out there?" He walks deeper into the house, leaving me standing in the hallway.

Bookshelves stretch all the way to the ceiling, filled with sheet music, their tall, recognizable spines — ivory Peters editions, goldenrod Schirmers, and evening-blue Henles — lining most of the three walls, casting the room in a greenish, underwater glow. The fourth has a large picture window, curtained to protect the pianos — Steinways, both of them baby grands, their curved bellies facing each other, wings folded. The brown one is weathered and scratched. The other gleams a black ebony. On the shelf behind it is a bruised violin case, and in the corner sits a small glass writing desk. Two low-slung chairs face each other in the middle of the room with a table between them.

I sit down in one of them and it puts me in a slouch, my feet dangling like a child's, so I sit back up again, balancing on its edge and touching the floor with my toes.

"I hope you like cream and sugar. I took the liberty." He hands me a mug, sets a plate of cookies on the table, and settles into his chair, looking at me like I'm a strange bird. He cradles his mug close to his chest, his fingers looking impossibly long, stretched over the curve of the cup. Paul is rangy, wearing loose pants, his shirttail out. "So, Fremont. What's that like?"

"Pretty boring." Fried chicken places next to drugstores next to Indian chaat houses next to pho spots next to grocery stores. And behind it, bland hills.

"Really? That's too bad."

"I guess so." The first sip of tea burns, but I try not to let it show, swallowing quickly. If he knows I've scalded my tongue, I can't tell, but his eyes are sharp and dead on me, so I'm guessing he does.

"You must be Filipino, then."

I shrug a yes. I don't see why that matters.

"And you'd like to play more seriously?"

"Well, I'm no prodigy. This is just, you know, for school. Scholarships and stuff." An answer grown-ups would understand.

"You know it isn't easy, teaching people if they aren't serious about it. It's not just about playing fast or the right notes—you have to really want it in order to truly play well. To be an artist. And if you're just doing everything you can to get into college—chess, horseback riding, volunteering with veterans—all that, then maybe this isn't for you." His eyes wrinkle behind his glasses as if to soften the criticism.

"I don't do any of those things."

"Sorry about that last bit. I didn't mean to be harsh."

"I do want this."

"Why?"

I feel my burnt tongue. "Because playing feels beautiful." The last word is hard to say. No one says that word at school, and I don't say it to anyone. I can't remember the last time I've said it, and here I am, saying it, all cheesy.

It's true though. Songs don't feel like they really die. They feel like they just go back where they came from. And when I play, it's like I'm a part of that.

His eyes don't leave mine. I get the sense he's drinking me in, along with his tea. He must be thinking about walking me right out the door.

"How long have you been playing?"

"Since I was seven."

"That's a bit late. Have you been to competitions?"

"Mm-hm. I did one. The California Piano Teachers' Association, South Bay."

"How was it?"

"Okay, actually! I got third." I look down. I personally think third is pretty good. But maybe he doesn't think so.

"Nice!" His tone is warming again. "And what did you play?"

"Bach, Ravel, Beethoven."

He gives a swift smile. "Let's start with Bach, then. But first you should wash your hands."

I look at them. They don't look dirty. He raises an eyebrow.

"Everyone has to wash their hands before they play," he says.

He gives me a clean hand towel to use. The soap is white, imprinted with flowers. Like out of *Little House on the Prairie*.

I scrub beneath my fingernails and paste my hair down with a wet hand. From the mirror, a grayed-out face peers back. I always look sick when it's cold out. Squishy lips, big eyes behind big glasses. There's nothing I can do about any of that right now though.

In the practice room, the bench gives an acquiescent creak beneath me as I move it back to the usual distance from the piano and run a few notes. Every piano has its eccentricities: some are like old, grave men; others are flashy. This one is warm and golden. Supple. I can sink my fingers deep into the bed of the keyboard, like I'm feeling for the underside of the note. The action is a little loose compared to the one at home, but it feels really well kept.

Here we go. The C-sharp Major, from Book II of *The Well-Tempered*.

Already my muscles are seizing up, and Paul looks like he wants me to get on with it, so before I lose all courage I take off at a speed I immediately know I can't manage. The piece has a processional quality, a thrumming in the left hand. It should not be like a hummingbird. My hands are skittering over the chords, and it's worse if I try to force myself to stop shaking. The fugue is rushed and it sounds like chattering chickens. I just keep speeding up and up and up.

"Hmm," says Paul as the last note fades. I flinch.

"It wasn't like that at competition."

He moves to the other piano and plays a fragment of the top melody—no sheet music. His piano is slightly brighter than mine. "You aren't opening it up, really. This," he says, playing a note, "links to this. *Pah-taah* . . . You see? But make it rise."

I risk a glance at him. No derision. Just focus.

He's being kind.

I try again. "More . . . tenderness in the right hand. Let the touch be like it's the only thing worth doing. . . ." He talks me through it, and the notes begin to flash like a cut jewel turning, the theme shifting, folding onto itself, like a choir of voices from the natural world, asking questions and answering them. We rip into the fugue and it starts to rock, every voice of the prelude in a frenzied weave. I get so excited, my fingers start to shake again.

"Better," he says. "Though I don't know if this is the right piece for you."

We run through a bit of Beethoven, but not for long. He waves me off of it in a few measures.

"What do you think?" I ask.

"I know it's difficult to play well in this kind of situation, at least the first time." A bit of a smile appears, though his eyes stay cool. "We could . . . work together for a month. Maybe do a competition, a small one. See how you do. There are some technical things I think that you can work on, but that's quite improvable. You sight-read well?"

"Yup! I mean yes," I say as quietly as possible, tamping

down my excitement—as if being too happy might make him change his mind.

"And you know my fees?"

I nod. One ten an hour, Andrew, his assistant, told me over the phone. Three times what we pay now. I have no idea how I'm going to ask my mom for the money.

"Okay. Well, then."

I pack up. "Send me some recordings," he says. "And I'd like you to get an exercise book. Czerny's *The School of Velocity*. Practice it an hour a day, after your scales for speed and control." He pokes the book of Mozart sonatas peeking out of my bag back down where it belongs. "You'll have to work for it," Paul says. "Everybody has to, of course, but . . . we'll see. I think it will be evident very quickly if this is worth your while." He puts his hand tightly on my shoulder and studies me, tilting his face in one direction. Nothing seems certain, and I'm sure it shows on my face. "Take heart. You have nice hands. That's a good sign."

"What do you mean?"

"They're articulate."

Outside the house, I do a little victory dance, complete with whoops and screeches, and it scares the pigeons and I catch a bit of side-eye from a fellow pedestrian, but who cares? Who cares! I skip downhill. The houses, pastel bonbons each one, line my way. I pull my phone out of my backpack, slip my earbuds in, look for a song to match the hour, choose one with a bright tambourine. The blue sky swims in *oops* and *bop-bops*. The drums smack and shove, and the falsetto words are sighed all daydreamy.

He likes me. Well, okay, he liked me enough, and enough is a lot in my book. And if he likes me enough now, he could like me even more later. I can't stop smiling at everything: the BLACK LIVES MATTER signs posted in windows and bicycles chained to parking meters, even the sidewalk cracks flowing by and a hipster girl, with a nose ring and her Afro-hawk dyed green and rolled-up jeans, who smiles back at me.

The song harmonizes and whispers that everything I did was right. I could be the girl in the song. The kind of girl a boy sings about. Who is vindicated. Who is right. With perfectly dirty hair. Who could say or do whatever she wanted, and people would still love her.

CHAPTER
—— *Two* ——

I get on the train and do the thing I'd been trying not to do before today: I look him up on my phone.

I find an old YouTube video. Vladimir Horowitz sits beside him, his hands together, as if in church. A master class with Horowitz. That's like having the pope watching to make sure you pray right. Horowitz's eyes glimmer over his papal nose. Even then he must already have been very old.

Paul's jacket doesn't fit well, hiking up at the shoulders when he brings his hands far apart on the keys. Sandy hair, longer and more ruffled up back then. The same straight nose and sharp blue eyes hovering over the keyboard, as if it's a map and he's plotting a course over sea. It's the third movement of Beethoven's *Hammerklavier* sonata. *Adagio sostenuto.* The one that sounds like a milky flood from some gushing star. The one Evelyn, my old teacher, said you shouldn't attempt to play before you've reached thirty, or unless someone you love has died—which means maybe I could play it, though it didn't sound as if she wanted me to.

I wonder how my mom will take this news about Paul. I didn't think he'd agree to work with me, so hadn't spent too much time thinking about her reaction before now.

The sky has become serious. Closer to home, every fourth house is a mirror image, colored like sand and dun. There are lawns like wall-to-wall carpet; windows alight with television screens, or dark with curtains drawn; and the sameness of every house, and every day.

By the time I kick the front door closed, all sense of elation has gone. The salty smell of fish sauce and softened onions floods the air, and the washing machine drones in the background. Mom's home. I guess she didn't go to prayer group tonight.

It's dim in the hallway, tinged orange from the dusty chandelier high above. Must be a bulb out. There's just enough light to see the statues standing at attention on the altar in the next room, greeting me with their carved holy smiles. My pencil-gray shadow lists on the wall while I shimmy out of my shoes and fling them toward the others that are piled like kindling against the wall.

The thud of my backpack on the floor echoes down the hall, and she calls at the sound. "Anak"—which means child, or daughter in my case—"come eat."

It's half a question, half a command. She sounds like she's in a decent mood. I pad sock-footed over the double thickness of Oriental rug laid over carpet into the kitchen. She's already in her light-purple house robe, scooping rice into a bowl for herself from our ancient rice cooker. "Did you eat yet?" With a flick of the spoon, a ball of rice drops into the bowl.

"No, I—"

"You should eat. And feed the dog. He's hungry. Did you do your homework?"

She doesn't actually require a response to questions. Sometimes she'll even ask me about school on Saturdays. But you can easily divert her with a newspaper article about someone getting E. coli at the grocery store, or predatory ants, or other topics that suggest conspiracy or impending doom. She's inclined to worry even when there's nothing to worry about. She'll cast about—*How is school? How is Tash?*—until she lands on something—*Oh, she has a crush? Does he like her back?* Once that's settled, she relaxes, as if she now has a handle on the situation, which she doesn't. *Well, I hope she doesn't get hurt. She's such a nice girl.*

I know it's just her terse Asian style of parenting and has nothing to do with how much she loves me, but sometimes I wish she were a little bit more like the moms in television sitcoms—baking cookies and dressing up on Halloween. My mother would never dress up for Halloween.

"It's Friday. I can do it tomorrow," I finally answer.

The kitchen has the kind of light that hurts my eyes, hyper and worn, especially after the pillow-soft light in Paul's practice room, and I feel like I shrivel down a size in the scalding light of our kitchen. Everything shrivels here.

Our dog, Dean, scratches at the sliding-glass door to the backyard—he always knows when I'm home—and I go to let him in, but Mom says, "After. We're about to eat." She shuts the lid of the rice cooker with a metallic clang and starts drawing up long, clear noodles out of a steaming pot on the stove. I study her profile, the intensity of her worry indicated by the depth of the lines in the corners of her eyes. She's almost my height, and we have the same face, though her cheeks are flatter, her lips a little less full. Eyes like pancake syrup when they're not tired, but she's tired now.

I pull a bowl from the cupboard and stand beside her. "Mom. Guess what?" There's nothing to do but just tell her, but I'm already tensing up for her predictable flip-out.

"What's wrong?" The slippery noodles have formed a bridge between the lip of the pot and her bowl. She coaxes them toward her with her fork until they splash into the bowl, the drops darkening flecks on her house robe.

"Nothing, actually. Nothing's wrong. It's just, do you remember when I did that piano competition?"

"The one you didn't tell me about until afterward?" A flat note of blame.

"I didn't want you to worry."

She sighs her frustration in response.

I smile, hoping to sway her mood to a more positive one. "I decided that maybe I could take it more seriously, so

I looked around and found a new piano teacher. An important one. He's like the best in the Bay Area?" My uncertainty turns the fact into a question. Her face snaps to me, her eyebrows raised. When she doesn't say anything, I start to babble. "Really, really, absolutely the best. I got his name at the other competition in fact. From one of the judges? His name is Paul. He's interesting. My audition was amazing. . . . My Bach was . . . it was like magic by the time he got through with it. I swear, I couldn't believe it was me."

I can't help smiling for real now, and she smiles, finally, tentatively. She puts her hand on my arm. "Wow, Claire. That's so . . . wow." Then, her hand begins tightening on my arm. "I hope he doesn't cost too much." And before I have time to answer, she asks, "Where are the lessons? How often? Did he seem confident about you? How successful you could be?"

I pull away. "No," I say, grabbing a fork from a drawer and slamming it shut with a hip. "He didn't say."

"Oh."

I prod the pale mess inside the stew pot, fork in hand. This is why I hate telling her things. She wants everything to be safe and secure. For every story to be over. If it isn't, it can't be good.

I stab a drumstick, pull it out of the pot, stick it on top of the noodles, and douse it with black pepper. "Do you know how hard it is to be accepted? You have to audition for him." I sidestep the trial period issue.

We sit down at the table, and she whispers a prayer. Hope for blessings, hope to be heard. "Where does he teach?" she finally asks, her tone dropping half an octave as she picks up her fork and spoon. Conversational. That's good.

"At his house."

"Where is that?"

"In the city."

"What city?"

"San Francisco?"

"You went there by yourself?" Her accent gets stronger when she gets louder—the careful flat *e*'s, the sharp *t*'s.

I feel a stab of guilt. "I'm home safe." I wiggle my fingers. "See, all ten fingers and toes. Virginity still intact." Her eyes widen, and immediately I regret the joke. Another stab of guilt. "It's a nice neighborhood," I say feebly.

"How did you get there? That's an hour and a half away."

"I took the BART."

"The BART?" She's repeating this as if she's having trouble understanding the words.

I chew, growing impatient. "It was easy."

"You can't just run off like that by yourself. You don't know what will happen."

"Well, I have to go if I'm going to go to a good college."

"But you're four-point-oh." A gleam of pride wiggles out beneath her knitted brows.

"That's not enough." We both knew that. Grades aren't enough. Math Bowl seems pretty average. But a thing like winning piano competitions, actual competitions, that will make you special.

We eat without speaking for a while, the slippery noodles laced with ginger and onion slowly filling my belly with comfort. She's probably thinking about all the things that could have happened, running through every scenario—bombs at the BART station, masturbators in alleyways, Armageddon. I wish she'd stop watching Fox News.

She delicately, methodically, tears her meat apart with a spoon and fork. I give up and just eat my drumstick with my hand.

"I was careful. It was fine. It's during the day," I say, reminding her with my voice that I'm still here. Nothing bad has happened to me.

"How much does it cost?" she asks.

"A hundred ten."

"An *hour*?"

"He's one of the best teachers in the area. Of course he costs that."

She shakes her head. Her face mirrors my own shock when I was first told his rates. Only, I adjusted. She makes no effort to. "Ay yi yi, Claire."

"Well, it's not like we're paying for Vassar," I say, standing up with my bowl. I dump the chicken bones and the noodles in the trash and get the water running.

Last fall, the inside of our mailbox shone with glossy college brochures. Sarah Lawrence. Wesleyan. Vassar. The University of Chicago. Reed. Oberlin. Each one looked like a different world of soft-cheeked, serious, pure-faced kids in hoodies and sneakers, perched on the stairwells of brick buildings. The Vassar brochure had particularly cute boys, but Oberlin seemed more like my place. It had a real conservatory, and snow. For weeks, I fell asleep looking at them, until one night my mother woke me up as she turned out my bedroom light. None of these, she said, were affordable, or possible. I cried, but I didn't throw away the brochures. I shoved them under the bed, and every once in a while I'd sift through them again. Maybe, at one of these schools, I'd be happy. I wouldn't be so out of place for liking books more than video games, and classical music more than hip-hop, and J. D. Salinger more than J. K. Rowling.

With piano lessons, and time, and work, maybe I could win a competition or two, or even a scholarship. A school like Oberlin wouldn't have to be a fantasy.

I feed the dog. The food's barely in the bowl before he digs in, his sun-faded pink plastic dish grating rhythmically against the concrete every time he licks it. He smells so real and funky, you can't pretend he isn't there, but his fur is nice and soft. My father's dog.

If Dad were still alive, these lessons wouldn't be a problem. He's the one who loved music, who insisted I take lessons.

When I was really little, the piano was just a toy, but I felt the notes in my body, rippling down my arms, pulling a twitch out of the skin between my first and second toe.

The waves of sound shimmered through my flesh into my bones.

Then it filled the quiet when my mother, who used to have more time for me, who took me to dance lessons and the park, who read me stories at bedtime, was consumed with caring for my dad. But the piano was there, alert, and it always responded to me. At that time in our house, it was nice to have a response, even if it only reflected what I was doing, no more. It was neutral. Made me know who I was, like a fish that needs the motion of water to know what the world is.

I was barely aware of what was happening to my dad at first, and then, around the time I was seven, the world finally became clear. He started staying in the guest bedroom on the first floor because it had gotten too hard to climb the stairs. Around this time I started to really play, and my dad took notice.

It was summer, before he was too sick to stand and was still himself, before he had to quit his job but would often stay home and sleep.

I was picking out the tune to the song from *Sleeping Beauty*—"Both hands!" he used to say when he told the story—and singing to myself.

"Do you know who wrote that? Tchaikovsky," he said. And he moved me over on the bench and played it from memory, and I sang the tune from the Disney cartoon. He showed me the left hand, and I picked it up. And that very evening, when Mom got home, he told her I should take lessons, and Mom, by then, couldn't say no to him.

We talked about music a lot—more and more as he got sicker. He made my mother take me to lessons. He played Bach, Schubert, Liszt, Scarlatti, Haydn on the stereo, looking at me meaningfully. Like he was filling me up with them.

By the time he died, I was twelve. I could play the *Sleeping Beauty* waltz—with pedal, both hands. I played Mozart fantasies, Bach cantatas, and the "Aria" from the *Goldberg Variations,* which he asked me to play more often the sicker he got. It had been so hard to learn. The timing, the way it sometimes seemed only just barely to hang together, and threatened at times to fall apart.

After he died, playing started to feel like an entire world. A gentler world. It soothed me.

I don't have a lot of clear memories of him from before he was sick—not as many as I wish I had. He would let me swing from his arm. He used to rest his hand on the top of my head, which he did, I think, more to calm himself than me. He had moody eyes that scared me if they stayed on me too long. He was quiet, but both my parents were, and now my mother and I are. Comfortably quiet together. Like we know each other so well, we don't always have to talk.

I never took myself seriously enough to think I could be an artist. Be the thing I deep down want to be. And now that there is that possibility, I really want to see if I can do it.

———————

I launch the second wave of attack on my mom in front of the television. "If you weren't so afraid, you'd see how good for me this could be."

We're watching television, sitting right next to each other, so close that half of me has sunk between the cushions like a tire in mud. Old issues of *Vanity Fair* gleam on the coffee table. Her robe is velvety and smells of powder, and it's almost too warm, the way it was when I was a kid, burrowed under her blankets in the morning.

"And how much is the train?"

I cringe. "Around nine dollars a trip."

She clicks her tongue.

"If you meet him, you'll see that it's worth it."

Her thumb is on the remote, skipping over the news, commercials for vacuum cleaners, pauses on a legal drama we sometimes watch. "Next week," she says, nodding.

I punch the air in silent triumph. She smiles, makes the sign of the cross, whispers a word.

On the television, a private eye spies on a woman taking off her clothes, and an older man grabs her breasts from behind. When the private eye takes a phone call, you can hear the couple mewling and grunting.

My mother and I don't say a word. We don't talk about sex. Thank God.

Later, I run upstairs, get into bed, and send Tash a text. *Guess what!* If there's one person who would be utterly gobsmackingly happy for me, it would be Tash.

Colonel Mustard. In the library. Lead pipe.

No.

Definitely lead pipe.

I'm being serious here. I tell her with a text, receive emojis on emojis back. Hearts and unicorns and fish and balloons and cake and stars. I rub the bottom of my feet on my fuzzy blanket and text her a smile and a star back.

CHAPTER
— *Three* —

Mom keeps the heater on full blast on the way into the city. I'm glad we drove. This way we pass by all the cute little Italian and Japanese places to eat, places that look like whoever built them cared about beauty. If she saw the homeless people sitting against the wall at the BART station, and some of the dingy streets on the way, no amount of pleading would have gotten her onto Paul's porch.

"Not too bad," she says, looking approvingly at the stained-glass pieces set into the front door. "Not too bad," in Filipino mom-speak, means it's good.

She raises her hand to knock.

"No, don't." I seize her hand and point at the window. "That's someone else having a lesson."

The girl sounds formidable, just like before, but my mother doesn't seem to notice. She rubs her hands—"It's cold here!"—and wraps her cardigan tighter around her dress. Even when it's cold, she wears dresses. She's never gotten used to the feeling of pants on her legs.

"She's really good," I whisper. I feel edgy, listening to the girl, about to see Paul again. What if he realizes he's made a mistake?

We look at our phones in companionable silence until eventually the girl pops out the door. I watch my mother from the corner of my eye as we go in. I can tell she's awe-struck by the girl's face, and then struck again when she sees Paul, bending down a little to come to eye level and shake her hand. His fingers seem somehow even longer today, the way they wrap around her palm. His bulky tweed sweater emphasizes the sharpness of his shoulders, his flat torso. I'm so excited to see him, some of my nervousness is forgotten. He doesn't seem surprised to see her, though I hadn't mentioned she'd be coming.

"Hello! You must be Claire's mother. It's so nice to meet you."

My mother's face instantly melts into a smile. "Elizabeth," she says in her best manner, her voice softer than it normally is. She looks dubiously at the carpet. "Should I take my shoes off?"

"No need," Paul says. Inwardly I cringe. She's embarrassing, in her big floral-print dress, which doesn't look quite right here. Like she's been costumed for a different play.

But Paul seems oblivious to her awkwardness. He asks if we got here okay, and if the parking was bad. "It was horrible! How do you drive here?" My eyes widen. Already she's complaining.

He just laughs. "It's like an extreme sport." He moves to

the back of the apartment. Cupboards close. A blast of the sink. My mother shoots me a meaningful look I can't read.

"What?"

"I can see why you like it here." And she flicks her eyes to the kitchen. "Ang guwapo niya." He's handsome.

"You think he's cute?"

Paul strides back in. Mom turns red, flashes a stiff look at me as he lays down a tray of cookies and her tea. Mortified, I dig into my bag, grab my phone, and check that it's on silent just so I can hide my face. I suppose he would be handsome to her.

"It's lovely to watch people dip their cookies," he says, his smile generous. He must have heard.

"That's how you should do it," she says. "Don't you think?"

"I do, actually. They both taste better."

I head toward the bathroom, lingering over the pencil drawings framed along the hallway, partly so that I can overhear them. I'm curious to hear what Paul might say about me to her.

"I hope you didn't take time off of work to be here," he says, his tone as soft as hers.

"No. My shift ended at three."

"Ah! Well, I'm so glad she's here. Does her talent come from you?"

My talent. That's nice. I turn the water on, just a teeny bit, so I can still hear her. "Well, her father played the piano for our church, and his mother was a music teacher. So it was like that, you know." I can picture her brushing something imaginary away, as if the talent in our family is no big deal.

"Lovely. And so he still plays?"

"He passed away."

"I'm so sorry to hear that."

When I come back, she looks as uncomfortable as I was, slumped in her chair. Her look softens when she sees me. Paul winks a greeting and we settle in—me at the beautiful Steinway again, he to sit in a wooden chair, slightly behind me. He asks if I'd seen his e-mail—he'd sent me a few pieces to try and a few competitions to consider. I chart the movement of her eyes—from him, to me, to the shelves and the drawing of a woman's profile on the wall.

"I do think the Chopin Étude opus ten, number—yes, number two—in A Minor would be good for you."

He reaches over to play a few measures. The highest voice—the highest line of melody—sounds like a bell that rings with more depth the more it sings. His hands spring like angsty bugs touching down on random flowers, but his face is placid. This is effortless. I sense victory when the worried wrinkles around my mother's lips soften, and her head moves in time to the music.

She puts her tea down on the table and turns slightly in her chair to watch us.

"What do you think?" he asks me.

"You make it look easy."

"Well, it's a good reach for you," he says, looking upward

and scratching his chin, "but not impossible. It's got just enough going on to keep you from being bored."

We move on to the Bach from last week. How to make two or three or four voices sing at once, to sing with the mood of the day with only two hands? I touch the keys carefully, trying to make each one sound clear. Definitive. Every note placed where it should be.

"Better," he says, nodding. "I can see how hard you've worked on it."

Paul is light with me, but I don't relax. I keep waiting for a criticism that doesn't come, partly, maybe, because my mom is sitting in the corner. I nod at his questions as if everything is fine, but it feels like everything is moving faster than I can. The rest of the lesson goes by in a blur. Besides the unboring Chopin, we settle on a Beethoven sonata for me to work on.

Paul turns to my mother. "She's going to do fine, Mrs. Alalay."

Words that relieve me as much as her. "Do you really think so?" she asks.

"Well, she can hear herself," he says, looking at me studiously. "Which is rare. She'll have to work for it, of course."

"You're going to work hard, right?" she asks, turning to me.

I flush. It's not like she didn't hear me practicing all week.

"I'm sure she will," he says. I keep my annoyance off my face as I pack up my books. He rubs the back of his neck slowly, as if it hurts. "You can always call me if you have any questions. If you're uncertain of anything."

"Why did you say that?" I ask her after the front door has closed after us.

"What did I say?"

We walk fast. I take a deep breath. The first one in an hour. "That you hope I work hard enough! Now he'll think I'm lazy." I'm sure that we've made a bad impression: the shoes, her tea.

"No, he won't. I'm sure he won't."

"Why wouldn't he?"

"Because I'm just—"

"You just insulted me."

"I didn't!"

"Everything has to be negative with you."

"You're so sensitive," she says. "Whenever it's someone you want to impress, you get so . . . it's like I don't even know you."

"Of course, I'm acting funny. There's so much pressure. . . ."

"I know. I'm sorry."

"You act weird, too!"

She sighs. "Claire. Let's just . . . not fight. Okay? I don't even see what there is to fight about. You are getting to take the lessons, aren't you?"

We're silent until we get into the car. She grips the steering wheel with both hands. I watch her nervously check the traffic, looking three times before taking her turn, tapping the brakes when a bicyclist dashes past on our right.

Eventually the air blasting out of the vents heats up. I smell lilac in the air and realize she probably put on perfume to come here.

"Sorry, Mom."

"It's okay."

"He's great, isn't he?"

"You know, he seems a little . . ."

Here it comes. There's always something. "A little what?"

"A little too easy-breezy. Like he's used to getting what he wants."

"I thought he was nice to you." He seemed extremely polite to me.

"He was," she concedes. "At least on the surface. But you never know."

"You're so suspicious."

"Well, he is a man! When you're as fortunate as he is, and that handsome, it's easy to be nice." Her laugh is dark. "Of course I'm suspicious. I should be suspicious."

"He's an amazing teacher!" Surely she isn't going to veto this because he's a man.

"Mom! See, this is what I mean. Please stop second-guessing everything."

I glue my eyes to my phone, so upset that I start going through my e-mails, pausing on the clothing sales and deleting all the junk. She isn't happy unless the sky is falling.

"I'm just being careful, that's all. If anything happened to you . . ."

"I know."

I look away, at the view of warehouses and fast-food chains flowing past. It is only us two. She wasn't close to my dad's family, and aside from a few visits from one of her sisters every few years, we don't see her family. They live in the Philippines, and it's too expensive to go there.

She touches the Saint Christopher medal hanging from the rearview mirror, crosses herself, and whispers a prayer. "What is his full name again?"

"Paul. Paul Avon."

She whispers his name, her accent hard on the *v*, and crosses herself again. "Will you at least text me when you get there?" I watch slices of light cross her glasses.

"Yes."

"And you have to come right home afterward."

"Of course."

"I really am proud of you. Dad would be, too." Her tone makes my stomach do a flip-flop. I feel more pressure when she's nice to me.

CHAPTER
— *Four* —

Changing my schedule is a breeze. I ask the photography teacher, Mr. Mullen, if I can leave class to play the piano in the auditorium. "My new teacher wants me to practice more." I say it loudly to make sure that when people see me in there, they won't think I'm a loner freak—though they probably already do. I've been at this school so long, there's no changing my label.

Mr. Mullen must hate school as much as I do, because he just lifts a faintly bitter eyebrow at me and waves me away. I lift my chin a little as I sail out of the room. Freedom. It's like I don't even have to ask. I guess when you're an honors kid, don't do drugs or anything criminal, and basically act like a mini-adult, you can do what you want. There really isn't much time to waste, though. The first competition, a small one in a Burlingame hotel, takes place in a month.

"Gangway, major ego coming through. Double wide, double wide." My head snaps to Ben Haden. Blond, his hair sticking up like an exclamation point. Blue eyes gleefully on fire. I don't know what he has against me, except my grades, but he's never stopped saying mean, hateful things. I've avoided him for years. I stick my tongue out to hide my shame, then scurry off.

The piano sits at the back of the stage, a dried-out shell that's well hidden in curtains of the same color. Sickly yellow lights hang from the ceiling. The empty seats scallop around me, extending outward to the walls like ripples. Behind the walls of the theater, I can hear the lunch ladies bang pots. It's so empty that my ears cling to anything happening outside the open door. Sneakers scuffing the concrete. Ryan DeGuzman's distinctive, relaxed laugh, like he's comfortable with himself. Ryan, who is gorgeous and a senior and who I've never had the guts to say hello to, even though sometimes, he says hello to me. And then I do the dumbest thing—I pretend that I'm confident and give him my best cooler-than-thou toss of the head. It's a total act, but I mean, what am I supposed to do, stop and talk to him? No way. I feel like everything I am naturally isn't good enough. There's no 4.0 on my body for him to admire, and he probably doesn't like classical music, and then there are my glasses.

I wish I felt I was more like the other students, but maybe deep down, they're lonely, too. Even people with tons of friends, like Jasmine Granger, quiet and feminine and beautiful, are probably lonely sometimes. But it just doesn't seem like I have much else in common with those kids, sitting in class, head in the clouds. Their heads are just not in the same clouds as mine.

Sometimes, playing so far from everyone else, the loneliness gets like an itch between my ribs, somewhere deep, where I can't scratch. The piano sounds terrible then, with its edgy ring, its grumbly low notes. And then there's the middle F, which sometimes sounds and sometimes sticks. It's not good for much but scales and these new exercises Paul wants me to do, so it feels like watching the same television program over and over.

What does Paul want me to sound like? I don't really know. I think of the lightness of the girl who plays before me—her quickness, her speed—and sing over my notes, covering up the sound of my playing.

My honors biology lab partner, Duncan, and I pour methylene blue into a test tube, and he mentions some shock jock on a radio station.

"I don't listen to the radio much."

I can see he's insulted. "I thought you were into music and all."

"I am. Just not Top 40, I guess."

"What, you think it's beneath you?"

Here we go. "A lot of it is catchy, but it's not very complex. It's all about wanting to get down, wanting to get some, wanting to be rich, wanting to get back with someone."

"What about Radiohead? They're complex. And emotional."

"And white," says Angela Diaz, smirking.

You can't be too white at my school. And you can't be too brown, either. It's so paradoxical. Your parents come to America so you can be successful. They don't even teach you their language so that you can completely assimilate, be successful, go to college, be a doctor or a lawyer or an engineer. So you assimilate as well as you can, and if you get anywhere, anywhere close to being smart enough, or successful enough at it, you get told you're too white.

But there's no point in getting into it with him. "I respect Radiohead, but it's not my thing. So whiny and depressing."

"They're being ironic," Duncan says.

"I guess I prefer a more natural sound."

"That's kind of the point. The music expressed the zeitgeist of the time. The fakeness of what people wanted. The artificial flavoring."

"Then why have more?"

"You'd rather listen to Beethoven," Duncan says. This is an accusation.

"Yeah, so?"

"My dad listens to Beethoven."

"Your dad has good taste."

"My dad is a dork."

Angela Diaz smirks again.

Well, at least he's alive. That's my comeback. But I don't want to say that. It's the pity line.

I sputter instead. "Do you even know what *zeitgeist* means?"

Maybe there's something wrong with me for not liking Radiohead. Or Duncan. He has all these friends, and I don't, but he's obnoxious. I don't get it.

At lunchtime, I find Tash near the new tech center, where we always hang out. They never cleaned up after they built it, so the dirt's white with concrete dust and whatever they make walls out of, and the plants look stuck into the ground, spindly and uncomfortable.

She's sitting with her eyes closed, earbuds in.

"Earth to Tash."

I wave my hands in front of her face until she blinks at the sun. She looks surprised. But then she tends to, because of the dots of glitter she wears at the corners of her eyes. With her white miniskirt, her orange All-Star sneakers, and tiny pigtails high on her head, she looks like a space fairy. And a freak, by our school's standards. Which is why we hang out. We're not preps who like hip-hop. We're nerdy. We're artsy. We're a clique of two. It's easier to pretend I'm not lonely when I'm with her.

"You have to listen to this," she says, handing me her phone. "Tom showed it to me." Tom is her recent crush, a boy from another school.

I look at the screen. Spiritualized. *Ladies and Gentlemen We Are Floating in Space.*

I've never heard of it. Apparently Tom knows all kinds of music—seventies Afrobeat, sixties French pop, nineties post-punk. Hence Tash's crush. I plug my earbuds into her phone—no one touches Tash's headphones—and listen.

It's a baroque round. A clear, bell-like keyboard drifts in, and a spiral galaxy of sound, debris aglow, revolves in my head. Heavenly. Tash looks skinny, her shoulder blades poking up a little on the back of her shirt. Where wings would be.

At the end of the song, she looks at me solemnly. "Right?"

I'm happy and sad at the same time. "Definitely."

"I think Tom likes me," Tash says. "Do you think he likes me? He wouldn't have me listen to songs like this if he didn't like me."

Atomic debris continues to drift around us. See, that's the thing about Tash. We dream similar things. If I were to tell her the sun changes color when I listen to Debussy, she'd get it.

CHAPTER
—— *Five* ——

Paul knows my weak spots before he even hears me play.

"Okay. Measure thirty-one. Let's go."

It's been a month. The ACTs have come and gone, and while other people are tanning in the late-spring sun, I'm paling. Soon I'll be as pale as the Korean rom-com TV stars my mother loves. But the torture—Paul's grueling exercise assignments, the long trips to San Francisco, and seeing Tash less and less—is working. My scales feel like they've readjusted, as if Paul's taken small wrenches to them, touching them this way or that, the way he might adjust slightly tilted picture frames on the way to his bedroom.

"Don't bite your lips, hmm? You're performing. It's a generous sharing of yourself with the world. You want other people to want to be you or be with you. No one wants to be with an awkward girl."

He sits beside me and a little behind, one hand conducting the air, sometimes twitching like a puppeteer, or cutting the air like an air-traffic controller. Or both hands hover like gulls over a bridge. It is reassuring, though, that someone's there to tell me where I'm going wrong—pointing out errors as small as pedal marks and bar rests. For all his little boyish ways—his bare feet, with their triangular toe pads, his choirboy politeness, and his undone shirt cuffs that hide part of his hands sometimes—he's unnervingly serious.

"Posture." He touches my shoulder, loosens my arms. "Relax."

The strap of my tank top slides down my arm, and he brings it back into place.

The feeling of his fingers on my shoulder lingers. I suddenly feel very, very awake. I press the weight of the melody onto the piano, the keys rippling. Dust motes shine and float. I don't know if it's the song or if it's him that is making me feel this way, but when I look at his face when the song is over, he looks unflapped. "Not bad," he says. "Decent. You'll want to work on this measure when you get home. . . ."

And I do. I spend half an hour on two seconds of music. There's no way I'm only going to be decent.

Parked in front of the community center in Burlingame, where the competition is about to start, my mom holds out a Tupperware and asks if I want something to eat. Cold pancit noodles or a peanut butter and jelly sandwich. This isn't her brightest moment.

I twitch my head no.

"It might settle your stomach."

"I'm not hungry."

"Have you eaten anything at all?"

I don't answer. She tsks sharply. She takes out the sandwich she made this morning. "Here."

"Later, Mom."

"How can you compete if you don't eat?"

I don't answer. I look out the window at the green manicured islands dotting the parking lot, the palms brushing the cloudy sky. It's so early that the lights of the hotel sign are still lit.

Everything seemed fine at Paul's yesterday. We went over the pieces I'm going to play—the Bach I first played for him during my audition and Beethoven's sonata *The Hunt*. They felt solid—accomplished even. Paul was encouraging. He liked the way certain parts of the melody were being sung—softer when they were typically louder—as if there was something hard about reaching those notes. "I just want to make sure you slow down a little—don't rush. Be in the piece, you know?"

"Do you think it's finished?" I asked, feeling a twinge of anxiety that these pieces wouldn't be perfect. There was always something that needed work.

"It's all a process," he said, shrugging. "You'll go on to play them. Even better than you play them tomorrow."

"You don't think I'm ready?"

"You know them by heart?"

"Yes."

"And you understand something of the piece." A thing that, I was only beginning to learn, meant to him that I understood why it worked the way it did. Something of its essence. The calculations that had been made to bring it to life. "Just have fun," he said at last. "Didn't you do well at the previous one? You shouldn't have any trouble with this one."

"It just matters more now."

He cracked a smile. "Picture everyone in their underwear."

"Does that really work?"

"Well, it's distracting, you know, choosing the right color for the right person in the audience. This one has olive-green boxers with crescent moons." He winked. "That one in a tropical motif. You know."

It was a bit of warmth that made the fear recede, but this morning I found my fear had rooted, stolen over my heart in my sleep, and it's making me act weird, move weird, stare at my mom like a deer in headlights.

"Where's your coat?" she asks.

"I forgot it."

Another exasperated sigh.

"Are you sure you want to do this? We don't have to, you know."

It's because I want to — so badly — that I feel so miserable. I leave the Tupperware on the floor and open the car door.

The reception area is large, like a library without books in it, painted in doctor's office teal and peach. My mother points at a round little girl, her glittering silver tutu skirt rustling as she walks. "It's like prom in here. Or First Communion," she whispers. I can't help noticing that most of the people around me are Asian, though no one as brown as me. It's just like the first competition I went to. I feel as if we stick out.

The girl waiting in line in front of us lets out a high-pitched squeal when she catches sight of someone across the room. They rush to meet and hug dramatically, like they haven't seen each other in a while. I wonder how long they've known each other. How long they've been going to these things. It occurs to me that the girl before me at my lessons might be here, but I haven't seen her yet.

"Claire . . . Alalay," the woman at the table says. "Oh! One of Paul Avon's students. Lovely. Welcome."

I brighten with the recognition. Finally, I feel a little thrill of excitement. She knows my teacher. I belong. She tells me where I can find a piano to warm up and where I'll be playing and when. It will be hours before I perform.

We blend into the parade of dresses and stockings and heels, eventually settling into two overstuffed chairs, loudly upholstered, in the air-conditioned lobby. I take my history book out, Mom a *Vogue*. I soak in dead presidents, internment camps, rations. She stews in asymmetrical hems; beautiful, fearful eyes; honey sunny hair.

Some kids look miserable; others have hard-set eyes that mirror their mothers'. Utterly stoic. Others are actually laughing. What I wouldn't give to be one of them.

"I think the *Apassionata*, Dad. No, definitely the *Apassionata*," I overhear.

"Seems a bit overplayed."

"But it's so dynamic!" The man's glance lingers over my mother, who isn't paying any attention.

"I just think your piece should stand out."

"Are you cold?" my mother asks. Her face has gone pale. Whatever cheerfulness she'd felt before is gone. Somehow, at some point, she switched into fear mode without my noticing. Her resting state. "We should have brought a blanket."

I shake my head no. She's visibly relieved, and even more so when I pull out the sandwich.

"Hey! You're the lesson after me." I look up. It's the girl from Paul's. Hair up, lips like a bow. Her long cheeks and light-blue eyes make her look a little feline. "I thought I'd see you at one of these shindigs."

Her way of playing always makes me want to like her—quick and clever, always on the attack. Even when the music smooths out into a rolling legato, there's an urgency. So annoying that she's pretty, too. When she smiles, her eyes melt and light up at the same time. I can't help looking at her dress—gray-blue and long with tiny greenish-blue polka dots—and bemoaning mine, which I'd bought simply because it was the right kind of thing—black, a simple A-line that fit me. I'd wanted it in blue, but it somehow looked cheaper. I give her my hand. Is that what I'm supposed to do? She shakes it.

"Julia," she says. "Have you gone yet?"

"No, soon, I hope."

"Well, go fast. Don't keep us waiting. I want to go *home*."

I laugh. "I feel like I've been here forever." She points to the bathroom behind us. "Gotta run. Good luck." I wonder if she means it.

"You too." A sleeper wave of nausea washes over me as I watch her leave. There's no way I can beat her. No way.

"She's a classmate of yours?" my mom asks.

"At Paul's."

"She's wearing leg warmers. That's smart," she says.

An hour goes by. "Are you sure you want to do this?" my mother says for the second time, looking up from her laptop. She's been binge-watching K-dramas.

Her eyes plead, and I suddenly understand that she's doubting, too. There are so many things she leaves for me to try to understand on my own, so many things she doesn't say. Parents don't have to explain themselves. They aren't necessarily straightforward about their feelings.

I think I know why she doubts me. I wonder if she's been replaying every slip of my fingers in the last few days, every missed note, panicking as badly as I've been. I wonder if, secretly, she doesn't think I can do this. Or if maybe she doesn't want to see me crack.

It's true, she's never seen me fail. Not really, not in front of masses of people. For a moment, I wonder if that's why she thinks I'm so pretty. So smart. So artistic. She's been protecting herself from really finding out. Willingly blinding herself out of love.

A burst of applause pulsates through the walls.

"No. I definitely, absolutely want to do this." I give her a confident smile, suddenly determined to perform well, if only to keep her from thinking ill of me, to keep her from falling apart.

It's time. We join the others shuffling in the hallway. A burst of applause pours in when a door opens. She whispers in my ear, "You're so brave."

We part ways in the auditorium as I look for the right place to sit—there are chairs marked near the front of the stage. I sit down and try a small smile on the girl sitting next to me. Chipmunk cheeks, a strawberry-red dress. She pulls a hand out from where she'd been sitting on it, waves. My mother has chosen a seat near the back, in the corner. There is a sense of expectation, like before the choir sings at church. My heart wants this so badly, there is nothing left to do but play. The girl beside me chews gum in my ear, the rhythm of her quiet smacks slowing when names are called out, speeding back up during the applause, and stopping completely if the player on the stage catches her interest. She seems so relaxed, it makes me realize how spun up I am. I look at my mother—she's too far away for me to read her expression—but just seeing her reassures me as I walk onstage to the piano.

Paul was really specific about what to do before I start. That moment of silence that deepens right before you play? Use that moment to collect yourself, Paul said. The room— the thin audience clustered in twos and threes—waits for me. The sharp sound of paper programs cuts through the air. I raise my hands.

It's a strange piano. There's no time to get to know it. Some keys are heavier under my fingers than others—the looser ones give in so easily, it surprises me the way it does when you're walking on a gravel path and the ground suddenly gives way beneath your feet and you slip a little—a turbulence that comes into the melody, shakes it off course. In a moment of panic, I think, for some reason, about my father, as if he could rescue me by discovering me playing by myself and put me on his lap, like a throne.

It starts to go lickety-split. Too quick, maybe. Not as emotional as I play when I'm alone, but fear is at my back, chasing me on. Paul would say I'm playing like I was admiring someone's children.

People clap—no more or less than for other people. I rush off the stage, suddenly thrilled. No mistakes. A few sparks, even. I didn't disgrace myself.

Now that I've finished, it's easier to listen to the rest of the players. The next girl—the one with the gum—has marvelous fingers but no power—hers is the quietest piano. Next is a boy, flashy in his white suit, who makes a Liszt étude sound bizarre. There's no music in his music. As I listen to him, it slowly dawns on me that I have a chance of winning. Why did I think this competition would be any different from the one I had done before? Was it because Paul gave me the name of it? I try to corral my expectations—it's better, my mother would say, not to hope too hard, but it frolics in me like a puppy anyway.

Hours later, in the dark below the stage, I slip the backs of my heels off, swing my feet. My shoes have grown too tight over the course of the day, and I'm tired of wearing this dress.

Winners are being announced for the younger divisions, and I try desperately not to be jealous of the beruffled girls and boxy-suited boys claiming their prizes. They seemed like normal enough people before, but now I am curious about them, as if they all have some glow of destiny. I examine their shoes, their outfits, and try to correlate their winning with their bodies, but nothing about them seems special, except that they won.

"In third place, Jeffrey Chang." My division. We sit up. A group of twenty or so stand up and applaud loudly. I swivel my head to see Jeffrey freeing himself from the audience, smiling as if he knew he would place all along.

"And in second place . . ."

I hold my breath, straining to hear my name and trying not to look like I want it as badly as I do. I glimpse the shame of losing. How would my mom handle it if I fail? She's never seen me fail before. Maybe this would be the end of lessons.

"Claire Alalay."

My mother yelps like she's been pricked with a pin. They've slaughtered my name, a minor bruise to the ego; it doesn't matter. I wobble up there, hands trembling as I take my ribbon and an envelope. The big meaty paw of a strange man in a nice suit is placed in front of me. I shake it and charge back, ribbon in hand, feeling like I could be four again, playing airplane, zooming up the aisle. I squeeze through the bodies in the row who can't seem to help smiling at me, and I can't help smiling at them.

"Ang galing!" my mother says, not bothering to whisper. I hand her the envelope. Three hundred dollars. My mother's soft, round face has melted into happiness. "God is merciful."

There is a quiet joy shining in my chest.

In the background, I hear Julia's name called. First place.

"Yes! Yes, yes, yes!" I bang my palms on the dashboard with every *yes*. A weight in my body has lifted; happiness comes in bursts, like a piece of toast popping. Two competitions to place on my applications. I yank my body against the seat belt.

"*Sst!* That's not very ladylike." Then, "Are you going to keep the money for college?"

"I want to pay you back for the lessons."

"No." Her voice is stern. A tiny seam of worry appears between her brows again. "You have to save it for college."

We stop at a drive-through and order burgers and fries.

"Why don't you put a napkin on your lap," she says, "so as not to mess up your dress?" I'm too happy to mind. There is a tiny whisper in my body: you really can do this. You could live the rest of your life working with music.

Stanford. Oberlin.

My mother drives with one hand, shoes kicked off. Eventually she hands me the wrapper that once held her burger. "When is the next one?"

She's planning. It's a good sign. I stuff the wrapper back in the bag, then dig down into the corners for stray fries. "In a couple of months."

"That's good. Two months before your next stomach flu." I jostle her, and she smiles.

I flip through the radio stations. Everything is just too calm. I settle on the Beach Boys. Their music feels like sunshine. By the time we left the competition, it was dark out, so I never saw the sun today. Their harmonies swirl around the car, into my eyes. My mother sings along. That's so rare. I fall into their perfectly harmonious rosy world along with her, thinking it's mine.

CHAPTER
—— Six ——

"Well done," Paul says later that week when I give him the news. He seems cool about it, but I know him well enough now to notice a glint of pleasure in his eyes.

I wonder if I should bring up our agreement, our trial period, then decide against it. He hasn't said anything about it since that first lesson, and I begin to wonder if that means I passed. "I really don't think I was that good."

"It might be better for you to think that. Perfectionists make better art." He walks to the bookshelves and plucks a slim, melon-colored booklet off a high shelf. "Here we are."

Chopin's Ballade no. 1 in G Minor.

It's one of the most beautiful, strange pieces in the world. I give Paul a look.

"Perhaps it could be a—I don't know—a set piece for you. For the Lener. It's a stunner when it's done right."

"The Lener?"

"Oh, it's ages away, but it's this competition in the fall. I think you should try to go." He looks around his desk, his glasses slipping on his narrow nose, and hands me a brochure.

On the front, gunmetal clouds and scrub brush. A building made of glass dwarfed by immense moss-brown mountains. First place for my age division gets five grand.

The fall? I guess that means I'm in. I've passed his test.

"Where is this place?"

"In Bishop. Near the Sierras. Very beautiful there."

I try to hand it back to him, but he tells me to keep it, so I do, trying not to get it wrinkled in the jumble of my bag, and then I awkwardly get out my own copy of the Chopin.

"Ah. You have the Cortot. Perhaps you should have the Mikuli edition, too? Just for reference."

He sits down on the wooden chair, pulling it up to sit beside me. I can smell him—soap, a faint woodsy smell. The notes swim before me, bobbing on their lines like fish in the waves. Sharps everywhere. The staffs jagged like mountains.

"Now, this could go badly. There's a lot of room for interpretation, which basically means there's a lot of room to interpret it badly. I think it has something to do with one's emotional personality. Some people are just more trite. Though I don't think that's you." He leans back into his chair and twiddles his fingers on the armrests. "Let's do the first few measures."

"Just start?"

"Half time?"

"Okay."

I trace the path of the notes, my hands knowing where

to go as I hop onto them like stones on a river. Four notes in, he stops me with a fingertip on my forearm and a sigh of exasperation. "No. Is that half time? Even slower, then."

My shoulders rise at the comment, but I do what he says. His hand curls slightly over mine, obscuring my view, to stop my hands yet again with a comment about the shape of the ascending line, and again because of the time I put between each note, the weight of each one beneath my hands. Nothing is right. I play the same introductory measures over and over for the rest of the hour. Wondering how do-or-die this is has become a gut reaction, and as I play, I imagine him saying, "No, no, I've changed my mind. I can't work with you." Even though I passed his test, I know I've done well, these thoughts appear.

"Allow yourself to be a little more dramatic. Take some risks. Don't worry. If it's too outré"—his hand, just off to the side, waves the time, makes outlandish gestures, odd movements, as if adjusting minor currents in the air—"we can check that later."

There's one off-kilter chord that we play over and over. "More strength in the pinkie finger," he says in a raised voice. "Hmm, maybe you should use the fourth."

I try the fourth.

"Again," he orders, like a drill sergeant.

I play it one more time.

"Again."

I try the phrase once more, wondering what he's looking for.

"Fine," he says, gesturing for me to continue, then stopping me yet again just two measures later.

By the time we're through, I feel like I've been slowly crumpled into a ball of paper, first by folding tiny corners, then folding those corners in. A systematic crushing. We've barely gotten past the first page. My cheeks ignite in shame. All the aunties are exchanging looks in my head.

He touches my arm and asks if I'm okay, and I shrug, pretending I am.

"Don't be so uptight. Think of it like praying. Like something that you lose yourself in."

"I don't pray."

He cocks his head at me. "But you wear a cross."

I make a face. "My mother makes me." I touch it. I know the way it feels—the warm metal, the dull points—more than the way it looks. I've worn it since my father got sick. For protection, my mother said. The few occasions when I've removed it, she told me to put it back on as if something bad would happen if I didn't. Crosses are magical to her. For me it's just a thing I have to do, like watering the roses. It's just easier to have it on than to ruffle her.

He nods. "Turned off by Catholicism, then?"

"Like a lightbulb."

He laughs. "I'm an ex-Catholic, too. Though so much of the music we're playing, even if it isn't religious, feels religious somehow. Nowadays our daily lives are so mundane. I can't imagine anyone writing, or having the sort of gargantuan all-or-nothing feelings people must have had back then. Not with YouTube. And pop-up ads. And all that Insta-whatever and I-things. You know. Maybe if we cloistered ourselves from the Internet, people might be a little deeper, a little quieter."

"Why did you quit being Catholic?"

"Well, it's a beautiful religion," he says. "But I didn't like some of the ways it tries to get you to be good."

"Exactly! Can't we just keep the beautiful parts, and get rid of all the purgatory stuff?" There's something about Paul that makes me talk about things I never talk about. Tash is a great friend, but religion is something we'd never discuss.

When my dad died, Tita Alta said he was burning in pur-gatory for his sins. At night I would think of my dad some-where, perhaps in the hot core of the earth, unable to see light. Finally, I had to reject the whole thing: God, crosses, sins. I was too afraid all the time.

My mother, on the other hand, prayed even more after my dad died. She lives life like it's a plank you walk until you either fall or jump off—a thing you do with caution. Like we're supposed to still our very breathing, as if we'd lose our ability to if we actually enjoyed it.

"I wish they'd do away with all of that," he says with a sharp look. "Purgatory, homophobia. It's very cruel." He rips a sheet of paper out of his notebook. "I also want you to listen to these."

"All of them?"

"Mm-hm."

"Are they on the Internet?"

"Some are, but there are a lot of recordings that have never been digitized. They're still on CD, or on records. The school has a library if you can't find them otherwise." The school. He means the conservatory.

"Don't you have to be a student there to use the library?"

"You just need permission, and then you have to call and they'll mail you a card."

He writes an email, and I call on my way home.

Chopin. The ballade. I finally get to play something I am completely in love with. I barely notice anything on the way home, barely notice I've made it to the door. Women's voices singing through the front door pull me out of my thoughts. Mom's novena prayer group meets every Friday, rotating from house to house. It must be our turn.

The room is stuffier than usual, and the voices meld softly together as I weave through the bodies. Prayer books rustle. Fans waft.

Mom touches my cheek in greeting. Rosary beads click as they sway. It smells of old lady perfume and hot wax. The thick flames of red votive candles, lit in glass cups, undulate to a rhythm that's not in the song, the last song for the night. I know because I was brought to these things every Friday when I was a kid, and bored, and then dragged to them when I was older, still bored. They've been singing the same songs in the same order every Friday, and the last song, in Tagalog, is the saddest one. I don't know what it means word for word, but I know what it means by its feeling.

Some of the women sound a little like they're speaking, their voices deep from singing from their chests. Some sing like birds. Some bleat. The lady beside me warbles, her singing gravelly and thin.

There's my dad's picture beside the altar, off to the side, the one of him with me on his lap, looking fat and dumb. A strange feeling comes over me when I see it, one hard to pin down. My mother's friends have crowded their small statues on the altar, close as chess pieces, porcelain and wooden dolls standing on pedestals with shiny fake hair, round cheeks, and red or green velvet capes embroidered and trimmed in metallic thread in doily-like patterns.

The song ends and it's like a gate's been opened. The women start to talk over each other. I weave past them and go straight into the kitchen, where foil-covered trays are laid out on the table. Score. I snatch up a paper plate and take a few spoonfuls of the sweet, custardy flan floating like a raft in a pool of syrup, noodles dotted with tightly curled little shrimp, some pork lumpia—this must have come from a caterer, because Mom never cuts the egg rolls so small—and some rice.

The women begin to trickle in. Tita Pat pinches my cheek and says, "Hey, how's the piano? Still playing?"

I give a silent, respectful nod and cringe. It's all that's expected—respect, silence. Docility.

A lola—not my actual grandmother—touches her cheek to mine and sniffs—a little perfumed air kiss.

I pull out a metal fork and a cloth napkin, a habit I've picked up from Paul. We waste too much paper.

I'm about to flee when my mother speaks into my ear. "Will you play for us?"

I stiffen. She just wants to show me off. "Do I have to?"

"Don't you want to?" The smile on her face loses a touch of happiness. "I thought you needed to practice performing."

"Well . . ."

"Please, Claire."

"Ooookay." I dash to the piano, play a haphazard Mozart sonata—fudging a bit and cutting a full passage—but no one notices a thing. I'm hungry. And the ballade is waiting for me. I retrieve my stranded plate and squeeze in between the aunties.

"Ang galing!" says Tita Irma when I come back. "Wow. You are getting so good."

"It's hard to play it right, though, on this piano. It's so cheap."

I sink my teeth into the crispy skin of the lumpia, tasting its sweet, peppery pork. The oil has stained the plate.

"Merong piano teacher. A new one. Paul Avon," Mom says. More Tagalog. I hear the word "competition" in the tangle of words. Second place. More words. She says Paul's name again, as if she is in awe.

"Walang first?" says Tita Isabelle, who has never liked me.

Mom presses her lips together and shakes her head.

"But who knows? She'll get first someday," says Tita

Anna, who does like me. She looks to me. "Right, kiddo?"

I blush. My mother says something defensive, quietly, in Tagalog, to brush the comment away.

So competitive, my aunties. If I got into Princeton, one of them would say, why not Harvard? I look at my mom and roll my eyes and she shrugs, though I see she's a little annoyed, too.

The conservatory is off a narrow side street from the Civic Center station, so tall its shadow darkens the sidewalk on the other side of the street. Banners flutter down its sides. There are wide stone steps that lead up to the glass doors, with kids standing around outside them, instrument cases strapped to their backs. I take a selfie in front of its facade and go to post it. No, even with a filter, I look too cold and windblown. Delete.

Inside, the wooden floors gleam golden, and a wide flight of stairs spiral up the middle of the lobby. I pause at the door, expecting someone to ask me what I'm doing here, but I flash the card that came in the mail and the security guard smiles as if he already knows me.

My mother barely twitched when I asked her if I could go back to the city the next day. She just wanted to know what time I'd be home. She's probably still annoyed with the aunties.

I find my way to the library on the second floor. It's not that large, but it's packed with books, and it has the kind of silence that's full of thoughts. I like how everyone is preoccupied with themselves in libraries. No one cares what you do. I don't have to pretend to be anything here.

Aisles of folios, carousels of libretti. Books of music whisper. Deeper in, records and more records, shelves crammed with CDs. I'm overwhelmed. I wish I could sleep here.

I pull out the list Paul gave me. It's long, with specific pieces, specific orchestras and performers. Specific years. I've already marked which ones I can listen to on the Internet, but Paul of course was right—plenty of them aren't available online.

I start searching the catalog, retrieve a few, but one, a string quartet from the thirties, doesn't give a code. Just says SEE THE LIBRARIAN.

I head to the front desk. "They have so many records," she tells me, going to retrieve it, "that a lot of them are tucked into odd corners, especially the older ones." I check it out from her and head for the listening stations.

I plop myself into a chair beside the turntable, clamping the headphones to my ears. Tash would like these. They dampen the outside world, like being underwater. Carefully I slide the first one out, the one the library had tucked away. Beethoven's Grosse Fuge, by a group I've never heard of. They must be long gone. The yellowed paper sleeve is fragile and slit at the creases. The record itself looks foggy, and I'm disappointed by its cloudy face. At its center, the word COLUMBIA is emblazoned—not the logo I see on new discs, but a dignified typeface in fat, clever gold letters.

I set the needle down. The tones are clear; I'd thought

since its surface was scratched, it would be hazy. But it's all there: the urgency, the agony. My chest warms and over-flows. While the record spins, I take a little video of it and post it on my Instagram.

A boy looks at the album cover in my lap and smiles at me as he swings past my knees to sit down at a record player nearby.

I smile back before I even realize I'm doing it. Then I stop when I remember where I am. It seems against the rules to look at other people in libraries.

The quartet rises and falls. Maybe Paul wanted me to hear this because he wanted me to play like this, tragic and dark and charming.

The boy looks about my age. Maybe. Definitely cuter than anyone at home. A lankier young version of the pia-nist Glenn Gould—dark tousled hair, a brooding face. He reminds me of how Tash and I used to cross the Dumbarton with her mother to go shopping for books. She thought it a wholesome, academic thing, but really, we would go to look at the boys in Palo Alto and marvel at the difference in gene pools between Fremont and Palo Alto, where generations of trophy wives have created modelesque boys with curly hair and soccer calves and golden skin. Not a stained tooth in sight. We'd drink cappuccinos and pretend we belonged.

I probably seem too obvious. I try not to look at him again.

Strings weep. The room falls away. Bursts of joy are

forged from the weave of instruments. Then it's done. A sense of mourning pricks my skin. I take off my headphones and slide the record back into its sleeve with a soft zip. It's only been thirty minutes, but I feel as if I've aged.

I'm shaking another record out of its sleeve when I hear a clear voice behind me. "It's helpful to look at the sheet music when you listen." It's Julia, scanning the record cover over my shoulder. She keeps smiling at me out of her upturned eyes, like I'm okay and a perfectly normal specimen of a human being, but I'm too surprised that she's even speaking to me to come up with anything to say. She waves at the boy, who waves back. He smiles at me. Another surprise.

"Does it?"

"Well, it helps me, anyway."

It takes me a moment to absorb this. "Then you can see how they're interpreting the music, I guess."

"Yeah. And sometimes they make mistakes."

"Really?"

"A lot of the older recordings have them."

I wonder if she'd practiced extra for the competition, then decide not to ask. I'm afraid of knowing. I start to flush. She looks at me so steadily, I start to wonder if I look like I don't know anything. "Congrats on winning," I say, my jealousy a slight ache that can't be ignored. But I want to mean it. There's no point in not acknowledging I'm not as good as she is, is there?

"You too."

I try to figure out how to get her talking—about anything really, but above all about whether it was as hard for her as it was for me. Is she naturally better than me? But she's already moving toward the books and out of the room.

I keep on moving through Paul's list until I'm too hungry to stay. The boy has left. I meander a little on my way out, peeking through the small lit windows of the practice rooms on the floor below. A tuba puffs out a bass line. Someone somewhere claps their hands in a quick, exacting rhythm. A cellist faces away from her door, her slow bow quivering, the frizzy bits of her hair catching gold. I think of what Paul said. It seemed like everyone was praying here when they played. Maybe I've found my own church.

Usually I have all of Saturday to play, but by the time I've gotten home, given Dean his belly rubs, picked out some videos of my playing, and e-mailed them to Paul—he wanted to hear what I had for competition applications—it's already five. I'm anxious to practice.

The piece isn't impossible, but it almost is, with its death-defying, blind leaps of the left hand down the piano, notes toppling on top of each other like dominoes—no time to think before your fingers move. Just earnest, passionate, clear abandonment of safety in the pursuit of love.

I play the right hand through to the end of the first theme, and then the left, trying to make each part full, as if it were the music in its entirety—half a choir sings through the fingers on one hand, then the other half. Breaking down the music this way is like tracing the piece with a pencil before you fill in the color. I burn the music into the tendons of my wrists, the shapes my fingers make into a memory, until it almost feels automatic.

Eventually I put both hands together. If I don't stop to think about it too hard, my hands will play it as naturally as aiming a spoon into my mouth—it just happens—though every time, I'm sort of amazed at the way every finger stretches to the notes they're supposed to, the way flowers stretch to open in time-lapse movies. Every voice goes in its direction, or tries to. It's easy to single out one voice over the others, to make it sing, but four voices at once, each one singing its own heart out—it's why concert pianists are brilliant.

The richer, the fuller I can make each voice, the more it feels as if the composer's thoughts are appearing in my mind. Their anxieties, their way of looking at the world. I get so deep into that world, I can lose my own for a while.

But at this point, I can only get glimpses. A small but growing list of issues is being written on an imaginary notepad in my head. There are always questions about expression. How should a song be sung? How loud should a voice be? I try different fingerings, make decisions I don't feel sure about.

I jump at my mother's approach. "You have to eat. There's chicken adobo."

"Oh, right."

I'm not hungry, not really, until the smell of garlic and soy sharpened with vinegar hits my nostrils.

"Did you go the whole day without eating?" She tsks. "Did you feed the dog?"

"No."

"I'll feed him."

I take the plate and sit on the floor, checking my texts, my Instagram account. Then I brush my teeth and crawl into bed. I feel like I have been soaked in music. It's ten thirty. There's moonlight. I was lost in music the whole day, and it felt like the best, smooth kind of day. A day without loneliness. A day with just myself and music to keep me company.

CHAPTER
— *Seven* —

A month later at Paul's, he wants me to play the ballade, the whole thing in one go. My instinct is to tell him it's not ready, but there's no way I can say no to him.

My heart is going rickety-tickety as I sink into the beginning, rise up on the swell of the first opening notes, and realize that once I begin, the notes wipe out my thoughts. They just come down like rain until it's over, and I'm relieved when I lift my hands from the piano.

"This isn't done," he says.

"I know it, though. The notes. I know how it should feel."

"It's not the notes. But . . . the expression? Every tiny little thing has to be considered." He gestures with his hands, lightly, as if he's conducting his own words, and gives me a knowing, amused look.

I *have* been considering every tiny little thing. I've been considering them over and over.

"Also, allow yourself to move with the music, to be . . . Your body is so tight over the piano. You're hunched like Schroeder. You need to move to the music."

I put my chin in my hands, lean my elbow on the piano, a thing I know I'm not supposed to do, but right now I can't help not caring.

He gives me a look like he knows he's gotten me in a huff. "Yes. Be more confident. Stop being so timid in front of me. How can you make Chopin sound vulnerable if you don't take the risk of being vulnerable? Sometimes I think— a lot of my Asian students seem to live so . . . stiffly."

I will myself not to cry. No tears. He studies me for a moment. A look like fear crosses his face, and then it closes. "It's important to take risks. On the stage. In life. Have some fun!" He pats my shoulder, but it doesn't make me feel better. In fact, it makes me feel worse. "What are you doing this weekend? Anything exciting planned?"

"Nope," I manage to say. "Just a competition."

"Oh. Oh, that's right. Well, good luck. I'm sure you'll do fine."

Our conversation turns back to the piece and I do my best to listen, but I can't. He continues to talk as I blink back tears until the music comes back into focus. I manage to make it through the rest of the lesson, but afterward I barrel down the hill toward the train.

I *am* taking risks. I *am* being vulnerable. I take a risk every time I leave home for the city, every time I leave class to practice. And it's not my fault if I don't seem like a ballsy, fun-loving teen. If I were, I wouldn't be playing so well in the first place, wouldn't be ready for lessons. I'd be like Tash, skating the A-minus/B-plus rail.

And I don't even feel that Asian, whatever that means. I eat spaghetti sauce that comes in a jar. I know every brand of microwave pizza. We listen to sixties pop in the car. I don't even speak Tagalog. My parents did try to teach me a little, even after my teacher at school said they should stop because she thought I was getting confused. Then my dad got sick, and Tagalog got swept to the wayside, along with vacations, trips to the Philippines, going to the movies, summer camp, circuses, Fourth of July barbecues, swimming lessons, Brownies. All the fun stuff. All the fun American childhood stuff.

Instead, all I've worried about since then is piano and school. Not that my mother browbeats me about grades. I just do well, so she doesn't have to worry.

It wouldn't be like this if Dad were here. We'd have more fun, I bet.

I'm not surprised when I lose at the competition the next day.

The fingers on my left hand keep sliding off—just a hair—from where they're meant to go. Notes that should be sharp and clear begin to get muddled, at first just a little, but then a lot, and then finally, I just can't stand myself. My fingers freeze. Right in front of me. I look at them, thinking, *Timid.*

I manage to keep going. After, during the half-hearted applause, I look at my mother, covering her face with her hands; then on my way off the stage, I steal a look at one of the judges. Her face is kind, which helps me get to the car.

"You need to pray more," my mother says on the way home. "I keep telling you to."

"Oh, good God."

She shakes her head and says something in Tagalog, then crosses herself. "Don't make fun."

"Sorry." If only Paul hadn't said what he said. I'm sure he didn't mean it in a bad way. I'm probably just being sensitive, making a big deal out of nothing.

I look out the window so she can't see how close I am to crying. I read the freeway signs and try to forget who I am, and what just happened, try to space out on the road speeding past.

"Are you sure you can take all of this?" she asks.

"Please, Mom."

"I just don't like to watch you suffer."

"I'm not suffering."

I hear her reach for a tissue on the dashboard. The tires clunk over the divider, and I look over at her; she brings the car back to the center again. She wipes her eyes and her nose, and crumples the tissue in her pocket. Guilt washes over me.

"I really don't know if this is a safe path for you," she says. "It would be so much more practical if you just went into tech. There are so many jobs. And it wouldn't be so hard for you. Don't you think?"

I don't answer her, hoping to bury her question with silence. Tech. It sounds like failing to me. Like settling for less than what I really want.

CHAPTER
— *Eight* —

At lunchtime, as I emerge from the auditorium, Tash pounces with "Come to the dance with me!"

Her face is bright, but then it usually is when she's talking about Tom. The boy who's been showing her music.

"Seriously?" I sigh, arching my back, which has begun to ache from hunching over the keys for the last hour.

"Yeah, well, normally I wouldn't go, either, but Tom's going. His friend is deejaying. Weird, huh? Don't you think it's weird? I mean, our school with a DJ he'd know. Anyway, I know you hate dances, but will you come with me? Not go-go. Just you know, hang out there. Just in case."

The end-of-the-year dance? Tash is sweet and dumb like that. She still thinks that a school dance could be what it looks like on TV.

"We said we'd skip junior prom for a reason."

"Yeah, because you don't want to go without a date."

I frown at her. "That's not fair. You have Tom to crush on. There isn't a single boy in school I like." There isn't a single boy in school who likes me.

"Come on. It won't be that bad," she wheedles. "I can't go alone."

"Why not?"

She frowns. "You've been such a sourpuss lately."

"Sorry." I haven't told her about my complete humiliation. Or what Paul said to me. I just don't see the point of telling her. She'd just call him racist. And then I'd have to feel bad that I like him so much.

"Okayyyy. I'll go," I say. "But will you help me figure out what to wear?"

She gives me a brilliant smile. "'Course!"

On the way to the Haight, Tash puts on the playlist she's been working on for Tom.

"You don't mind, do you? I want your opinion."

Tash's playlists are massive undertakings. They're like little kaleidoscopic worlds. Sonic dioramas. Usually we pick apart every song choice, every transition, listen to it with earbuds in the car and around her house, to see how it fits into different kinds of moods.

I feel a cold stab of guilt that I haven't once offered to help.

It's good—good transitions—but it's made of songs I know too well. So dull. Like I've listened to them so many times, there's no life left.

"What do you think?"

"It's good!" I say, feeling another stab of guilt that now I'm lying to her.

At a vintage shop in the Haight, Tash flits from one rack to another, like a butterfly attracted to certain flowers, while I slowly flick dresses past me, working my way through the pale yellows, slowly deepening to mustard, zigzagging into the spring green, to forest green, to moss, to brown.

One is bad for my boobs, which are so small they're mostly make-believe. One shows my tummy. One makes it so I can't wear a bra. One fits perfectly but isn't my color.

Dances are torture. Why did I say I'd do this?

"Ooh. Very 'Future Sailors,'" Tash says, holding up a nautical halter. She means the silly song from *The Mighty Boosh,* this old TV show we used to watch religiously. I laugh, quote a lyric.

"You should try it on," she says.

"It's not too sexy?"

"Heavens no."

I try on the top.

"Cute!" she says, her eyes drawing themselves up and down over me.

"It's definitely not embarrassing," I say, talking like my mom, trying to hide the fact that in fact, I feel shimmery inside.

The moment I see the open gymnasium doors, I hear the words slip out of my mouth—"Can I go home now?" No shimmers here. Just quaking in my shoes. Music too loud. Shoes too tight. Not enough people. Too many people. Why did I come? Clothing isn't enough. Feeling ridiculous can't be remedied by a shirt. All confidence has been obliterated by the sounds of Taylor Swift.

Tash's already farther ahead, looking for the coat check, looking for Tom.

In her wake, I feel tiny.

On the basketball court, the preps are repeating the same dance routine, over and over, no matter what song comes on. In the corner, by the window, the one badass hip-hop dancer at our school shows off, trades off with other, lesser hip-hop dancers as a handful of boys watch. Everyone else is just standing there, looking awkward, yelling over the music. On the stage is the DJ—I guess it's Tom's friend—and Tom. He looks clean. His long bangs are falling in his face.

Tash drags me off to the side, close to the stage, where she can see Tom and Tom can see her, but not so close that he might think she's stalking him, she says, which he might be thinking anyway. . . . Tash doesn't hide. She can be seen in her yellow dress through the inky light. A gentle glow from cell phone screens bathes the blank faces of kids sitting along the walls on the bleachers. Tash tries a shimmy. I slide, pretend I can't lift my feet from the floor. She laughs.

I turn around in place so everyone melts together, blurring the melting pot that our principal calls our school. There are the hoochie girls with their tight, stretchy clothes and awkward makeup. The preppy kids in V-neck T-shirts and particular shades of denim. That's a large contingent, and not all Asian, just a mix of preppy types who I swear iron their jeans. Ryan DeGuzman is here, looking beautiful. I feel a jolt of nervousness just seeing him.

Timberlake segues effortlessly into Queen and Bowie's "Under Pressure." I feel a throb in my belly in answer to the hand claps. That soft, precise bass line. Only Bowie can make a finger snap sound urgent. Without resistance, my heart starts to feel like a helium-filled balloon inside me. I dance before I'm fully aware of it. "I can't believe they're playing this!" I yell to Tash, who nods, gritting her teeth and dancing like it's the last thing she'll do.

Then David Bowie comes in, his voice all warm and velvet, and I sing along—no one can hear me singing that I have a terror of knowing what the world is about.

Tash points to the stage, an obvious question on her face, and I nod to the beat as she leaves, but it doesn't take long for me to stop dancing, now that she's gone. The floor looks emptier, too—I guess the DJ pushed a bit too far with Bowie, and some of the dancers deserted.

I join the other wall clingers and look at my cell phone, but really, I'm just thinking about how invisible I feel.

To pass the time, I burrow into the college websites. I've never heard of the New School. It looks interesting. Small, radical. Completely different from home.

I wonder if Paul would think I was timid, standing here.

I wonder if everyone here thinks I'm timid.

I'm just about to get up and do something, anything, when a slow bass changes the magnetic pull of the floor.

Clingers come free of the walls. I feel a brush of fingers on my forearm and look up, expecting, hoping, to see Tash. It's Alex Lin. A skater friend of Ryan's, with discernible lashes and one dimple. I barely know him, but he always says hello in the hallways. Polite as an old man from another generation. "Do you want to dance?" he asks.

I don't see why not. I get up and follow him out onto the basketball court. He reaches for me. Tentatively, I wrap my arms around his neck. Heat radiates from his skin. We rock back and forth. I sneak a peek at his face — it's as puzzling as a Mensa test. Unreadable. I suppose he looks happy, but then he usually does.

Tash and Tom are going strong nearby. Body to body. Tash, her eyes closed, doesn't see me.

"Do you remember when I gave you a dragonfly?" he asks all of a sudden.

"Back in middle school?"

We had a lot of dragonflies on the baseball field. I don't know why. The Hmong boys had made these slingshots, intricate ones out of rubber bands. They were shooting dragonflies out of the sky, until a teacher found out and made them stop. I was in seventh grade. He was in eighth.

"I left a dragonfly on the picnic table at lunchtime."

Something clicks. "You were one of the dragonfly killers?" The Hmong boys were younger, like, in the sixth grade. It seems strange to me that an eighth-grader would have hung out with the Hmong boys.

"No. I just picked up the ones in the grass."

"Oh." Then, "I thought someone was trying to scare me or something."

"No. I was just being lame. I had a big crush on you."

We rock back and forth. I can't breathe. I'd never really thought about Alex. I'd never thought I should think about him. He always was kind of half-invisible. Nice, but invisible.

"I had no clue."

"I know. That's why I'm telling you."

"Why?"

"I don't know. I guess I wanted you to know."

My head is spinning. "Weird." I have no idea if we're moving to the music, or just swaying, reasonlessly swaying. "You have a girlfriend, don't you?"

"Yeah. She didn't want to come."

And now he's graduating. "That's too bad."

I close my eyes, let him rock me. I smell mint, orange, and dust on his sweater. To think, the whole time, someone had noticed me. He'd liked me, and I wasn't even trying.

The music fades.

He touches my neck—this funny weird touch, as if he were gently scratching it. "Thanks for the dance."

Impulsively, I kiss him on the cheek. And then he's gone.

Tom drives us home, me in the back seat and Tash in front of me. I'm in shock. Tash turns in her seat and raises her eyebrows like I've offered her a cookie as I tell her.

"No way! He's such a sweetie," Tash says. All kinds of

things are behind her eyes, but mostly joy. Tom's playing the mix she made for him. A good sign. I don't really want to go home. The night is warm, so warm that the vapor in the air can be felt, and still I don't have a single goose bump. A night made for dresses. A night you could swim in. A night that asks you to stay up and be with it.

"Do you guys want to stop and get a coffee somewhere?" I ask.

Tom says, "Well, I have to get up early. For work."

"Yeah, I'm tired, too," murmurs Tash.

I look at their two heads leaning in unison into the turns that lead to my house. They're quiet. And when I get out of the car, she doesn't mention hanging out this weekend, which she usually does.

As they zip off, it dawns on me: they were just waiting to get rid of me so they could make out.

My mother's already in bed. The television in her bedroom is at low volume. I slide into bed, put in my earbuds, and press play. Ravel's string quartet trickles into my head, all sinuous and promising, and I feel this hope, this painful, astronomical comet tail of hope. The second movement is the shrug of a cocoon off a butterfly. So strange, what just happened. I never would have imagined. He liked me.

CHAPTER
— *Nine* —

Tash looks different the next time I see her at school. Something in the angle of her shoulders, and the edges of her eyes.

They spent the whole evening together, she tells me. After the dance. "All we did was kiss, all night. We couldn't stop kissing. Oh, and we listened to music." She squeezes my shoulder.

"That's great," I say, half-heartedly. She was MIA all weekend. It was strange. We usually chat or text at least once.

The bell rings, and she squeezes my shoulder again, turns around, doing a floaty, bouncy walk down the hall.

So weird. She's not a shoulder squeezer. Or she used to not be. But maybe that's what happy people do; they touch other people.

At lunch, she tells me too much: what he's like as a kisser, and what they ate and where they went after the dance to make out. How she had a beer. My eyes pop. She got to have beer without me.

"He thinks we should start a band."

"You don't even play anything."

"Well, Tom said he'd teach me how to play the guitar."

I raise my eyebrows. "He plays music?" This all seems fast.

"Do you want to join? I mean, I know you're busy, but it might be fun. We're going to call it the Cloudcastles. Or Sunchaser. Something shoegaze-y. He has this analog keyboard you could play. It's old, and there's something wrong with it, but, hey, it's rock 'n' roll. Anyway, you could be our songwriter. Or we could just jam. I mean, whatever you want to do."

"Jam?"

"Yeah."

"I don't jam."

"Well, write songs, then."

"I don't think so," I say automatically. I don't even have to think about it.

"Why not?"

"It takes ages to start playing decently, much less write a song. I mean, fuck, I don't write songs. I can't." I think of all the melodies I've made up, strewn all over my head, that don't seem to really go anywhere.

"I bet you'd be amazing at it."

"Yeah, well, I already have the competitions."

Crestfallen face a-glitter, she kicks a shoe idly on the concrete pavement. "But it's almost summer," she says.

I open my lunch, withdraw an apple. The fact she's

even asking rankles. The idea of being in a band watching Tash and Tom love-birding throughout the summer doesn't sound like a good time. It would take me away from what I really need to focus on. And we would sound horrific. I can picture it now, everyone struggling and no one in tune or in sync with each other and me wondering why I was spending so much time at something with no point. We'd be G–C–G-ing it for ages.

And there were other issues, too. It bothers me, the thought of Tash playing guitar. Actually playing music. That's not what she's supposed to do. It's not her thing; it's mine.

The uncomfortable thought is like a worm inside me. Well. If she's going to play, she should at least learn properly.

"Can I just say something, though?" I ask.

"Shoot."

"Are you sure you want to have Tom teach you? You don't want a real teacher?"

"I want this to be fun."

"Well, you say that now." I take a bite out of my apple. "Sorry, but I just can't imagine you wanting to be in a bad band. Why not do it right?"

"There's nothing wrong with the way I want to do it."

"If you say so."

Her face goes cold. "You know, you don't have to get all snooty. You could just say no and skip the drama." And she opens up an *Aperture* magazine and pointedly ices me out.

———————

I don't think I was particularly mean, but maybe I was. I text her an apology but she must not think it's enough because the next day Tash is still stoic, and the next. I even ask her about Tom one day after chemistry, just to try to be nice, but she's monosyllabic. I follow her to her locker.

"Come on, you must understand how I feel," I say. "It's so much better with a real teacher. I just want you to be really good, and I honestly don't think you can get there on your own."

"Well, did you ever stop to think that maybe I don't want a hoity-toity teacher that sucks up my time and becomes, like, an obsession?"

I draw back. "Paul's not an obsession."

She just rolls her eyes and huffs and yanks on her combination lock, which doesn't budge.

"He's not an obsession," I repeat.

"All you care about is Paul," she says, not looking at me. She starts yanking out books and stuffing them into her bag. "It's Paul this and Paul that. He's like God. You barely spend time with me. You're not even interested. It's like you're too good for me now."

Her last sentence stings. I have kind of felt that way lately. I brush my feelings of guilt away. "That's not fair. I have a lot of work to do to be able to compete. And you don't know Paul."

"I know that he makes you unhappy. All you do is practice to try to please him."

"That's what I'm supposed to do!"

"You don't think you've gone overboard? You're always on edge about what Paul is going to think at your next lesson. What's he doing to you?"

I roll my eyes and fold my arms up tight. Who is she to criticize me? Or Paul for that matter. Not everyone wants to cruise through things like she does. "Think whatever you want. Music is my life. I don't have time for crappy bands. And you've changed, too," I say. "The only reason why you're picking this fight is because you have Tom now. You don't need me anymore." It feels true when I say it. The hurt is, anyway.

She opens her mouth to say something, then closes it.

Maybe this is just the price I have to pay for following my dreams. The last days of school crawl to a close, and it's a relief when they're finally over.

CHAPTER
—— Ten ——

Other summers, I'd wake up, go downstairs in a T-shirt and undies, eat a vanilla ice-cream cone for breakfast, and read until Tash called to go hang out at a café, hide in a bookstore, or watch Netflix and do sheet masks.

But that seems ages ago, when I was a different Claire.

During the last few days of school before we fought, Tash seemed different, too. More relaxed. More touchy-feely. Lucky her, to have love change her. She's probably going to be doing all the things Paul thinks I should be doing in the summer. Drinking beer, partying.

I play a Bach prelude to delicately sharpen up my sleepy head and settle down my thoughts. Worries about Tash and Tom are nudged backstage in a measure of quarter notes, where they can stay. My own summer rushes up in my mind—warm, glorious days filled with playing music, deeply colored and clear. Ravel in the afternoons. Chopin and Brahms at twilight. Bach for the mornings. Beethoven at any time of day. Tash was wrong about me being unhappy.

I can hear Dean's toenails scraping the concrete outside. It is a little quiet, though. Too quiet. I go downstairs and let Dean in.

It's been a week without Tash or school. I text her, but no response. I guess she needs her space. Honestly, I think I do, too.

In her absence, my lessons with Paul seem more vivid.

"To play someone else's music is to live in someone else's mind for a while," Paul says at the following lesson. There's a crease in his collar, stubble on his chin. He's in his socks, black and inside out—you can see the seam at the toe. "Sometimes, you get a glimpse of their soul. But there are many, many infinitesimal calculations behind that impression."

The sheet music for the ballade is in front of us. "Now, what do you think this piece is about?" he asks.

"Love." Obviously.

He purses his lips in disagreement. "And what's love?"

"Joy. Not having to worry about things. Knowing that everything will be all right because you have someone next to you." I think of Tash.

"Cute. I wish it were. This"—he taps an area of the score with the eraser of his pencil—"is painful. There's always something of tension, of struggle, in G minor. Now, the beginning, the very beginning"—he hums it—"is not in G minor. It feels a little unformed, confused. And it unsettles the listener, makes him long for some kind of resolution, you know?"

He lets the notes scatter like leaves.

"There's the tension. Always tension. This isn't about love. It's about wanting love."

I watch him play, committing to memory his movements, the feel of him, the particular colors of his music.

He shifts his chair back, beside me, and slightly behind.

I lay my heart on the keys. His hand prods along one of the inner voices.

"Excellent," he says.

I beam.

I take the train to the conservatory early one morning. It's different at this hour—the commuters don't look at one another, and the city is even colder today than it was in the spring. Now that school is out, the conservatory is as sober as a bank. The high ceilings make all the sounds echo and blur into a quiet, muffled stream—footsteps, laughter, oddly no music. The school library's closed, and the day, which had seemed so promising, now seems a little too quiet. I start hoping I'll run into someone, Paul or Julia.

On the hallway walls are pictures of students in orchestras, opera programs beneath glass cases, bulletin boards tiled with flyers for used instruments and practice ensembles and trips abroad. On one is a poster for the Lener. A deep-blue sky, stark brown hills. I recognize the building made of glass, like a church. THE PLAY'S THE THING, says the caption. It's in Bishop, California, just east of the Sierra Nevada. There are different ways of setting up competitions. Some have qualifying regional rounds. Others have multiple challenges — a musical obstacle course. Maybe you have to play with an ensemble. Maybe everyone has to play the exact same piece to get to the next round. The Lener is most interested in expression. In uniqueness of voice.

In the hallway of practice rooms, a violin's raw voice passes into sweetness as it sings on and on a single note — the *Kreutzer Sonata,* the second movement. It pours into the long, silent hallway, and I'm drawn to the open door.

I can only see the boy from behind — his dark curly hair parted to one side and curling up on the edges at the nape of his neck. I think he's the one from the library. The one who smiled. The Glenn Gould lookalike.

His fingers are spindly and clever and firmly grip his violin. Every line is clear, lilting. The piece can be drippy — more trite, Paul would say — but the way he plays it, it actually feels a hair too sharp, and he doesn't slow down and linger where I'd expect him to. He marches straight through it like he's blowing down doors.

An Asian boy with shiny black hair combed straight back accompanies on the piano. He doesn't see me, either — his back faces the door. There's no delight in his playing. It's all effort. I cringe, remembering what Paul said about Asian musicians.

The violin boy sounds like the afternoon. Notes waft steadily like dust motes, as if they had nowhere they needed to be, the way I've been feeling all morning.

Suddenly he twists and shoots a glance over his shulder at me, like he's sensed me watching him. Full lips, fox-faced. He lowers his bow.

It is the same boy.

The accompanist turns — overbite, baby-skinned — looks questioningly at him, then at me.

I attempt a wave as the playing subsides. "Sorry. Didn't mean to bother you."

"How long have you been hanging out there?"

"Not, like, stalker long. I just love that movement," I say, looking at the frayed cuffs of his faded green corduroys.

"Me too. When I'm not feeling frustrated by it."

"You don't sound frustrated." I risk a glance.

"Guess we fooled her," he says, turning to his friend.

I laugh, but it comes out like a high-pitched giggle.

"I'm Lee."

"Claire."

"You're Julia's friend," the violinist says. He remembers me.

I'm sure I look horrible. Especially in comparison to Julia. I hide one sneakered foot behind the other. "Well, not friend exactly. We know each other. How do you know Julia?"

"School."

He smiles like I'm not a dork, which is pretty amazing in

my book. He's perfect. "Why aren't you friends with Julia?" he asks, pushing his hair out of his eyes.

For some reason, I keep thinking about my shoelaces flopping on the floor. They're extremely dirty. Girls are supposed to be clean. "We only just met. We take lessons at the same place."

His eyes flicker with interest. "With Avon?"

"Yeah." I stand up straight, suddenly finding a little courage. The accompanist glances at my hands.

"Sweet. You must be pretty good." His tone becomes knowledgeable, his words clipped. He cracks a lazy smile.

I shrug a shoulder. "I'm okay."

"Avon doesn't have bad students."

"Well, you haven't heard me play." They both laugh, to my surprise.

"Are you going to practice? Play with us," Lee says. The other boy shoots him a look, but Lee keeps his eyes fixed on me.

It's so sudden. "Nah, I can't."

"Okay. Well, maybe sometime."

I turn to go. I should leave before I embarrass myself.

"Wait. My phone died, but . . ." He grabs a pen from the top of the piano, takes my hand, and writes his number on my palm. It tickles unbearably, but I make myself stay still, as if boys wrote on my skin all the time.

"Let's play. Maybe with Julia or something."

The other boy rolls his eyes, impatient. I write my number on his hand, too, trying not to fall over. I suppose I could just text him, but then I'd have to make the first move. Plus this is more fun. Like out of a movie or something.

I walk down the hall, tucking my hand into my pocket, like a talisman.

At home, I play with purpose until the sun starts to slant through the window. I'm sharp to the way my hands feel, as if something's opened in my chest and now my shoulders are set differently and my arms are moving more fluidly and my fingers seem to be more at ease. Some of the trickier fingerings I've been trying to get down seem more sure.

It feels lighter. More like what I imagine Paul wants of me, everything pouring out with fire and grace and speed, like Julia.

I take out my phone and set it on a shelf, take off my glasses, and, hoping I still have some magic left in me, keep going, trying to record exactly how I felt, listening to Lee.

I don't miss Tash at all. I have a new life.

I enter Lee's number carefully in my cell phone before I shower, then I lie down naked on my bed where the sun has spread itself out in a hot thin polygon. I fan my hair out on the bedspread and lie open, like a snow angel. It's a secret thing I do. The pleasure of sun pooling on my belly, slipping down the insides of my arms. With my eyelids closed, I feel like I'm not really small. I'm not really a child. I rub the smooth ball of my shoulder against my cheek. The impossibility of such softness. The beginning of a melody blinks on and off in my head like a sign in the dark. The shadow of the number was still there after I showered, and I look at it in the sun.

Whenever I get bored with TV, or I'm walking the dog, or my eyes burn from looking at sheet music, or on the train, or whenever I just get tired of waiting for something to happen, which is maybe every thirty breaths or so, I check my phone to see if Lee texted. It gets to be so often, my mom notices and asks who I'm waiting for.

"No one."

Three days. Nothing.

Maybe the number washed off before he could write it down. Maybe he forgot. I suppose it's exactly the kind of thing a boy could forget.

Or maybe he's just like me. Too shy.

At least it happened.

CHAPTER
Eleven

I'm meeting Paul at the conservatory—his assistant, Andrew, called to change things around at the last minute. There was a mix-up, and he was very sorry, but I wasn't.

I can't help but look for Lee in the halls of the school, up the stairs. In every practice room I pass. I feel like an assassin—always looking down halls, peeking around corners for a boy with dark curly hair, carrying a violin.

Paul is playing something simple but unsettling, with strange notes that catch me off guard.

I open the door. "Is that Satie?"

"It's something of mine," he says, lifting his hands off the keys with a start.

"It sounds post-Romantic."

"*I'm* post-Romantic." He pinches the sheet music off the piano with his thumb and forefinger and puts it away. "It's not really worth anyone's time. It's just a toy."

"How do you know?"

"I know," he says wearily. He plops himself down on the chair beside the bench and folds his arms, turning his face away, revealing his profile. "How's it going with the ballade?"

"It's . . . going." I look one more time through the window for Lee before settling into the music.

Paul stops me just as I'm digging in. "You're breaking up the line here. *Paaa-taaa.* That's the same voice, not separate from what comes before. It's a whole idea. *Puh-tah-dada,*" he says. His choirboy singing voice overexaggerates. "Not *Puh-tah—DAH-da.*"

A few measures later: "No, no, don't imitate. Use your own voice."

I begin to sweat. I have no idea what he means by that. My voice is gone. It's hiding. The world condenses into this tiny room. I try again.

"Perhaps," he says, "we might grant Chopin the favor of going at tempo. Hmm?"

I would die if Lee were watching.

The thought bids every note I've learned by heart to evaporate from my fingers. Soon I'm tripping over the keys, halting over my own notations.

Paul's hands draw huge shapes in the air, as if that will help me get what he's trying to say, or help it end.

When I'm done, he's looking down at his hands on his thighs. Maybe he's so annoyed with me he can't even look me in the face. "Right, then," he says. "Let's move on to Scarlatti."

An easier piece, but my hands are shaking and I falter. His

comments are gun bursts. At one point he stops and takes my hands off the piano and says, "I feel as if you are wasting my time. Is this the real Claire? Or is this a robot Claire, sent in her stead, and the real Claire is off in Bora Bora?"

I look at him, dumbfounded.

He sighs. "Spiritless. Okay, let's just carry on." He gestures to the piano impatiently.

The end of the lesson is a mercy.

"I watched the recordings you sent me for your Lener application. I don't think you should send them in," he says just as I reach for my backpack. "Nice try. No really," he says, when he sees my face. The tears are beginning to surge. He scratches his temple. "I just don't think the tone of the piano you played them on does you justice."

My shitty, shitty piano. Of course. Maybe that's why he's being so sharp with me today.

"Try playing the ones here to record. They'll suffice. They're in tune anyway."

I barrel out of there, hoping I can get to the bathroom to cry unseen, but I see Julia down the hallway. Julia again. Strange to see her here after my lesson. I can't bear to have her talk to me now. I give her a quick wave and a fake smile, as if the tears aren't already there on my face, and blow past her before she has a chance to speak.

On the train, I stare at my reflection in the window, shake my head, and look elsewhere. I feel humiliated.

Everything he said was true.

Use my voice, he said. What's my voice?

"Hey," says a man, standing in the crowded aisle. "Smile! It's a gorgeous day."

My head snaps in his direction. He's taller than me, and there's something in his eyes — too friendly, too strange — that threatens me.

He waits for my response. I'm momentarily reminded of Jack Rieber, from PE class, handing me a baseball bat and asking me suggestively if I knew how to grip it. I'd pretended he didn't exist. I'd looked past him at the geese in the sky. So he said it again, adding maybe I'd like some lube to make it easier, and how he'd give me some. And then he got up close to me and tapped me on the shoulder with his own bat, and then on the chin.

I switched gym periods.

I find the puppet strings that control the corners of my mouth, and jerk them outward, as asked.

He laughs. "All right."

I refuse to look at him again. Somehow, I feel ashamed. I'm ashamed that I smiled. That I didn't tell him off, the way other girls might have. And I'm ashamed that my smile was so fake. Like I should be appreciating what a great day it is like everybody else, even though for me it's been wretched.

I look out the window, clenched tight, still as a fly on the wall, waiting for him to leave. I look reflexively at my Instagram. Pictures of Tash with Tom. I touch the heart button. If I could talk to her, she'd probably help me laugh off this intrusive guy, and smirk at everything Paul said. But deep down, I don't know if I ever really could dismiss anything Paul says to me. He's always right.

I try to skate past my mother, who's in the front yard in her housedress, her church necklaces looped around her neck, and wearing her old bent-up straw hat, but she calls me like there's no question I'll come over, so I do.

"They're getting aphids again. Help me." She dips a yellowish sponge into a plastic bucket of soapy water and hands it to me. I shudder.

"That sponge is disgusting."

She ignores the comment and wipes the top of a leaf.

"It will just take fifteen minutes."

"I can't. I have to practice."

"How can that be? You're always practicing."

"Yeah. On a shitty piano."

"What?" She cradles a glossy leaf, stuck all over with little gray, unmoving bugs, in the palm of her gloved hand. "You make it sound beautiful."

"Paul thinks it's mediocre."

"Paul thinks." She tsks. "It's not a Steinway or whatever, but it was your dad's and I'm not giving it away." She dab-dab-dabs at a single leaf.

"Yeah, well, lots of things of Dad's were mediocre."

"*Sst.* Claire!"

"We should get a new one."

She rips a sigh out of her chest. "What do you want me to do? Marry rich?" She squats beside the pail and pushes her sponge back into the water. The aphids release from the sponge and float up to the surface. "The piano is fine."

"No, it's not. It's not and you know it. It's barely in tune!"

"Well, we can tune it."

"I guess. Though it still . . ."

"What? Still what?"

I shake my head and storm off. "Never mind."

CHAPTER
— *Twelve* —

I don't sleep well. I'm wrung out and dried up stiff in the morning. Nothing I played sounded like music last night. Just notes strung together. I couldn't figure out how anything should sound. I feel so weak, nearly crying in front of him.

Paul's a jerk.

I go into the city early, not because I feel like it, but because my thoughts get worse, stewing in my room.

In a café a few blocks down from the conservatory, pretty, escapist pieces seep into my head—Ravel's *Boléro,* Tchaikovsky's *Pathétique*—but I can't focus. Was it just me or was Paul in a temper? Maybe he was taking something out on me. Or maybe he was frustrated because I'm not getting better the way I should.

Julia, in her windbreaker and carrying her backpack, walks past. I knock on the window, catch her eye, and wave. She smiles. A few seconds later, she's inside. "You okay? I saw the look on your face when you got out yesterday." So she did see me leaving yeserday. She offers me her packet of M&Ms, the corner of it torn neatly off. "I like dark chocolate better, but the machine's out of Special Dark. As usual."

Chocolate in the morning. I hold out my hand and she pours some in.

"It's not your fault. He was awful to me, too."

"He was?" It's hard to believe. She's too good.

"Uh-huh. I heard it was because his girlfriend was in the apartment, packing up her things."

"He has a girlfriend?"

"Or whatever it is you call it at his age."

I think of how uptight his assistant, Andrew, sounded in the message he'd left. "How did you find out?"

"Paul's friends with my dad. Word got out. Dur-rama!" she says, pincering another M&M between her thumb and forefinger. "Anyway, I just thought I'd tell you. We probably weren't the only ones he's reduced to tears this week." She shakes her head. I can't help but think, *So he makes you cry, too?* I feel relieved, and strangely bonded to her. We're going through the same things.

"Whatcha listening to?" She nods at my phone.

"Tchaikovsky's *Pathétique.*"

"Ah. The dream," she says. She pushes another M&M neatly into her mouth with her thumb, which is bandaged around the tip.

"What happened to your thumb?"

Her tone turns matter-of-fact. Businesslike. "The *Waldstein.* My fingers are getting destroyed. I've been having to tape them. Those octave glisses. I've spent hours on them. Literally hours." Her *t*'s are hard, like Paul's. She uncovers the Band-Aid on her thumb and shows me the raw purple at the very tip where she's bruised it over and over again, sliding them on the edge of the keys. My jaw drops. "At least I'm not bored," she says, and laughs.

I follow her out of the café and into the conservatory, where we part ways — she for the library, me for the studios. So Paul had a fight with his girlfriend. I guess that explains it. But still, it wasn't like anything he said to me wasn't true. I need a tougher skin.

With the taste of chocolate in my mouth, I duck into every unlocked practice room and sample the pianos, trying their voices, wondering which one is best.

Tash texts. I feel a thrill. *Hey, how goes it.*

Not bad, I text back. *Lessons.* [poop emoji] *You?*

Lol. Feel like a break? We're making cookies. Maybe we can catch up?

I immediately feel disappointed. I want my friend back, but "we" means I'd have to see both Tash and Tom. Sounds awkward.

Can't! I'm seriously sucking right now, I text. *Sorry. Soon though?*

Okay. Sure.

Have fun, I text back, feeling more distant from her than ever.

———————

The following Friday, I hear Paul and Julia working on pedal through the door. The notes blur, wavering in the air, stop abruptly, then levitate again. *Attaca-tacca-tacca. Ratatatat. Ra-tatatata.* Julia spits fire like a machine gun. There's silence after—as if Paul and Julia are quietly inspecting the body.

"Oh, no! You're here. That was horrible! Could you hear me?" Julia asks when she and Paul come out. "I feel like I've been caught with my pants down."

I shrug. "I thought it was a good show. Very decent underwear," I say, blushing.

She and Paul both laugh. His blue eyes turn to me as her footsteps meld into the general noise of the street. "Well, then. You're getting to know Julia."

"I guess so," I say cautiously, in case he's got something bad to say about it. It's only been a week since his cranky, low-grade tantrum with me, and I don't want to set him off. But it is true that Julia and I have been running into each other more—by the vending machines, in the library. We even sat together in the school café.

"That's good, that's good. She's so focused. I think her understanding is very fine for her age. Though of course, I taught her, so I guess I'm biased."

He seems more relaxed today, his chair closer to the piano than usual.

"This here," he says, pointing to a measure with the tip of a pencil, "should be softer, more delicate. There should be a sense of returning but also moving forward at the same time."

The lesson is going fast. His chin, dark with stubble, lends his eyes a deeper blue.

"Are you growing a beard?" I ask, taking advantage of his mood.

"Kinda," he says. "I hate shaving. I only do it for the ladies." Hmm, he only shaves when he's with someone. "Relax your shoulders, and when you come to this part, lift your chest up, lighten. Every time the notes climb." He touches my shoulder briskly with the pads of his fingers. I jump, but he doesn't seem to notice. "Then, on the downstroke, let your arms get heavy. Use their weight—yes."

I breathe carefully, moving slowly, looking up from time to time to see if I've gotten it right by the tiny changes of light in his eyes, the height of his eyebrows, the way he moves his hand. It starts to feel natural, and I can hear how my body's slight change makes the music breathe, the notes go deeper.

"Playing is a physical act. It reflects how your body's feeling, even if you don't mean it to. The more you relax, the better, at least for these lovely open parts. And then when the melody repeats . . ." He shows me on my piano, sliding in next to me. I move so that we don't touch. He plays past the theme into the graver development and the dark crash of a waltz. His long fingers appear jointless. The feelings swim in the air.

All of a sudden, he lifts his hands off the keys.

"You're getting better." His stubbled cheeks stretch into a smile, making me forget in an instant my days of picking over every measure of the ballade that's been giving me trouble. His cranky attitude last week. All of that. I thought it was improving, but when he says it, I know it's true.

CHAPTER
—— *Thirteen* ——

A few days later, I run into Julia at the conservatory, sitting in one of the black leather chairs in the student lounge, a paperback open on her knee. She gives me a nod, then looks back down at her book.

Part of me wants to leave her in peace, and part of me wants to stay. Staying wins. Staying means I can tell Paul that we hung out.

She looks perfectly composed, even though her hair is tousled all around her head. It's perfectly tousled. Little diamond earrings peek through her hair. Probably real.

"What are you up to?" I ask, and it sounds normal enough.

"Nothing. I'm tired."

"Me too."

I sit down next to her and she makes room for me, swinging her foot to the floor. I notice she's left the Band-Aids off her hands. The bruises have faded.

"Do you want to get out of here?" I ask, taking a chance.

"Um, sure!" She shuts her book so quickly, I feel touched. "What do you feel like doing?"

"I don't know." I haven't thought much further than this.

"Wanna go shopping?"

We walk down Market, past men with better hair than the girls back home and homeless people that look right through us.

The thing about Julia is that she's not just smart and clever; she looks like she's playing someone smart and clever on TV. In a sci-fi movie, she'd be the governmental head of a matriarchy of lithe, slim-boned, fierce women. Too strange to be pretty, with intense, light eyes, a too-upturned, narrow nose, and the kind of lips that look colored in. Even if she were a less-gifted musician, she'd probably do well, just because there's so much to look at. She's only wearing a T-shirt, jeans, and asphalt-colored Converse All-Stars, her hair clumpy like she didn't brush it that morning and doesn't care. But people walking past us look at her all the same, and then, maybe because I'm right next to her, me.

"How old are you?" I ask.

"Seventeen. What about you?"

"The same."

She looks at me wide-eyed. "No waay. You don't look it at all."

"I know." I make a face. I look like a cartoon character in a Disney movie.

"You could try contacts," she says. "Or wear makeup."

"Makeup makes me look dumb." I hate makeup. I hate

makeup counters. I hate the women at makeup counters—
the way they look at me, like I'm a pebble stuck in their shoe.
And I hate the smell.

She stops me in the middle of the street and studies my
face. "No, I don't think it would. That skin."

We move into a gradually building tide of people, and
the shine of the stores begins to take over the sad, depressed,
newspaper-gray blocks that surround the conservatory. Julia
keeps up a steady stream of chatter, about music, about
Paul, about the school, as we pass tables filled with jewelry
on the sidewalk. She'd rather be a dancer, she tells me, but
her mother thinks that career has no longevity. "As if being a
musician does. But it runs in the family. I don't remember a
time when I didn't play," she says.

A surge of envy. "Have you been with Paul a long time?"

"Since I was maybe nine? He's a family friend. My mother
was a singer for a while. He wasn't that big a deal at the conservatory or anything at the time. I mean, he had promise
but that's not enough. Even a record album isn't enough."

"I wondered what he looked like back then."

"Why, do you have a crush on him?"

"No way! He's too old to have a crush on."

A cable car revolves in place, stately, like a merry-go-
round after the music's gone off. A hot dog stand gives off
putrid steam. A woman asks the general crowd if they're
registered to vote. I duck to avoid a man shooting his arm
out in greeting, eyes looking way past us, face shining, calling to a friend, his voice loud in my ear—"Why don't you

take your time? I'mma goin' in here!" And when he sees me looking at him, he looks me up and down appreciatively. "Hello . . ."

"Ew," says Julia. He looks at her, and his face freezes. Like he's afraid of her.

Shame pours over me. I get this kind of attention all the time. If I wear something, anything that makes me feel sexy, a tight pair of pants, or a fitted top, I get drivers honking at me. It's like an assault.

She gets admiration. I get lust. Maybe everyone's intimidated by Julia. She doesn't seem the least bit intimidated by anything. Like Barneys. She eyes the shop windows, the Balenciaga dresses, the Saint Laurent, and walks right in, like she belongs there.

The clothing is spaced far apart, in colors that don't suit me. Movie-star clothes for blond women. It smells weird in here — an ethereal, cloying spring smell that irritates me until my nose gets used to it. A woman smiles with her teeth and glares with her eyes. She probably half wishes we weren't there. Like we're going to spit on the suede or something. Maybe gather a bit of it with our teeth to make a nest.

Julia turns a corner with a ballerina-esque pivot and floats up the steps, and I follow her, feet firm on the floor.

She pauses at a navy miniskirt and eyes my figure.

"Really?" I say.

"It would look so cute on you."

I look at the price tag and leave it on the rack, but Julia tries it on, along with other things I'd never even dare to look at—cherry-colored silk tops, full skirts in kelly green, tissue-thin cashmere cardigans, pornographic-looking shoes for rich Italian ladies. She takes forever in the dressing room, and I'm left looking at dresses, the kind that end up in magazines.

Julia finds me in front of a pink dress—a shade that suits my skin. So rare. It costs over a thousand dollars. I'm almost afraid to touch it. I'm embarrassed to look the salesgirl in the eye.

"Did you find anything?" asks Julia, a bag beneath her arm.

I shake my head.

We look at the perfumes—an entire room of small, jewellike glass bottles glinting on mirrored trays that compound the twinkling. An older man, balding, in a light-gray suit and a rose-patterned tie, pointedly ignores us.

I have an urge to flee, but Julia picks up a spherical bottle and spritzes her wrists, then lifts her hair and smooths the inside of one wrist to the back of her neck. She brings her wrist to my nose. "Smell."

Nighttime flowers. The balcony scene in *Romeo and Juliet*. A Brahms intermezzo. "It smells like it's for old people."

"I like it," she says.

"Well, maybe not old old," I say.

I take another bottle, pull my sleeve up and spray it on my wrist. It smells cool, easy, fun. Debussy's *La Mer*.

Julia takes my hand and smells my wrist. "Hmm. That's lovely." She looks at the bottle. *"La chasse aux papillon."*

"Butterfly hunt."

"Is that what it says?"

"Mm-hm."

"You speak French," she says. She's impressed. I relax a touch.

The man comes over. "Just looking, I assume?"

"Actually, no," she says, instantly aging ten years. "I'd like this." She hands over her credit card.

His facial expression softens, and he even smiles as he presents the package, tissue wrapped. "It's a lovely fragrance," he says in a rapid-fire, clipped diction. "Jasmine, linden blossom, tuberose."

She takes the package. As soon as we're out of earshot, she screws up her face into pseudo-importance. "Just looking, I ass-yoom?" I bust up laughing. I like Julia, I decide. A low-ebb warmth. She's very direct, but it feels comfortable.

"Try this." Julia hands me a glossy black tube of lipstick.

In a lighted mirror, I smear it on.

"Not the right color," I say immediately.

"You're just not used to it yet."

"No, it's terrible," I say, wiping it off. I'm suddenly depressed. I look up at the many halogen lights above us.

"It looked nice."

I look at Julia, who is, I've decided now, beautiful, and then at my face. My lips are still stained a dark red. I shrug, not sure, but I believe her. "Cool."

I buy the lipstick and watch the salesgirl carefully wrap the box in tissue, as if it were precious. Suddenly I wish I could go home. I'm exhausted, though it doesn't make sense to be so drained after just shopping.

"I should go," I say.

"Do you have to?"

"Well, my mom is expecting me." She looks genuinely disappointed, and I'm charmed again. "But maybe I can stay for a little while longer."

I text Mom to tell her I'll be late.

Not two seconds pass before I get her answer: *Why?*

I think about it. Train delays. Dental emergencies. Barn burnings. Flag burnings. *Just hanging out with a friend.*

Tash?

No. Her name is Julia. You met her at a competition.

How late will you be?

Six.

Okay.

Julia's house squats a little way back from the street. Crooked rosebushes lick the bottom of its windows. A curving path lined with chipped flowerpots leads to the door.

Inside it smells of burnt coffee and books. A girl, maybe twelve, is tucked into a corner of the overstuffed leather sofa, reading a book and eating a Nestlé Crunch. She's oblivious to the dog following the candy bar's every move, peering intently at it through its shaggy fur.

"That's my sister, Gabrielle," she says. "And that's Horatio."

The quince-and-gold rugs on the hardwood floor are frayed. In the kitchen, the windows are warped, fogged.

There's a drip of marmalade on the counter, crumbs, a teapot.

I'm never going to bring her home to my mother's fake flower arrangements and lace doilies beneath Oriental vases, our shrines to Jesus and ancient rice cooker flaky with the dried drips of gluey water.

Julia's dad is in the kitchen. A few gray hairs glow in the light. His hand is large and rough with a cushy palm and engulfs mine. "I'm Seth. Happy to meet you. I've heard über-tons." He turns his attention to the African violet in the sink.

"Nice to meet you."

"Staying for dinner?" he asks.

"Um." I look at Julia, who raises her eyebrows in the affirmative. "Sure." Cool.

Julia's pouring iced tea. "Can I have a joint?"

I stare as Seth fishes in a kitchen drawer. "You'll smoke it here, of course?"

"Of course." She lifts an eyebrow at me.

I'm agog. "It's a trade," she says. "I file papers at his office; he pays me in weed."

"You're not supposed to tell anyone that," Seth says, his voice trailing behind him as he strides out the kitchen door and down a hallway. He doesn't sound serious, but he isn't smiling, either. I can't tell if she's in trouble.

"When is dinner?"

"Seven."

I text my mom back. *Can I stay for dinner?*

Julia carefully tucks the joint into her small brown leather bag, sending a meaningful look my way. She grabs the iced tea and leads me to her bedroom, where a pink tutu hangs from the wall over the bed like a massive chrysanthemum. A bra strap peeks out from beneath a pile of dirty towels. Ballet shoes are piled in the corner of the closet, whose door is wide open. How does she have time to play *and* dance? The closet blooms with dresses. A neat pile of sheet music waits on the nightstand.

She spreads out on top of the plum-and-navy quilt on her full-size bed and stretches to turn on a speaker on her nightstand. Beethoven's Sonata no. 13 catches my breath. No friend has ever played classical music for me, let alone in a room filled with pink tulle. Hard to believe there are other people my age who would do exactly the same thing I do when I get home. Listen to the same music, work on the same things.

"I didn't see a piano."

"It's in the music room."

"You have a music room?"

"It's on the opposite side of the house from where my parents sleep, so we don't wake them up," she says wryly, shoving a small pile of laundry off to the side as she rolls over to plug her phone into a charger.

"My mom's just got earplugs."

I push some clothes to the side of a chair and sit down while she fiddles with her phone. Soon I get a notification. Not mom. Julia's just followed me on Instagram. I follow her back and then instantly start scrolling through her pictures. Julia in a ballerina bun and pointe shoes. Julia with a flower crown beneath a redwood tree. Julia eating bao in Chinatown.

A soft knock, Seth's droll voice. "Julia, turn it down, please. Your mother's sleeping."

"She's always sleeping. Always," Julia grumbles.

"Well, she does have cancer," Seth says.

I get chills. Julia just huffs and turns the volume down to a normal level.

"Thank you." The woodwinds are discordant in response. I look over at Julia. She sits on the bed with her arms crossed and her knees up.

Partly because I want to give her space, and partly because I'm curious about her wardrobe, I peer into her closet.

"So many gowns." I leaf through them. Aquamarine, chartreuse, sky. Fairy dresses in Easter colors, colors for blond people. Black netting. Sequins. I wonder if I should tell her about my dad, if it would make her feel better, but before I can convince myself I won't sound like a dork if I told her, she asks me if I have a boyfriend.

"No."

"Me neither. It takes too much time. I had to break up with a boy because it took too much time away from other stuff."

"Really?"

"He's nineteen. No, twenty now."

"Is he cute?"

"Pretty cute. We still hook up. Nothing serious." Julia eyes herself in the mirror, then snatches up an eye pencil.

Suddenly I feel much younger than her. Babyish. I've only kissed boys at middle school parties and Math Bowl.

She carefully lines an eye, then leans away from the mirror to see herself, blinks a few times. She starts the other eye. Her dresser is covered with little boxes and bottles, carefully arranged. Pearly nail polish, glitter eye shadow, lip gloss.

"There is a boy," I tell her, picking up a bottle and looking at the label. "Lee. At your school. Do you know him?"

She puts her pencil down and looks at me with her newly darkened eyes. "Is something going on there?"

"No!" I think for a moment, to make sure this is true. "No."

"Do you want something to happen?"

"No!"

She looks at me, laughs, then picks up her phone.

"Don't!" I say.

"Why not?"

"I'm shy?"

She keeps texting. Zombies couldn't tear me away.

Still no text from Mom. I take it as a yes. Dinner is at seven sharp, and I sit where I'm told, at a large walnut table. Julia's mom perches birdlike, knees to her chest, wrapped in a bathrobe, her tiny magenta toenails showing, while Seth sets the table. I try not to stare. Cancer. Death in her face, gaunt, the same leonine shape as Julia's. My dad's was similar, but her head is wrapped in a blush-pink scarf, and my dad just went bald, and later, a fine mist of hair thickened over his scalp. It wasn't the same kind of hair. I wonder if she is after or during. She extends an arm out to Julia, who goes over to her. The other she extends to me.

"I'm Danielle." We shake hands. "Staying for dinner?"

I nod.

"Wonderful. You can help eat all this food. Julia and Gabrielle eat so little."

Seth puts down a tray of roast chicken and potatoes, where the potatoes have shriveled in the pan and the carrots are blistered and glowing. In the water pitcher, slices of lemon float like lily pads. There are little purple flowers in the salad. Fleetwood Mac plays. I think of my mother and me, who often sit in front of the television together, me eating pizza, her eating leftover rice and soup. I've never seen a dad set the table.

"Seth mentioned you also study with Paul?" Danielle rolls his name on her tongue. If Julia and Gabrielle eat like ducks, Danielle eats like a sparrow. A flake of chicken is speared on the tines of her fork, and a translucent orange bottle of pills sits outside the edge of her placemat.

"Yeah."

"She's new," says Julia, a lump of food tucked into her cheek. "Good, though."

"Jules has been with him for years," Danielle says. "How many years has it been?"

Julia doesn't look up. "Eight."

"You're very lucky," Danielle says to me. Even though she speaks clearly, you have to listen hard to hear her. "How many hours a day do you practice?"

"Four? Six? Six on weekends."

"You see, Julia?" She tilts her heart-shaped head at her daughter.

"If I practiced that much, I wouldn't be able to dance."

"I don't play straight through. I take breaks."

Danielle turns her head to me, which she does slowly, as if choreographed. "Do you dance, Claire?"

"No. I'm not a leotard type of person."

"You're Filipino, right? I thought they all loved to dance. Dance and sing."

"Nope." I look at Julia. Her eyes apologize. "I mean no."

"We had a cleaning lady once. She was Filipino. So nice. So hardworking, and so quiet, you barely knew she was around. She'd bend over backward for you, you know? Eager to please. She had a beautiful voice."

Seth chews his food. Gabrielle mashes a potato with a fork. No one acts like this is anything but normal, for Danielle to slice me open, as if I'm a cake, and pick around my insides. So I pretend it's normal, too. Does she even know she's insulting me? I keep my face a perfect blank. As blank and as unreadable as an impeccable, quiet maid.

"Well, you must be very good if Paul took you on," Danielle says to me, placing a morsel of chicken in her mouth.

"Maybe."

Julia rolls her eyes at me apologetically, then turns to Gabrielle. "Stop feeding the dog under the table."

"Oh, yes, Gabrielle," says their mom, "must you do that?" And the conversation takes a turn, to my relief.

"Sorry about my mom," Julia says once we're back upstairs. "She's like that with everyone."

"That's okay," I say, pretending that it is.

"I think your hair would be prettier up," she says, coming behind me. She does it neatly. One elastic, three clips, and seven bobby pins later, my hair is elegant. But it's so heavy, it pulls at my scalp.

"I don't look like a librarian?"

"Hot librarian," she says, looking at me critically. "You could wear a little mini. Knee socks." She fishes things out of her dresser.

With a flouncy skirt and knee socks, I look like a doll. I frown.

"Good God," she says. "I hate you."

"I look ten."

"Boys like that."

CHAPTER
— *Fourteen* —

Later, we slip out the back door—she doesn't even ask permission—and, dodging the raised garden beds, we go through the back gate and onto a street so full of trees, I can't see the sky. For a moment, I revel. Summer. Freedom. Cool air on my thighs. No mom—she still hasn't texted. I fight the urge to wipe the lipstick off my lips. It feels claustrophobic. I get déjà vu, search my memory until I settle on one: Halloween, my face covered in green makeup, wearing fishnet stockings so I could be a sexy witch when I went trick-or-treating at thirteen.

A few more blocks, and the trees are replaced by electrical poles. I point at a pair of shoes dangling from the wires. "What are those doing up there?"

Julia looks up. "Oh," she says. "Drug dealers somewhere around here. Probably that house." She points.

"Huh."

"You don't get high, do you?" she asks.

I shake my head.

"I wonder what you'd be like high."

"What are you like?"

"I dunno. You tell me."

I can't tell if she's being serious or not. "You're not high right now, are you?" I ask.

Julia laughs. "You're funny."

The boy standing on the next corner has hair like whipped egg whites — stiff blond peaks going every which way. He and Julia know each other and say hi. They go to school together. He introduces himself to me: "Xach — with an X," he says. His old army jacket doesn't quite fit at the shoulders.

"How do you know Julia?" he asks.

"Piano stuff," she answers.

He raises his eyebrows. "Cool."

We jaywalk, making swift diagonal cuts across the streets. They walk far faster than I do, Xach nonchalantly walking with a long stride, chin up, though he talks rapidly, nervously — more rapidly than Julia does. He's telling her about the tattoo he wants to get, if his parents let him. He keeps close to Julia, bending his head toward her and running his hand in his hair, and every time he says something sort of witty, he checks to see her reaction. Clearly, he's into her, though I can't tell if she likes him back.

At the end of a cul-de-sac, a set of stairs leads down between houses. "What is this place?" I ask. The stairs are narrow, and we push past overgrown plants with our legs.

"You'll see," says Julia.

They end at a large concrete expanse, lined with trees on either side, and a view — house lights and streetlights tracing the downward slope of the hill, and the black, formless void of the water. Sitting on the edge of the concrete, where it drops away, I make out someone waving us over. Julia points at the dark shape. "That's Lee."

I feel a thrill. But it takes me a moment to recognize him. He doesn't look as handsome in real life as he did in my mind. Not that he isn't handsome. He waves his hand. "Hey." His hair looks wet in the light.

Trees hem us in. We sit on the cold concrete, lined up on the foundation's edge. At our feet, farther down, a splotch of rooftop of the nearest house can be seen. No stars, just fog. Beyond the black expanse of water are more lights. I wonder where my home is, which twinkling light might be near my house, but I can't tell.

Julia digs in her bag and hands Lee a dog-eared book.

"Finally," he says teasingly, looking up.

She shrugs. "I'm a slow reader."

"What's that?" I ask.

The Mysticism of Sound and Music," she says.

He sits beside me but doesn't look at me.

"I like Rumi better," says Xach. "Can't help it. I'm a poet."

"It's all poetry," says Julia. She's settled in with her bag as a pillow, carefully lifting the tip of a lighter flame to the end of the joint.

"What kinds of things do you read?" asks Lee, turning to me.

The glowing tip hovers, arcs to Xach.

"T. S. Eliot." I think for a minute. "Ferlinghetti."

"We are the stuffed men," says Xach, smoke creeping out of his mouth. He coughs and passes it to me. "He makes me feel like the world is going to end."

"The world *is* going to end," Lee says.

"Do you really think so?" I ask. I try not to think about it, though I feel like week to week, things feel darker. It's been too hot. Too dry. There's barely been a winter. In my hands, the joint is as light and dry as a twig.

"She's never been high," murmurs Julia.

"Really?" says Lee.

Take some risks, Paul had said. I put it in my mouth and suck in like a straw.

"Oh, my God." Tears, coughing.

Julia giggles.

"You have to hold it in," Lee says. He takes the joint, shows me.

It goes around again. Xach is telling us about a girl he hung out with, one of those Burning Man–type girls who had a piercing in her tongue. I'm glad it's Julia who asks how that felt when they hooked up. He rolls his eyes and tells us he couldn't stop shaking.

I take another hit, but smaller this time. My mind begins to slowly spin, like a merry-go-round. My body is vaporizing.

"You should probably take it easy," says Julia, not unkindly. "You know, first time. Go slow."

"No one wants to go slow their first time," says Xach. Lee laughs.

I laugh a little late.

"Where do you go to school?" Lee asks.

"It's down in Fremont. You wouldn't know it."

"Oh, yeah, I heard the schools there are really good."

"Oh, that's Mission San Jose. That's not mine." *Mine's poor,* I think. "Mine's just a regular old school," I say.

"I wish I went to a regular old school," says Xach.

"No, you don't," says Lee.

"You're right. I don't." He lies back and stretches out a little. "No one wants to be ordinary." He eyes the tip of the joint, carefully rotating it so the paper burns evenly.

"What is this place?" I ask.

"My old house," Lee says. "Where it used to be. It burned down."

"Wow." His face is stoic, and I can't tell if he's upset. "Were you in it?"

He nods. "I was like, fourteen." There are patches of light from streetlights and the neighbors' windows, and I can just see his silhouette. Something about it makes my heart move closer to the bones of my ribs. We can hear people shifting in their kitchens. Dry voices from a television. A cupboard shuts.

"Were you able to rescue the cat?" Xach asks. "Family photo album?"

"My violin. My parents. Not the cat. Which is fine by me. I hated the cat."

"Did you get hurt?" I ask.

Xach laughs. "Tell her yes. Girls like damaged types." Julia smacks his arm.

"Well, it wasn't like we were stumbling and blind and, like, Terrence Malick–ish about it. It wasn't epic in a good way. It was like your head's like a Ping-Pong machine, just misfiring all over the place and you're trying not to heave."

He shifts closer to me, and it would only take a small shift for my cheek to touch his arm.

I should be practicing right now, I think. The thought reverberates in my head. Julia is mainly in shadow, and to me, her silhouette is flat, like a black piece of paper, and the vague texture of the trees behind her looks like another cutout, and the sky another. My head is as flat and as blank as a sheet of paper, too, and the idea of this terrifies me. I feel like I'd be unrecognizable to the people at home.

I really am high. I'm high and it's weird.

"Are you okay?" asks the black shadow that's shaped like Julia. "You look really stoned."

"I'm okay," I say thickly. This isn't what I thought it would be like.

"How are you?" I ask Lee, turning to him as if everything is normal. Like he didn't not call, and it didn't bother me, and I've been doing great. My eyes don't leave his.

"Good."

"You're doing Beethoven. The *Kreutzer.*"

"That's right. Though the day I met you I was a bit off." He seems abashed.

"I'm always a bit off."

He laughs, goes on. I can't catch much of what he's saying. I'm floating, and my body is farther away than it usually is, anchored to my mind by a thread.

Eventually his voice trails off.

"Are you high?" I ask. I am so loud in my head.

He pauses, then nods.

"Me too."

"It's good to be high once in a while. I get too wound up at school. I don't get to dream. It's all work."

"It's mostly work for me, too. But it's good with Paul. He lets me dream a little."

He nods. "That's what a good teacher is supposed to do."

Lee tilts toward me and I toward him. We touch arms. The silence between us goes metallic. I start to wish that everyone else would go away.

After a while, Julia picks up her bag. "I'm freezing, Claire. Let's go."

"Okeydoke." Slowly, stiff kneed, I get up, and Lee does, too. He kisses me on the cheek. "Let's play sometime."

"Definitely." I've never played with a violinist before. Or anyone as good-looking.

We walk down the hill. I'm still spacey from the pot and Julia's been really quiet and I can't tell why. I can't talk to her, not like I could with Tash.

As we turn the corner onto her street, she says, "So, you and Lee." She says it as if it's a business agreement. A flat reality you negotiate with a ballpoint pen and a spreadsheet.

"I guess?"

"He's a bit lackadaisical with girls."

Lackadaisical Lee. "He seems nice."

"Oh, yeah, he's a great guy. But he's a little, I don't know, easy come, easy go." I search her tone for jealousy, but it's hard to tell. She giggles when she sees my face. "Don't worry about it! Just, you know, have fun. Don't take him seriously."

"Oh. Okay."

My nose starts to run when we get inside. I'm back on earth again. The clock on the oven says 10:12.

"I really need to get home."

I must have said it too quietly, because Julia doesn't even notice. "Have you ever slept with anyone?"

I shake my head. "Have you?"

She starts opening cupboard doors and taking things down: a carton of Häagen-Dazs covered with ice fuzz, a can of whipped cream—organic, it says—and a large wooden spoon. She warms a bottle of chocolate syrup under running water. I sit down at the kitchen table.

She nods, as if she had checked something off a list. "Twice. With Joe."

That must be her ex-boyfriend. "What was it like?"

She spoons a heap of vanilla ice cream into her mouth, ejects a poof of whipped cream from the can right after, then quickly, with an expert tilt of the head, follows that with a squirt of chocolate syrup. She closes her mouth and her eyes.

I start clapping. She collapses into silent giggles and struggles to keep the ice cream in her mouth. "Shh!" she says with chocolate syrup on the corners of her lips, and points upstairs.

She hands me the spoon.

"It was crazy. Glad I got it over with, though." Julia looks down at her hands. "It wasn't that big a deal. It didn't hurt. Not even the first time. I did gymnastics when I was young, so."

"I did gymnastics, too," I say, ice cream in mouth.

She giggles at the sight of me studiously filling my mouth with whipped cream. As it melts into chocolaty richness, I wonder why I haven't thought of this before.

"Good, isn't it?"

I nod. I reach into the ice cream again.

"Uh-uh," she says, grabbing the spoon. "My turn. Can you still do stuff?"

"The splits."

"Both ways?

"No, just the one."

"Oh, I can do both." And she shows me, legs sliding wide apart on the kitchen linoleum, muscles straining. "It's from ballet."

CHAPTER
Fifteen

Going home, the train lights pushing into my eyes like cold screws, I wonder why Mom never texted back. She never got back about shopping or dinner. It's strange. Her danger sensors are always on maximum when I'm in the city.

I call her cell phone. She doesn't pick up.

I check my Instagram, look at Tash's pictures of baby birds nesting in a shoe, her new guitar, Julia's night pics from the hill. Then I check Facebook, which I haven't done in ages, but our family in the Philippines are on it. I skim over my cousin Virgil's post about how to make molten chocolate cakes in the microwave, then see a flood of messages to my mother and me. *My heart goes out to you always, but especially today.*

Love and light. Your father was a caring man, so musical, and I'm glad you are following in his footsteps. He is always near when you play.

Right. My dad died today. It's been five years without him.

———

I hop up the stairs to her room, unwilling to run, even though part of me desperately wants to.

No light in the crack beneath my mother's bedroom door.

"Mom?" Her room is stuffy and smells of scented tissues, sour breath. In a moment, I hear her breathing. She's probably been this way all day. Unable to get up.

"Claire?"

"Yeah?"

A pause, like she's rousing. "Where were you?"

"In the city. I . . . texted you. Didn't you get my texts?"

"No."

"Have you eaten?"

The noise she makes is noncommittal. "Don't open . . . the light."

I know what she means, but I turn it on anyway. She tsks. Her room is a bower of real and artificial flowers — on the bedspread, flanking the altar, on the cotton nightgown she's wearing. Jesus's mild, suffering face looks down on the bed. Pillows have been piled high on the side where she likes to lounge, watch Korean television, and pray. On the nightstand, small, multicolored novena prayer books are stacked beside a nest of rosaries. The other side of the room is clean and neat — an empty hollow where my father used to sleep, where I would come to sleep after he died, or stay up watching romantic comedies and, sometimes when she was feeling more melancholy, *The Sound of Music,* which held some significance she never explained to me.

She's buried in blankets. The plastic water bottle on the bedside table is empty, surrounded by balls of pink Kleenex. She's on her side, squinting in the sudden brightness.

Her cell phone's dead. I go to plug it in next to the TV in the corner, avoiding the gaze of the many Virgin Marys and Jesuses following me. Then I go downstairs to heat a can of soup for her. At the sound of the microwave beeping, Dean scratches at the glass door. Anger floods me. I should have remembered. But then I shouldn't need to remember.

Right after Dad died, she was in bed for months. At least now it's just a few days sometimes.

The dull yellow soup rotates in the microwave. I pry open a can of Pedigree and give it to Dean with a pat. My life seems nothing like Julia's. If Mom is like this in the morning, I'll ask Tita Anna to come over.

She slowly props herself upright, takes the soup. The spoon hovers closer to her mouth, full to the brim, then sits there. "Mom," I nudge her, and she blinks, opens her mouth.

I used to be scared when I saw her this way, but not anymore.

I know she might not eat if I leave, so I settle in beside her, in the place where Dad used to sleep, mold my body to her like a bookend that keeps her from toppling over. The newscaster recounts a gun death like it's an anomaly. I switch the channel, look for something happy, settle on a Harry Potter movie. My mother's spoon clinks. She won't talk to me about what's wrong. She never has.

After I check on her in the morning, I get my phone and text Tita Anna for help.

Tita Anna's hair is short, her fuchsia dress loose, with a pattern of tiny yellow-and-black diamonds on it.

"Where is she?" Tita Anna asks in a hushed tone after she presses her cheek to mine.

She kicks off her black block-heeled shoes and goes right upstairs in her stockinged feet.

Tita Anna is one of the church ladies who gives communion in nursing homes and teaches Sunday school. They've been friends for years. Through the door, I hear the tone of my mother's voice change, become more animated. She'll be okay.

I go outside to check on Dean. His dog tags scrape the cement when he hears me call softly for him. The complicated smell of fermented shrimp paste, at once so good and so strong that I can practically see it in the air, has hopped the fence from our next-door neighbors' house.

His breath comes too fast. He sniffs the salt of my hand, gives it a lick, but then he hears something I can't and goes to the hole in the fence that is just the right height for him to poke his nose into. He huffs once, twice. It may be the old Sikh grandparents from down the way, pushing their grandchildren to the park, or a mouse in the plantings.

Dean comes back and I pet him until I feel better, then we go inside and I give him breakfast.

I mount the stairs, Dean at my heels. My ears are tuned

to Mom's bedroom door. The mingled Tagalog and English is soon loud enough for me to hear through the wall, the lilting Tagalog taking a pause for Tita Anna to intone, in clear, accented English, the words "celebrate his life by living. Not by punishing yourself for still being alive," and then lapsing back into Tagalog.

I shut myself in my room, turn the pages of a college brochure. Lee-like boys. Glowing girls. The more I think about it, Stanford should be my first choice. Even though I'd like to see snow, what would my mother do without me?

Swifter steps than my mother's advance to my door. "Hon," says Tita Anna, "will you play something for us? Something your father would have liked?"

I go downstairs and start the slow, meditative beginning of the "Aria" from the *Goldberg Variations*. Quickly Tita Anna appears, shakes her head, and makes a gesture, as if shooing a fly. "No. Something happy. Something he listened to when he was healthy."

"Like what?"

"Don't you know?"

"I can't remember. Not right this minute."

I feel like I've left him behind somehow.

"Well, just something happy, then," Tita Anna says.

I give her something from Debussy. "The Children's Hour." I can hear her clapping when it's done.

CHAPTER
— *Sixteen* —

Later that week, in Paul's bathroom, I splash cold water on my face, put on some lip gloss, check my teeth, braid my hair in pigtails, and change out of my sweatshirt into the Future Sailors top I bought with Tash and the one little mini I own that reminds me of Julia's. I can't believe I'm going to meet up with Lee. A real date. He just texted yesterday — a little last-minute, but I'm bursting with excitement. I almost texted Tash to tell her, but it felt too awkward, so I didn't.

My clothes hook Paul's gaze like a fish, pulling it along as I saunter past. "Bye," I say, unable to stop from smiling.

I skip down the steps and bounce onto the bus, which drags. The city is turning blue, and car headlights glow sleepily. The Chinese lady sitting across from me with her big shopping bag looks tired, rocking with the bus, her eyes somewhere else.

I text my mom: *Running late today. Going to have dinner with friends.*

Not three minutes pass. *What friends?*

Julia.

You have to come home right after.

At last we're close. Near the front doors, the huge windshield gives me the sense of looking out from the prow of a boat sailing into port. I catch the driver glancing at my legs and I turn, giving my skirt a special flip as I step down.

I find Lee against the railing of the long staircase up to the school, reading a book, which he's folded backward in two. *Franny and Zooey*. Love Salinger. Immediately I like him just a little bit more.

"Do you ever get that way, where you've been practicing so much, talking feels weird?" he asks.

I laugh. "It's like your tongue has atrophied."

"Or like the talking part of my brain never got charged up."

"You need to do tongue push-ups."

He laughs. "Maybe later."

There are free shows in the small auditoriums on the first floor. We walk from one theater to the next to read the program notes that are posted on an easel beside each theater door. "No. No Mozart. Pretty as it is . . . Mmm . . . Beethoven . . . Oh. Hey. Here we go."

We duck into a small theater.

The string quartet has already begun.

"Philip Glass?" I whisper. Hard not to know the composer in the space of a few measures.

He nods, leading us down the back row. Stage lights

throw strange shadows from the oblong acoustic panels along the sides.

The strings wheel like birds, change course as one. The cellist drives her bow with such force, she sometimes comes off her seat. Impressions in a deluge: shards of water, crust cracks in the earth. Dust whorls. We're plunged into a sad dream. Her bow shivers on the glinting strings, drawing slow, ragged tones, as if it's lost its breath.

I'm jolted. Goosefleshed. Overwhelmed. I'm in love, though I'm not sure with what. Something.

He leans forward, his back ever so slightly curved. He holds his hands loose between his legs, soft like the way he sways when playing, and his eyes are lit as if inside him are filaments that flicker and shift and burn.

Intermission. The world is ordinary again. The lights are up. People are filing into the aisles. Carefully polite, cheery conversations. Lee sits back and sighs, and I know exactly how he feels, because I feel the same way. We've just glimpsed something rare—like a strange land you can only visit in dreams.

"What was that?" I ask.

"String Quartet number five."

"I've never heard it before."

We just sit there, not feeling like moving. People walk up the aisle on stiff legs, check their phones, state opinions loud enough to climb over other opinions. I feel surly, annoyed with them. With anything that pulls us back to earth.

Lee looks at me with a question in his eyes. "Can we . . . ?"

"Yeah."

He takes my hand and we move out of the auditorium, to the lobby, and then outside, into the cool air. Cars shear the night. There's no one outside. His T-shirt is nubby and thin, as if it's been washed a million times, and we're so close I can feel how warm his body is beneath it. He kisses me.

I'm in someone else's life.

We walk down the street, into another neighborhood, not talking much. Should we be talking more? I don't feel like talking. If we did, it would break the mood. I read the street signs and feel the air on my knees, try to memorize what my hand feels like in his.

"I'd rather be a quartet player than a soloist," he says. "I like the repertoire better. Plus it's nice to play with other people, don't you think?"

"I don't know. I haven't tried much."

"You should. It makes it more fun. Less crazy-making."

"The cellist was amazing, wasn't she?" I say.

"She was. They all were."

"Her especially. She was fierce." I wish Paul had seen her. Maybe it would change his mind about Asian musicians. Our steps make light, tapping, almost hollow noises on the side-walk. I let go of his hand and rub my arm, which has gotten cold. He puts his arm around me.

"Jealous?"

I don't answer.

"Come on. Admit it."

"Are you?"

He shrugs. "Totally. Comes with the territory. If you really want to be good at something, you end up being jealous of everyone around you. Even people who aren't playing your own instrument."

"I wish that weren't true." I think of Tash. I didn't even want her to play.

A homeless man asks for change and I shy away, feeling bad for him but not knowing what to do. Lee shakes his head no. Guilt on guilt. I lean against Lee, let my feelings pass. We walk by old movie theaters and nail salons, taquerias and diners. There are so many people on the street. Men in puffy jackets and Japanese denim, girls in unstructured, bland, earth-colored tees, tight jeans, long tribal-inspired shawls that for whatever reason are always on white girls but never brown ones. At home, you'd be lucky to run into someone walking their dog. Here, people are everywhere.

"Have you ever played on the street?" I ask.

"Yeah . . . sometimes for music department fund-raisers. But never, like, in the BART station."

"Why not?"

He laughs and doesn't answer. I guess it's a dumb question. Maybe only certain kinds of musicians do it, and others don't. I have no idea which one is which, but I'm pretty sure that he must belong to the one that doesn't, and this is somehow better.

We go to one of those yogurt spots where you can put on your own toppings, and he laughs at my choice of Fruity Pebbles. It's endearing that he even notices. After we finish, we meander around the streets.

"Fremont must be cool. I bet there's all kinds of really good food there. I love food from other countries."

"I guess we do have that: Asian bakeries next to boba tea shops next to Mexican bakeries. Indian supermarkets."

"Don't you guys have a Little Sheep?"

"The hot pot place?"

"Yeah. I love that place. There's one in San Mateo."

I don't see what the big deal is, but okay. "Maybe you could come out sometime."

"Maybe." He laughs. "We could go on a food tour. There isn't any decent pani puri around here." I wonder what pani puri is, but let it go. He walks. "There're probably some cool Filipino restaurants, too."

"Home is better." Not that Mom makes much of an effort anymore.

He tells me about the book he's reading about positive thinking, about the music he's composing, a song cycle inspired by the different emotional qualities of fire. He would love to be a music director. Go down to LA, write scores for Wes Anderson movies.

Lee is perfect. I could see myself with him. Living in Laurel Canyon.

"I'd love to play for movies."

"Yeah?" He stops and looks at my face and we start to

kiss. His hands are underneath my top, palms flat on the surface of my belly, cold and tickly.

"My apartment is nearby." I'm not looking him in the eyes, but at the stubble that covers his Adam's apple.

"Um . . ." If we go somewhere, it would feel like—I don't know.

"Never mind," he says before I can decide. One last kiss, a promise for another time, and he's gone.

The next morning. Luminous. I'm all lit up inside with kisses. I find the *Kreutzer Sonata* on my laptop and listen.

A handsome boy likes me, and I like him, too. I really do think that the way you play shows the quality of your soul. It shows the way you think, what you feel, and what you are capable of feeling. And there's such a sweetness to the way he plays. It reminds me that the world is a caring place.

Deep down, he's a good person.

There is something about having been kissed that changes everything. A real kiss. Not like seventh-grade spin-the-bottle games. Or for three months in the eighth grade, there was Matt Rogers, a boy in the neighborhood that was my boyfriend, which meant we talked on the phone every night and held hands. But this kind of kissing, with the kind of person that makes me feel not just normal, but super-normal. Like maybe I'm not such a freak, with barely any friends and who replays songs, or conversations, or whole movies in my head because there isn't that much else to do. Maybe he likes me because I am exactly that kind of person.

Happiness flows in. The bedroom is shining. Even the small, struggling trees in the neighbor's yard shine. I read *Siddhartha,* swallow it down like a sweet, heavy fruit. In the walls, the water is running. Mom's taking a shower. She's holding it together. Her depression passed like a storm. Her directions are back to rapid-fire speed. *Clean this; do that. You're home fifteen minutes late.* It's almost comforting.

The sound of the shower is the signal. It's time to take off for the city. Do the recordings. I don't feel timid or voiceless today. And I'm so going to kill it at the competition next week.

CHAPTER
—— *Seventeen* ——

I put on a dress that Julia let me borrow, a tangerine, tissuey dress with spaghetti straps, pin up my hair, pack up my recording equipment, and head to the conservatory.

The rooms are deserted, so the Yamaha I like best is free. I start in on the Bach Prelude and Fugue in C-sharp Minor, from Book II. Wait for magic, but nothing is coming easily with my phone mounted to a tripod, recording everything.

I try to forget the phone, think of Lee. Lee who is the perfect height. Who knows who Philip Glass is. Who goes into tunnels in the park to play. Who reads Salinger and always seems to know where he's going. Who wears the softest jeans.

Beethoven rises to meet me, flies from a distant galaxy to touch me. My arms are as flexible as chewing gum. Fingers scurry like insects. I play flat out, as if racing to some finish line, as if I can't wait. Don't think. Just do. Do things like Lee might.

He texts. My heart beats in double time. *Hey. Free later? Wanna kick it?*

I'm in the practice rooms. Come on by.

I play back my performance, wince, take off my glasses, try again.

I move on to Brahms, then Shostakovich — hardly sexy, but it's flashy. It'll be a good one for him to walk in on, but he doesn't. I'm playing the ballade when he walks in.

"Impressive," he says from behind.

I jump and look at him, then down at his violin case. "Hi."

"Nice dress."

"Thanks. It's Julia's."

He glances at the phone. "Smart to do this in a practice room." He sits abnormally close. A bit of my dress is pinned beneath his thigh.

"Do you feel like playing?" I ask. "I'm not sure how we'd do that. I don't have any of the right sheet"—he kisses my neck, and my little bird heart starts going thumpity-thump— "music. The phone's still recording." I giggle. I turn it off and put it in my bag, though not before I take a picture of us together.

I kiss him back, wondering how my body knows what to do. It's like when you start singing along to a song on the radio that you didn't know you knew. All I have to do is follow his lead and brush away my fear.

Time slips into another gear. He goes and flips the light switch and locks the door. I'm a little bit scared but not enough to stop anything. The melody from the piece I just played repeats over and over in my mind, like it's never stopped.

The kisses deepen, his teeth graze my lips, but I guess I always knew that he kissed like this because of the way he moves when he plays. The fabric of my dress brushes my legs as it moves up. He's picked up the hem, slid his hand beneath it. I press against him. Our breathing makes a strange antiphonal call and response, one breath of mine following at the heels of one of his. He finds his way between my legs.

"You're okay with this?"

"Mm-hm." At last. My voice has taken a strange, high-pitched tone.

He puts his hand beneath my dress and a finger slips beneath my panties. I lean into him, rest my forehead on his shoulder. The music has stopped. "You are so wet." His finger pushes inside of me and I hold my breath. "Are you a virgin?"

I nod, and because I'm not sure he can see my face, I tell him so. "Yes."

I'm disappointed when his fingers withdraw.

It's true what they say. Nobody wants to be someone's first.

So he puts my hand between his legs. I pretend not to be scared, like I know what I'm doing, and touch him through his jeans, which he unzips, and I do what I've seen on the Internet, what people who don't talk to me at school talk about in the hallways. Or at least what I think they do. When his breathing gets louder, I go on with it, figuring it out as I go by the look on what I can see of his face and me thinking, knowing, that this is what I've been missing all this time. And I don't mind, actually. It's kind of nice. There's a strong odor of sweat, and then he comes, his hand touching my arm, like he's reaching out to me.

We hear footsteps outside, and for no reason I can logically comprehend, it makes me giggle. I grab a Kleenex from my bag and touch it to his thigh; the semen slides along his skin, slimy, and doesn't soak into the tissue. He doesn't move while I do this, as if he doesn't want it to spread. It's disgusting, and the look on his face is slightly revolted, too. For a moment, I think he may be revolted with me but then he takes over, wipes his thigh briskly, folds the Kleenex carefully over it as if trapping a dead, crushed bug inside.

He zips his pants up, and in a sweet, serious, slightly possessive way, he kisses me, and asks if I'm hungry in a low, different voice. I've never heard that tone before.

As we walk to a nearby burger place, he holds my hand lightly, so lightly I keep wondering if he's about to let go. For his four steps, I take five. A thing has happened. I don't know how serious it is. If he will stay with me after this. I feel as if we are loosely, invisibly tethered to each other.

He gives a wave to the hostess. "How's it going?"

"Hey," she says. Her smile is small and cool and familiar. She turns to lead us to a table, her gaze drifting to me, my dress, which must look odd here. I wonder how many girls he knows.

We eat French fries, dipping them into the same puddle

of ketchup, but he doesn't eat burgers because he's vegetarian, so I don't get one, though I'm starving. The lights in here make me feel spacey.

His gaze strays past my shoulders and in a rush to keep it, I ask how Salinger is.

"It's eh. I don't know. Too close to home sometimes. I'm reading Dostoyevsky now. Ugly, pure. It's not like American things. Like this place?" He gestures around Burger Box. "It's like they don't want you to feel things anymore. Just eat your hamburger and get fat and watch television and die not having done anything or having lived. Do you know what I mean?"

"Totally. I feel like if I stayed in Fremont, that would be exactly what my life would be like."

"You should leave."

"I hope to. I mean, the main reason I started playing seriously was so I could get into college."

"Well, you're obviously talented," he says seriously. "You're with Paul and everything. He can't take just anyone."

"I guess that's true." I chew. "Yeah, lessons are different. I've never had any like them before. It's like, every time I go, I change."

He pops another French fry into his mouth. "Has he started to quote spiritual literature at you yet?" he asks. "Julia told me he does that."

"No. Though he does get poetic at times."

"Yeah. I hear that gets to the ladies." He rolls his eyes.

I look askance. "He doesn't do it on purpose, does he?"

He shrugs. "Probably. Doesn't matter. It works."

"Well, not with me," I say. "I'm dating you." Oh, God, did I say that? "Seeing? Seeing, dating. Whatever." I stare hard at my French fry.

"Definitely whatever. I don't really define things according to what other people think things are supposed to be like. Do you know what I mean? It's just a label."

"Yeah," I say. "Totally." I start eating fries two at a time.

"Anyway, as for Paul"—he shrugs—"I'm sure he can't help it if women like him." He opens his hands, as if helpless. "They throw themselves at him."

"Has Julia . . . ?"

"I don't know." He wipes his mouth a little primly with a napkin, then shakes his head. He looks annoyed. "Not my business."

I wouldn't be surprised if Paul has dated students. Not that he seems like a lech or anything. It's just, you can't really tell how old he is. It just doesn't matter with him. What he is during our lessons—that's what matters.

Lee walks me to the train station after we finish eating. He's so quiet again that I start feeling weird. Like maybe he's bored.

"We could play next time," I say. "If you want."

"Sure, we could do that."

"Friday? After my lesson?"

"Uh-huh." He gives me a quick kiss good-bye, one hand on his violin and the other in his pocket. I rattle down the stairs as fast as possible, giving a hop to take the last few.

CHAPTER
—— *Eighteen* ——

A few days later, I take the bus to the mall to buy a proper bra. A sexy bra. And panties to match. I'll see Lee again on Friday, and I don't have any nice underwear.

The mall hasn't changed at all since I've grown up. It's small, three colors of beige, with a huge parking lot. Shabby, especially compared to the kinds of places there are near Julia's house, or near Paul's. And garish. The bra department at Macy's greets you at its entrance with shiny purple and rose-colored bras. Sturdy. Loud as parades.

I wish Tash were with me. I almost texted her, mostly to share the news about Lee. But then I thought about it and realized that maybe she would disapprove of what I was doing with him, and I don't need that.

I squish the foam cup of a bra between two fingers, turn the price tag over. It smells like wet cardboard and honeysuckle in here.

"Can I help you find something?" An older lady with a name tag and a ton of hair spray squints at me through her spectacles, as if trying to tell if I'm here to steal underwear.

"No, thanks!" Please don't appraise my breasts, thank you very much. Please don't tell me I shouldn't be doing what I'm doing.

I move away, trying to look innocent. Inches away, another girl—a woman, actually—is looking at the same candy-pink, polka-dotted bras with ruffles along the top. They're French-cut, the label says. We carefully avoid looking at each other.

I go for a white mesh one without padding. It looks a little sexy but not too porn star. What am I, a 32A? I've read magazines that tell you to get measured, but there's no way I'd ever ask one of the ladies carefully winding straps around plastic hangers to examine my boobs like a picture they're about to frame.

I make a swift dash for the dressing room as if God is watching me doing something wrong. On the way, one of those extremely puffy bras that are supposed to give you massive Marilyn Monroe breasts beckons. So I grab it.

The dressing room air is stale and sour. The curtain in my stall won't close all the way. Keeping one eye fixed on the gap for passersby, I take off my shirt, free the mesh one from its hanger, and put it on.

I barely fit the cup, but it's really not too bad.

I lift my hair up, off my neck, and pile it on my head. My skin shines where the little bones of my rib cage arch up. I still feel nerdy, so I remove my glasses, and look again. In the mirror, my body and my face are a blur. I like the way I look.

I try on the padded, machine-gun bra, put my shirt back

on, and start laughing. There's a curving ridge through my T-shirt, a sharp outline of the top part of the bra. It's a topographic map of a mountain range. What would a boy think if he saw this? It's like a padded room for my boobs. It's like boobs on top of boobs.

I go back to the rack with the mesh one to try to find matching panties, but they're all G-strings. Butt-cheek city.

I grab an extra-small pair, head to the register, and try to smile. The lady is all business, like, yes, of course, sexy clothes, whatever, you have sex. Maybe she sees people like me come through all the time. Like maybe this is normal, and no one talks about it. No one I know personally anyway. Certainly not my mother. It's like there's something wrong with it. Something to be ashamed of.

Muzak softly playing in the background, the woman takes my money, barely looking at me, completely oblivious to the unveiling of underwear before Lee's eyes that would soon, hopefully, be taking place.

On the way out, I spy a beauty shop. Facials, thirty-two. Brazilians, forty. I check my wallet. Still flush. Bracing myself, I go in.

The garage door is open, and my mother is standing behind her parked green Toyota Corolla, trunk open, smoothing out the curve of her grocery receipt as she reads the coupons on the back for haircuts and car washes. She calls me over, tearing one carefully out.

"Help me," she says, not looking at me, instead placing

the sliver of the receipt carefully into her coin purse and snapping it shut. She doesn't wait for a reply and begins heading inside. All of this is to my relief, as I'm walking gingerly from the waxing, mincing my steps, and I don't want her to notice it.

She shuts the garage door behind her, and I'm left with the grocery bags and the sharp smell of laundry detergent. Hostess Donettes are balanced on top of the cereal boxes. Dean dancing around my legs, I haul the food in as fast as possible, hefting as many bags as I can in at a time. But then I can't enjoy the order, the system, and the simplicity of putting away the food, the way I usually do — the ice cream in the same bag with the quart of two percent, which props up the bag of frozen corn. Maxipads are perched on top. Nunnish pads.

"Mom," I call, dumping the bag on the kitchen floor.

"Yeah?" Her voice sounds as if she's in her bathroom.

"Can you get me tampons next time?" I shove the ice cream into the freezer, resisting the urge to stick my head in.

She emerges from the hall. "Why do you need those?"

"I feel gross with pads."

I feel her looking at me, trying to understand, but I don't look back.

"But pads are healthier."

"But most girls use tampons."

All of a sudden, I realize that I just told her I was willing to put something, anything, inside my vagina. That I even have one. We both stand there, two people acknowledging that they have vaginas after many years of pretending they didn't.

When I got my period, we didn't talk about it. I just grabbed a pad from beneath my mom's bathroom sink and she eventually just started getting two boxes, I think, instead of one. There really wasn't much to talk about, anyway. School, the Internet, and television took care of all of that.

She unearths a cantaloupe from one of the bags.

"Playtex. The slim ones," I say.

"You can get an infection."

I laugh. "That's only if you leave them in for days."

She looks at me again, piercing me from another angle.

"It's just more comfortable, I think. It seems like it, anyway."

She laughs grimly. "Just wait until you try them."

Eager to escape, I leave the rest of the bags on the floor of the kitchen and get a glass of ice water—more ice, less water—and go to my room. I dig my new bra out of my backpack. The light goes right through it. I hide it under my bed.

CHAPTER
—— *Nineteen* ——

On Friday, Julia opens Paul's door, waving happily when she sees me.

"Guess what! I'm going to Interlochen!"

"Huh?"

"The music camp," she says patiently.

He's even more beardy than last week. "One going to Interlochen, the other going to the Lener. I'm absolutely bursting with pride," he says, smiling.

"The Lener, huh?" She purses her lips. "Hoy-tee-toy-tee."

"Well, I haven't been accepted yet."

"I'm sure you will be. Anyway, let's hang out soon. Catch up before I go."

"Right, then," Paul says when we're alone. "I have more notes from last week. Now, it was lovely, really," he says when he sees my face. "But you really aren't there yet."

"The beginning of the ballade last week had a dark glitter to it," he says. "So elegant. But as it got darker, you began to lose its emotional through line to the next part of the piece. It's like you were anxious to get through it." He speaks slowly, as if under a great weight. It's strange.

"Is there something wrong? Do you have a headache or something?"

He laughs. "Oh, I'm fine. I mean, I'm not, not really, but thank you for asking."

"Well, if you ever want to talk about it."

He gestures with his pencil. The piano again. "Now, you have to really get into the darkness to find what will propel the piece back into the light. Otherwise it won't feel spontaneous."

I swim into it, a few measures before the second theme. A burning rhomboid of afternoon light has broken free of the curtains and landed on the wall opposite.

Paul touches my upper arm lightly, and I drop my shoulders.

"Neck," he says.

I straighten it, pull my chin back. The arms should be heavy, the weight of them poured into the keys. The textures of the piece adjust, settle into the feeling of the room—a warm, generous afternoon, every moment ticking and falling away, round and shining.

"Close your eyes."

My underwear is a secret against my skin.

He touches my shoulders, and for a moment I feel as if my arms are just extensions of his. It's like I don't have to try. If I think about it, the piece will startle awake, lose its feverish, dreaming core.

The end floats away. A devilish grin spreads on my face, because it's good—finally, really good.

He looks at me. After a moment he says, "Your devotion shows."

I pull my shoulders back, basking in the words.

"It's easier when you're young," he says offhandedly. "You can just let it happen. It's harder when you're older to re-create that feeling that everything is new. You have to be vulnerable. And it's hard to be vulnerable when you're older." Pride glints in his eyes. "You have to practice even more when I'm gone."

I droop. "Where are you going?"

"I've been asked to sit in for a short tour over the summer. A piano trio. Paid vacation," he says. He sees my face. "Oh, come, now, it won't seem that long—I promise."

I pack up, saying nothing. I don't want him to go. Not now. "Oh, I tried to do another recording. For the competition." I dig my phone out and hurriedly e-mail it to him, a wave of nervousness coming over me as I push send.

"Excellent! I'll listen to it directly. If it's anything like what we did today, I'm sure it's fine. We're submitting late, but I know these people."

After my lesson, I stroll down the hill toward Civic Center. My earbuds dangle around my neck in case I feel like listening to music, but I don't. I want to hear everything around me: cars and buses and cell phones and dogs' claws scraping the sidewalk, the ticking sound of a bicycle, homeless people talking to themselves, troops of hipsters. Wind in trees. Any other time I'd be worrying about the Lener, but since I'll see Lee soon, I want to be in the world.

I drop a dollar I can't afford to give into the case of a guitarist who plays sloppily on old dull strings, but I like the song, an old bossa nova tune. I doubt Paul would like it. Or Lee.

And then I put a quarter in the cup of a homeless person, who nods and says thank you. A thing I've never done before, and it feels strange and good.

Jasmine smell oozes from flowers wriggling through the slats of a fence. Pastries make eyes at me from a window and I enter the shop, come out with a mouth full of cookie. I linger in front of store windows. I'm in awe of a dress, of a pink clutch, a gauzy, rose-colored scarf. I check the time. One hour to go before I meet Lee.

A worn bookstore. Jazz plays politely over the speakers. The books whisper. A journal with its heavy cream pages and fine, blue-green lines looks meant for me. I tuck it under my arm and wander over to the art section. I check the time again. Would it be better to be late? Lateness seems more romantic, so I drift over to Dostoyevsky, run a finger over the thick, important-looking spines. These are the books he likes? How does he find the time to read?

I leave the journal and buy *Crime and Punishment* instead.

———————

He stands in front of the AMC Metreon, which looks a bit like a space video game that's been turned into a building. It glows like a television. The sides of the building are made of glass. Inside, people slouch in sleek armchairs, staring at screens, playing games. Other people cluster at their sides, also staring, mesmerized. The chairs are full. It's supposed to be a place for entertainment and shopping in one, but watching people stare at screens is really, really boring, even depressing, and all my excitement of standing next to him leaches out.

Our faces are cast in blue.

"Do you really want to go in here?" I ask.

"I do, actually."

"Me too." I don't want to like the place, but everyone around us seems so hell-bent on being here, I'm curious.

We're swept up in a tide of people, lights in the floor flashing like pinball lights. I keep thinking we're going to break one when we step on them, or that they'll make a sound. A hand slides along my back and around my waist. He looks down to see my reaction. I lean my head against Lee's shoulder, muffling the sound of all the conversations rising up with us on the escalators. We look at the books on their carousels at a bookstall—cookbooks for ninjas, Hello Kitty coloring books—and the stores full of photo booths and stickers. It's too loud to talk. Everything is glossy and cool, like a magazine—the floors, the plants, the large store signs.

"I don't get it," I confess, turning to check Lee's reaction.

He shrugs. "Maybe there's nothing to get. There's a movie theater up there. I think that's where most people are going."

His arm, which has circled around my shoulder, tightens. We kiss. I feel my body softening so that when he presses his hands into me, they press harder. "Feel like a movie?"

"Not really. I want to go to your place."

His gaze is heavy. "Okay," he says. There's a strain in his voice, and I feel a flash of warning; it subsides.

I'm so excited about what's about to happen, I don't even realize we're outside until we are.

Our strides match in the reflection of a storefront glass. Those are the eyes of a girl that's just been kissed. I catch the glance of a boy on the street, knowing his eyes have been on me as we approach.

"It's like *A Clockwork Orange* in there," he says.

"Like people don't want to be human. They looked so happy, though."

"They're probably faking it," he says. "Who could be possibly happy with just a superficial, anesthetized life?"

"My mom would like it."

"I bet." He smirks.

I feel stung. "Well, she'd rather be in the U.S. than back in the Philippines and poor."

"Have you ever been back there?"

"No. We don't have the money. But my mom says I wouldn't like it anyway. Too hot."

"I'd like to go there someday."

"Maybe you could come with me." Oops. "Not that I'm going anytime soon."

He laughs. So embarrassing.

His apartment building is plain, not gingerbready like Paul's house. I'm a teeny, tiny bit disappointed.

"Are your parents home?"

"Nope. They're out for the night." Of course they are.

He whistles on the way to his room, like he's more relaxed. A metal music stand holds music in the corner. His violin case is at the foot of his bed. Paperbacks are scattered beside it, the sheets neatly done. He's tidier than me. I watch him from the edge of the bed while he busies himself with the stereo.

"You have a turntable."

"Uh-huh. It's the best way to listen to stuff."

I flip through his records, pretending to be interested.

"I think my dad had records."

"Yeah? Anything good?"

"I don't know. I don't know where they went."

"That's too bad."

I sit down next to him. It's so cold, it chills me through my skirt. I'm staring openly at his lips, just waiting for him to touch me, but he's still talking—about records, and how

156

intimate they sound, compared to digital music or the radio. "Analog recordings store information in natural sound waves, and CDs and MP3s are just zeros and ones. They aren't natural to the human ear."

"Aren't they?"

"Yeah. That's why they sound harsher," he says, his eyes taking on a cool glint before he puts his palm between my shoulder blades and pulls me toward him.

The end of one kiss predicts the beginning of the next. They slur together like notes. His hands press on the small of my back and I can feel my nipples tighten against his chest. I pull off my shirt. There's no way I'm going to stop this. It's definitely the way things should be, even if it's supposed to be something I shouldn't do. In this case it feels really good to be doing something I shouldn't be doing. I'm digging the music and the feel of his bedsheets—soft and old—against my back.

My skirt comes off in one tug. He doesn't say anything about my underwear. I don't think he even notices it—it just slides right off, after the skirt. I turn to face him. He pulls off his shirt, his eyes running over me at the same time.

"You're beautiful," he says. Two words and I change. Suddenly I feel safer. His body is long and white, his spine curved like a bow. He kicks free of his jeans. I look between his legs, wishing I could take a longer look without seeming pervy.

The next song isn't really to my taste, but I try not to

think about it. We get under the covers. His sheets are cold. I wiggle closer to him to warm myself. I can feel his erection against the ridge of my pelvis, between my legs. I feel kinda weird. I feel like we should be talking more. His lips are unbearably soft, and all I can think about is where we touch. Beneath my hands, his shoulder blades are smooth, curved like river stones. I imagine he's soft inside, the way he feels outside. I'm nervous—there's nothing to stop us but me saying no. Not that I would. There's something bright here, something that keeps me afloat. The music. The fact that things feel good. How nice it is not to be alone.

I feel his fingers between my legs, and my eyes widen. They're cold and rough at first, but I don't want him to stop. I can't get close enough. I want him to go slower. I want him to go faster. I slide a hand between us, and he holds his breath when I reach into the dark space and grasp him, damp and soft skinned as a baby, and firm. I forget my part in things, and let him do all the work. Sweat collects between my forehead and his shoulder.

"Are you sure you want to do this?"

A yes beats in me like an insect's wing. I nod. He turns over onto his side and reaches into his bedside drawer. An awkward, almost formal pause. He struggles to open the wrapper and push the condom down around him. It looks silly and gross, but I don't laugh.

He turns toward me again, and his fingers return. No, not his fingers. His breath catches. All the bonds between the cells of my body break, and I'm not me anymore. I'm the space between stars. I'm the color of my eyelids, when I've shut them against the sun.

"Are you okay?" he asks.

I nod, pinned down and holding him to me at the same time. He starts to move. I shut my eyes tight. It feels like I'm not breathing, even though I am. I'm amazed by the noises I make. I don't know where they've come from—I've never heard them coming from me. It doesn't hurt. I'm surprised it doesn't hurt. It feels good, though not the way I thought it would. The fear doesn't leave me, but it doesn't matter as much as what's happening. Bright dark burning shining wetness ache need to be loved. It feels like I'm finally doing something I've wanted to do for a long time.

The record starts to skip. His eyes flick to mine, but he breaks his gaze when he catches me staring at him.

He won't look at me for the rest of it. After a while I give up and look away, too. For some reason, it's easier.

He makes a noise like someone punched him in the gut, and stops. I look over his shoulder at the ceiling, continuing to hold him because there isn't anything else to hold on to.

The fridge's buzz from the other room kicks on. The soft sound of a car as it passes. Normal things that don't sound normal right now.

He looks at me. I look at him. He smiles without teeth, touches my cheek. I try to keep very still, as if it would keep him from moving away from me. Then with an awkward movement, so that the condom stays on him, he rolls over. There is a small mole on his back that looks penciled in with a brown crayon. A moment with a tissue. Then he reaches and flips the record.

Music. Back to regular life. "Where are you going?" I attempt to put a smile on my face, but it won't stay.

"Nowhere." He gets up with a grunt, fishes his boxers out from under the sheets, and stretches the neck of his T-shirt as he shoves it over his head. Fumbles with the buttons of his jeans. He feels me staring and he looks at me, gives another smile. The space between us hangs like it's on crutches. For a moment I remember, of all people, Julia. Is this what sex was like for her?

"Here it is." He stoops down and picks up my skirt.

Moving takes so much time. My back is stiff, bruised. My shirt feels dirty, putting it back on, both the shirt and my skin. My body doesn't feel quite like mine. I want him to say something. Something sweet. I want him to hold me.

"Was that any good?" I can feel the sound reverberating in my head. Why do I feel like my head is stuffed with cotton?

He lets out a puff of breath. "Yeah!" He kisses my cheek. The sweat he's left on my skin is cooling. Goose bumps. My throat is dry.

He sits and watches me button my skirt and tie my shoes—it seems so hard all of a sudden, tying my shoes—and when he walks me outside, there's no mention of seeing me later. "What are you working on?" he asks. His eyes have a glint in them. He's interested.

This is it. This is what it's like to get involved. It seems so thin.

"Oh. You know. I guess you heard some of it already."

"All you have to do is walk down this street, hop on the 21, and you'll be back at Civic Center again."

"Okay. Got it." I keep smiling and follow his lead.

CHAPTER
— *Twenty* —

The summer pales. I try to fix the mistakes Paul pointed out last week, all the while sending out subconscious signals into the sky, west over the bridge, toward Lee, imagining I'll get an answer back. He'll text; of course he will.

Everything will be fine. Everything is already fine. I think it's fine.

So why do I feel this way? It's supposed to be okay to sleep with people and move on. To be light. Have fun. This is what other people do.

I wish I had someone to talk to. There's no way I'd tell Julia. And Tash, well, even if we were on good terms, it's still embarrassing. I don't know how I'd explain to her that I wish there had been more. I didn't know that I would want more. It's irrational, but there it is.

I don't love him, but at least it would be nice to talk to him. Make sure it's okay, what we did. That he's not disrespecting me. Purposefully ignoring me. It seems strange to have sex and then not hear from someone at all.

Plus I've felt a little hollow since then. Like lonelier than I was before we did it.

I let Dean in when my mother isn't looking — she might protest since he's overdue for a bath. He comes in, relief shining in his eyes, and gives a quick sniff of the air to take account of things. I rub my cheeks in the soft fur between his ears, and he stays still for me and presses back and fills my heart.

I stay home, lounge on the couch, watch Netflix with my mom.

"Something's wrong," she says.

"Why do you say that?"

"Because. I can tell."

"No. Nothing's wrong."

"You sure?"

"Yeah. I'm just tired."

She sighs. "Fine. Don't tell me."

Her watch beeps on the hour. Time to pray. She puts the television on mute, crosses herself, and mutters under her breath. For some reason, I thought she'd take one look at me and know I'd lost my virginity. Like it would be obvious.

Not that I would just tell her or anything. She'd get weird. Maybe try to take me to a shrink or a priest. I'm pretty sure she'd be upset with me. Like I did something I wasn't supposed to do.

I don't want to see the look she'd get on her face.

And she wouldn't want me going to the city anymore.

I know I'll never tell her.

I shift a little away from her, so we aren't touching.

A few days later, Julia wants to see if we can sneak into the erotic Picasso exhibit at the de Young, so I take the train in and meet her there.

"Isn't that eighteen and over?" I'd asked when she mentioned it.

"Yeah, but they can't be serious."

At the counter, a girl asks for IDs. Julia pulls out an ID, tossing a furtive glance my way, and hands it over.

"I forgot mine," I tell the girl.

"Well, you can't go in, then."

"I've seen naked people," I tell her. Julia stifles a laugh.

She shakes her head. Her eyes have taken on a special, stubborn gleam. No.

"Just go in," I tell Julia.

"You sure?" I nod and go outside, check my phone. Paul's assistant, Andrew, texted, asking to see the photo I'm sending along with my application. No other messages. Nothing from Lee.

I'd just feel better if he was friendly to me. He doesn't even have to want me. He could just say hello.

A whole week passed with no word from him. Then I texted him to see how he was, and he waited a whole day to answer. *Good. Busy with summer plans.* No asking to get together. He didn't even ask how I was. It feels worse than rejection. It feels like he hates me.

It's sunny out. There are skaters and couples and old, well-dressed men with ice-cream cones and pale people in shorts — obviously not from here — with fanny packs. There are jingling hippie girls swathed in orange. Gaunt goth boys wearing anime T-shirts. Tall, lanky boys in oxfords and cardigans. Glossy, glammy Asians in full makeup and comfortable shoes. It's a big, mashed-up stream of humanity, strolling and Rollerblading and laughing and strutting and clomping and sick and unbearably happy, the kind of happy that makes me jealous.

After a while, Julia comes back. "Oh, my God, there were so many couples there. It was disgusting!"

"I wonder what they'll be doing tonight."

"The best piece was the one with the woman giving a blow job."

She shows me a postcard, giggling, of a man reclining, a woman's head buried facedown in his lap. Her hair hides her face. He smiles dreamily, as if he owned the world. Both of them have been dipped in blue. I try to giggle, but it sounds weird, even to me. I don't know how to respond.

I think about telling her. I'd like to. I've been feeling odd lately, like there's some clear glass wall between me and the rest of the world. It's been hard to feel things. So much so, I wonder if that's what Paul had meant when he said it got harder to make things feel new when you get older.

"Was it boring out here?"

"Compared to inside? No one was mating. So, yeah."

Then we're off to Stow Lake — she wants to see the

ducks and ducklings. The baby ducks are beautiful, with their mottled, mussed-up brown feathers. They're the size of tennis balls, turning about in the water with vicious thrusts, or else hiding behind their more grave-looking mothers resting on the sidewalk along the lake.

We take a selfie. "Nice," she says, looking over my shoulder at my phone. I upload it to Instagram. "Can you text it to me? I want to post it, too."

"'Course."

"My dad used to take me to see these guys," Julia says. "When I was younger." She's brought a crinkly plastic bag full of old bread, and she's starting to throw it into the sudsy green water piece by piece.

"And now?"

She shrugs. "He's too busy with Mom right now."

"I know what that's like," I say, remembering. She looks at me curiously. "My dad died when I was a kid."

She opens her eyes wide. "That sucks."

"Yeah."

"Do you miss him?"

I wonder if she thinks her mother will die. I recognized the look in Danielle's eyes. The resignation and the guilt. "Sometimes I feel like I've just gotten used to missing him all the time. Like it's there even when I'm not really feeling it."

Julia plops bread in front of a handsome, sleek new duckling. I want to pat her shoulder, but maybe she's the type to hate that. It can seem so fake. When my dad died, all these people wanted to hug me. I think they just felt bad themselves, so I let them.

"I think I know what you mean. They want me to live my life like I would if things were normal. Though honestly, this is normal. This is my normal. It's been like this a long time. There's no point in shipping me off to camp." She shrugs. "Things are fine. I'm practicing. I hung out with Lee and his new squeeze."

"His new what?" I watch a piece of bread submerge just beneath the surface of the dark water. A duck seizes it with a fierce thrust of its beak, then makes a sharp U-turn, its head turning this way and that.

"Yeah. One of our classmates. They're sickening." In the water's reflection, she checks her hair, and tucks a strand that's come loose from her ponytail behind her ear.

I don't know what to say. I feel as small as a penny. Silently, shuddering with my exhales, I throw more bread into the water, the ducks quacking with joy.

"What's she like?"

"Gorgeous. Plays oboe. They've known each other for ages. Very strong-willed. She might actually tame him."

"Then it's serious?"

"He seems serious. Though you know him. So hyperactive. He looks at every girl like they're peaches at the farmers market. Just has to sample every variety. And he's traveling this summer. Vietnam. I asked him if he would try to hook up with anyone over there and he said, 'Who wouldn't mind seeing a country through the soul of a girl?' It's like he's on the It's a Small World ride at Disneyland, the X-rated version. Though he said that before he hooked up with Georgia, so maybe he'll be different now."

The thing about sadness: when you play music, it has a place to go. It goes into the keys and then it goes into the air and out the window and on the wind and then into the ground like the dead. You can play until you're completely empty.

So fast. Was he seeing her at the same time? He must have been.

She's probably prettier than me. Better at music. More sophisticated. She probably knows where to get pani puris, has read all of Salinger. And Dostoyevsky. I put the thought into a broken chord, willing it away.

I look through photos of me for my application. Not one of them is remotely good. Sleepy eyes. Dress straps askew. Reflective nose. Uncomfortable smile. Toothiness. Shorts. Glasses. That timid look, the one that makes me look like my mother.

"Mom!" I knock on her bedroom door.

"What?"

I open it. I peek in to see her kneeling at her altar. Her beads drip along her thigh. "Do you think I can get contacts?"

"Why?"

"For performance. You know. Paul says that a lot of what people hear is affected by how you look."

"But I like your glasses."

"They make me look dorky."

"I like you dorky."

"Well, that's just you," I tell her.

She nods. She begins to whisper to herself again, which I take to mean she has no objection.

CHAPTER
—— *Twenty-One* ——

It's not until I get to Paul's and that familiar sense of doom comes over me when I peer through the windows, hoping to get some sense of how hard on me he'll be, that I start to break down.

It's just too much pressure. The week was a mess. Tash liked my photo on Instagram, commented: *Glad you're having fun! Want to meet up?* But I didn't respond. I haven't been practicing, I haven't liked listening to myself, so I just stopped. I'm frozen. Depressed. This, the day before a competition. I don't feel ready. Not even remotely.

I'm glad Julia is gone, and that I don't have to face her, too.

"Uh-oh," says Paul, after a glance of me waiting on the steps.

He puts his arm around me and draws me inside, where he hands me a tissue. "I'll make some tea, okay?"

I wipe my eyes, blow my nose, and put the Kleenex in my coat pocket, then start looking around. I'm in his living room, on a sofa facing a shelf of records and a record player.

Around the room, artifacts: an abstract painting, an Oriental-type silk triptych — like the kind my mother has, though this one is prettier, with lily pads and carp — a picture of a young Paul, sitting at the piano, a silver medal in a case — I wonder what it's for? A glassy-eyed cat perched in the corner eyes me from a distance. There's also a television, which surprises me. It's hard to think of Paul doing something so mundane as watching TV.

He comes back with a mug of tea and an egg tart, smaller than a cupcake, its lemon-yellow custard center smiling on a plate.

"Something rather magical about egg tarts. Very hard to be upset when you're eating them." He sits down beside me on the sofa. "You don't have to talk about it, you know. Do you want to talk about it?"

I shake my head. It's utterly embarrassing to tell a handsome person what a loser you are.

"Boys suck," I say.

A smile pops out, then vanishes. "Well." He clears his throat. "Well, yes, they do. But heartbreak is good! It's good for the soul. You can put it into your music, you know, that first part of the ballade . . ."

I shake my head, fighting my urge to smile. It's always music with him.

He nudges me playfully. "You should have teased him mercilessly. Played with him."

"I don't know how people do it." I pick up the tart and take a little nibble.

He leans back, settling into the couch. "Even when you're old, you can't keep people around. It always ends," he says.

"And you don't get lonely?"

"I'm always lonely. I mean, I'm just used to it. It stops mattering."

"Huh. That's terrible."

He laughs. "It gets less painful, I think." He watches me take a larger bite of the tart, sweet and crumbly and silky, then gets up and grabs one for himself. When he returns, he says, "You can't expect love. It's elusive. I bet half the time, when people show you love, you barely even know it. And when you show love, they don't, either. It's always masked. People aren't ready for it. Maybe they want it but not all the time, or they just have other things to do, or . . . I dunno, it's a cloudy day that day." He finds a record and places it on the turntable. "Anyway, there's going to be plenty of lovers. Boyfriends. Whatever. You're very pretty. You'll break hearts. You should. It's all part of it. No one can stop getting their heart broken. It happens to everybody. It should happen to everybody."

"Even you?"

"All the time, I think. Or at least I used to be that way." He sets the needle down with a practiced gesture.

"What happened?"

"I don't know. I just don't love as many things as I used to. It's hard to when you realize it's mainly just games we're playing. Anyway. Don't take boys seriously. Men, either. We're fucking idiots. We aren't worth it."

Horns, buzzy and drunk, do loop-de-loops in the air.

"Who is this?" I'm curious, despite my determination to keep moping. My voice feels thick and weird. I sound ugly.

"Billie Holiday," he says, sitting back down on the couch, his hands on his lap like a schoolboy.

"I didn't know you liked jazz."

"She's a genius with rubato. She pushes the melody, plays with it, gives it an internal motion, as if the melody moves slightly with a puff of wind, or a surge of the sea. She makes it organic. Imperfect. More human."

She flutters her voice like a tropical creature. The tightness in my shoulders, in my arms, begins to melt. "I like her. I don't usually listen to jazz."

"This recording—it's like having her close, in the room with me. All the delicacies of her become more palpable. She seems more fragile, subject to forces all around her. It's in her body—she's rather beautifully tragic—and I think we hear it instinctively because the voice comes from the body.

"The thing about rubato is, it's like a comment on your own feelings. The shift in the weather, the time of day. Your disappointments. Your joy. A singer might not sing a song the same way, night after night—maybe the players are in a different mood, or maybe it's pouring outside. Or maybe something happened—bad news on the radio. A typhoon in the South Pacific. Nine eleven. That stuff can be there. You affect the rhythm because you feel moved to."

Paul loves what I'm doing with the ballade. "See? There's more in it now. More feeling. And the arpeggios right before the second theme feel firm." A pause. "You know, I listened to the recording."

"What did you think?"

"It's . . . well, it's pretty good." He has a sly look in his eye. "It needs some editing—there's a bit at the end where I think your ex-boyfriend features."

I feel my face burning. "Oh, my God."

"No, no! It's fine. You're fine. Don't worry about it."

I can't look at him. I can never ever look him in the face again. What a stupid mistake! This is what I get for having my head in the clouds over a boy.

"Oh, my God," I say again. I cover my eyes.

He shrugs with an apologetic smile. "It's okay. There's nothing to be embarrassed about. It's just a kiss. All very natural. And I stopped watching as soon as he appeared."

"Really?"

"Really."

I peek at his face through my fingers. He's smiling encouragingly. There isn't a single bit of derision in his face.

"The recording was good."

"Really?" I look at him squarely. After everything that's happened, at least one thing is going well.

"Yes! You certainly have a chance at getting in. We'll see.

But even if you don't, it's so close to being ready for other things. Other competitions, conservatory applications. It would be really helpful to get this coda up to speed. It needs to roll downhill like a rock slide. You can practice here if you like, while I'm gone." He rubs his scruffy chin. "Actually, that would be perfect. I need someone to house-sit. Not overnight or anything, just someone to come in every day, feed the cat. Let in the piano tuner. Do you think you can do it? There's money, of course. . . ."

"That would be ecstasy."

"Would your mother mind?"

"Probably not. I mean, as long as I get home before she does every day, she's cool."

He laughs. "Mothers. Andrew will call, arrange it all."

"You're not just saying this to cheer me up, are you?"

"Not at all. In fact, if that were the case, I wouldn't be telling you that the photo you sent is subpar."

"What's wrong with it?"

Seeing my face, he says quickly, "I just don't think it expresses who you are."

"It's just a photo."

"Well, no one's going to tell you the picture matters, but it does. And the one you sent is too casual. Too naive-looking, you know? I mean, this photo, it doesn't say anything about the way you play. Your intelligence. Your sensitivity."

My eyes have gone round. "Maybe you can take my picture."

"I don't see why not."

"Now?"

"Sure! I have a little time." He leaves, then returns with a real camera. He surveys the room, then me. "The light is rather nice right now. Perhaps you can put your hair up a little? Show your neck."

I put my hair up in the hallway mirror while Paul watches. For once, I'm not nervous. I turn to look at him, twitching my nose, rabbitlike. He laughs.

"You should be playing—don't you think? Musicians are at their most revealing, their most beautiful, when they're playing music."

I walk over and sit down at the piano, aware of his eyes on me, aware that I've changed my walk because he's looking at me. He brings the camera between our faces. I flash him a smile.

"Okay. Play."

I put my hands on the keyboard. Bach. Bach like a marionette.

"You know, your lips look a little dry. Maybe . . . do you happen to have that lipstick you sometimes wear?"

I shake my head.

"Lick your lips?"

I do.

"Huh. Well, there are a few things in the bathroom." He puts his camera down.

I follow him down the hallway. "Why do you have makeup?"

"Women leave things sometimes."

"Oookay."

He laughs.

In the medicine cabinet—lipstick, Chanel. My lips bloom a rosy red. He watches me, leaning against the door.

"What do you think?" I ask. I use a finger to spread it evenly to the very edges of my lips.

He doesn't speak. He just nods. I'm reminded of Julia's dad, Seth, the way he just sits back and observes things.

"That bad, huh?

"No, it has a mystique. Lipstick does in general." He shrugs and walks down the hallway.

I follow after him, sit before him, straighten my back, lengthen my neck.

"Don't smile at the camera! Look away. Look moody. You're heartbroken."

I start to laugh.

He sighs. "Come on. Be serious. Let your lips be relaxed. Not open, just . . ." I pout them a little. "Better. Okay. I like it when you have that slight frown."

I play, listening more to the camera's soft click than to the music. "Perfect. Your skin is pretty in this light. See? Like caramel."

He shows me one of the pictures he took.

I look older. Deep black eyes. The light glows along the tops of my arms.

"Do you like it?" he asks.

"Yes." I've never seen that look on my face before. As if something is about to happen. "I like my hands."

"That's you. That's you and the fantasy of you at the same time." He looks at the photo on the screen of his camera, smiling. I wonder, not for the first time, if he likes me. "If you're going to do a thing, even a little thing like taking a picture, do it right."

I pack up.

"You have a competition tomorrow, yeah? The one at Mills?" he asks.

"Yeah."

"Beautiful building. You'll have a great time."

And for the first time in a week, I feel that that may actually be true.

The aura of Paul's apartment clings to me as I roll languidly down the street. Where the sun's warmth had been on my arms, I now feel a slight touch of chill, but I leave them bare and take my time going downhill, happier than I've been. What happened with Lee seems unimportant, and I can pay attention to what's going on around me — the rhythmic push and skip of syncopated bass from a passing car, the solemn tap of my shoes, the strain of a man's voice, talking too loudly on his phone.

At Mills College, I sit on the grass between sessions with my mom. It's pretty — old buildings that remind me of Catholic mission-style churches, the arches of doorways hulking. Nothing fragile. Old trees. It's so quiet, so systematized, that the announcement that I've won—first place for the teen division—is a shock. I can barely eat on the way home.

My Cal and Stanford brochures are now back in plain sight, unearthed from beneath the bed. I dream of Curtis. The Royal Conservatory in Toronto. Spending weeks on the Mediterranean, playing music in galleries, in museums, in concert halls arraigned in chandeliers. Of knowing the scent of a different ocean. Of performing under the vault of a cathedral in Prague. Of sipping coffee and joking around in recording studios. Daily manicures. Beautiful, poetic boys. Salads with flowers in them. I'd buy my mother a larger house, somewhere in walking distance to a church. She could live a whole new life.

My body is so full of dreams, I just lay in bed for hours in the morning, thinking.

I e-mail Paul that I've won and get a speedy reply: "I had no doubt. You work so hard and so well—you truly have the temperament to really hear yourself (and also hear criticism, which is so important). Well done!" He sends me a hug emoji.

I can't help beaming. I send him a hug emoji right back.

Carefully I fill out my application for the Lener, attaching my new photo, links to my recordings, and a list of competitions. I edited the newest recording—I took out everything after Lee appeared, making sure that all that trash would be gone forever and ever—and uploaded it to YouTube.

I think Paul was being easy on me — that kiss was still more than I would want other people to see. More than I wanted to see. At least I can go on as if it never happened. Paul certainly didn't seem to be treating me like anything I did was weird.

Instead, he was nice. I felt special at his house, with his camera and his record player.

I work on a playlist for Paul for his tour — for the airports and restaurants and bus stops. There will be moments of silliness, of drowsiness, of excitement! I've never traveled, but I have ideas from the movies — sunshine and dust and indifferently friendly people. Of grace.

That's the concept, anyway.

Andrew calls. It's a genuine freak-out — there's a faint strain in his voice, like a string being bent a smidge too sharp. Usually he's bored, placid — his voice is so smooth, you can't believe it's real. Paul's pressed for time, and therefore so is he. Could I come tomorrow? I needed to get the keys, be shown how to take care of his cat and plants.

"There's a lot going on, but it's my only day at Paul's — his party — how disorganized, I know. Please don't think ill of me."

"There's a party?"

"Well, a get-together. Kind of a warm-up for the tour."

"Yeah, sure, why not," I say as casually as I can.

"Fantastic," he says.

Mom is okay with it, especially since my ribbon from

yesterday's competition is now hanging on the fridge. Anything with Paul is okay with her.

I put Philip Glass on the playlist. Why not? Never mind that it was spending time with Lee that gave me the chance to know it. It still brings me to a painful place in my mind, but it isn't so bad. The music still feels like love.

CHAPTER
— *Twenty-Two* —

I've never seen Paul's place in the dark, with all the windows lit. Strange to find the door unlocked.

It's warm inside. So many people. They're lining the hallways and sitting in front of the musicians on the carpet or perched on chairs, looking scrubbed and pruned and well ironed. When I come in, they shift slightly, as if I've disturbed the cabin pressure.

Violins bounce over the dew-clear ring of piano. I find a place to stand and watch, feeling a tremor when I get a good view of Paul at the piano, supporting the two string players. The bones of my rib cage shift. I feel unsteady, and tense my toes like I need to grip the floor. I'm nervous.

Paul is right. People are at their most beautiful when they play. He is, anyway.

His eyes dart up to greet me — or, no, he doesn't see me at all, or if he does, he's giving me the oddest look.

The violinists rock their instruments as if they had souls, and the music marches, solemnly twisting, and each turn is like the planet rotating a fraction, like a second hand on a clock.

At the end of the piece, there's an excited buzz in the room as people begin to move and talk again. It's a similar crowd to the kind I'd see at the conservatory—whiter than at home, more paler-skinned Asians and few brown ones. I can't help but look at the earrings of a lady near me and wonder where she got them. I'd never find anything like them anywhere that I'd shop.

I try to make my way over to Paul, but a tall boy with a prep-school buzz cut approaches me.

"You're Claire." He extends a hand. "I'm Andrew, Paul's assistant."

"I know your voice."

He laughs and gestures to the kitchen in the back, and we walk toward it.

"Did you enjoy the piece?"

"It was gorgeous."

"Love Vivaldi. Look, I have a few things to do, but have some food. We'll talk in a bit, okay?" He points to the kitchen table.

Vivaldi. Of course. "Okay. But where's, like, the normal food?" I scan the trays of vegetables and shrimp and wrinkle my nose.

"My goodness you're young," says Andrew. "Honey, eat your vegetables. They're good for you."

"There isn't any real food," says Paul, laughing, from behind me. I stiffen. "There's cheese, though. Sorry—you'll have to blame Andrew for the spread."

Andrew shrugs. "There's cake." He gestures to the far corner of the kitchen where a cake, decorated with a frosting keyboard, wishes Paul a happy birthday.

"It's your birthday?"

He shrugs. "Yeah. Kind of."

"I didn't know that. How old are you?"

He laughs, pats me on the shoulder, then goes to find someone more interesting to talk to.

"If you want to find out how old he is," Andrew says with his lips closed, "just count the keys on the cake. Or eyeball them. You know."

I find a glass of wine — a woman throws daggers at me, but no one's mothering me here — and look around the kitchen. I've never been inside it. African violets on the windowsill in brushed-chrome pots. Brushed-chrome faucet fixtures. It's very clean — and noisy, everyone's voices bouncing off the hard surfaces — so I sit down in the living room, having selected the libretto for *Apollo et Hyacinthus* from the shelf of pocket-size scores. I try not to stare at anyone or feel like a social failure. At grown-up parties, I never know if I should try to talk to people or what.

"It's ridiculous, this whole airport security thing," says the lady sitting on the floor in front of me. "I felt like I was being molested last time I went through."

"Oh, come on. You liked it," says the woman next to her. Her hair is curly on one side, slicked back on the other.

"It was like Ellis Island," she continues. "Like they were going to check me for head lice."

While the two of them laugh, the one-side-curly-headed woman looks me over. I already don't like her. "Are you one of Paul's students?"

"Yup."

"Really?" Her smile is false. "What's that like?"

"Well, he's the best."

She laughs. Her wineglass is half empty. "Oh, that's so cute! Isn't that cute?" She turns to the woman next to her for agreement.

"Well, you must play for us," the other woman says, a little less entertained, and looking at my jeans and shoes.

I blush.

They laugh — a high-pitched, contrapuntal harmony of twitters.

"I'm not dressed."

More twittering. I'm reminded of T. S. Eliot, how the women come and go, talking of Michelangelo. Women devoid of feeling. I can't imagine Paul liking them.

"Are you trying to get Claire to play?" asks Paul, squeezing my arm as he sits down beside me.

"She doesn't want to," says the first woman in a low, round voice. "She's being shy."

"That's a shame," he says. "I don't see why you shouldn't. Everyone's just kinda jumping in, you know."

"But everyone knows each other."

The women raise their eyebrows at me.

"Mostly. They're friends," says Paul airily. "And wives of old friends."

"And paramours," the lipstick-clad woman says.

"Some of whom are ex-wives."

They laugh. The second woman stares at Paul really obviously. It's disgusting.

"You can tell the musicians by the bad hair," says Paul. We touch arms.

"You don't have bad hair," I tell him.

"Well, if you aren't handsome, bad hair can be a distinguishing characteristic," says Andrew, who's come over to us. "I'm ready for you." He looks at me expectantly. The women continue to talk to Paul, who nudges the second with an elbow. Her face instantly turns sweet.

I don't want to go—if she's gunning for Paul, I want to see what happens—but Andrew is bent on showing me around. He leads me back into the kitchen, showing me phone numbers, the orchid on the windowsill, the plant food under the sink, the cleaning products, the cat food.

"If anyone comes by, leaves a message, whatever, just shoot me an e-mail. Try not to text me unless it's urgent. And definitely don't text Paul. He gets touchy when he's traveling. Use the house as much as you want, but be sure to be here when the piano tuner comes. That's the first Monday of the month at noon." He gives a conspiratorial grin. "Paul actually doesn't care if you have a friend over, but you know, don't trash the place. Restock the cookies. Clean up. You know."

I nod, pretending to know.

Facing Paul's record player, he takes a deep breath. "Look, I'm not going to pretend that you aren't going to try to use this. It's too tempting. Do you have one of these at home?"

"Nope."

"Good, then you don't have any bad habits. Always treat this record player like a crystal bomb. That needle costs a fortune."

He shows me how to remove a record from its sleeve, how to clean it, how to put it back. There's cleaning fluid, brushes. "Don't skip around. Just . . . play a whole side. Commit. Okay?"

I suppress a smirk.

"If you think I'm nuts about vinyl, you should see Paul."

Back in the living room, he shows me the desk next to the piano, where the check for the tuner is kept. Beside us, a musician is examining the violin behind the piano.

"Don't touch that," Paul says, springing across the room, to the dismay of the two women he's been talking to. He smiles graciously.

"Oh, yeah," Andrew says to me. "No one touches the violin."

"Why not?"

"It just bugs him."

Paul puts the violin back into its velvet-lined case, cradling its neck from its base with two fingers. If he's upset, I can't tell. He laughs easily when another woman across the room calls, "Paul, get your sexy butt over here."

"Are you trying to harass me again?" he says as he walks rapidly over. "Well, you can't. It isn't your turn yet."

Andrew is shaking his head.

"Is that his girlfriend?" I ask Andrew.

"Who, her?" Andrew smirks. "She wishes."

I like Andrew.

The noise of the party rises and rarely falls, but no one's talking about anything particularly interesting. I can never figure out what people at parties have to say to each other. Bursts of laughter like jets of steam releasing pressure. I can barely hear the music. So I just sit there, next to Andrew, pretending to listen to the conversations on either side of me — on one side, a man is saying we already live in a fascist country because our government is infiltrated by business. On the other, a woman is explaining how she cleans her shoes. I'm keeping an eye on Paul, who drifts from one group of people to another. He's not with anyone for long. He catches my eye as he kisses a woman on the cheek. He smiles at me, reassuring me, and I smile back. Then his eye is caught by another person, and I recede into his periphery again.

"This tour will be good for him," Andrew is saying to a shiny-faced, shiny-haired man who's walked up to us. "Get him out of his head a bit."

"It took some wrangling," the man says dryly.

"But it's good timing, what with that thing with Anna,"

Andrew responds, tipping his head toward the man. "Who'd want to linger? But you don't have to twist my arm. Vienna. Sheesh. Turin."

"Everywhere is the same to the brokenhearted."

"Oh, you're such a poet," says Andrew, nudging him with his upper arm.

Paul's voice is suddenly loud in my ear. His fingers gently touch my shoulder. The air changes density. "Several guests would like you to plaayy." He twinkles his fingers in the air. "No pressure. They're curious, I think."

The slick-haired man's eyes flicker over me. "You play?"

"Claire is a student of mine," Paul says, putting his arm around me possessively. I shiver with joy. "An excellent student. This is my manager, Henry."

"Claire. That's a nice name," Henry says.

"I think so, too," says Paul. "As if we can peer into your depths." I melt.

"Where are you from?" Henry asks.

"Fremont."

"No," he says, looking impatient. "I mean, where you're — your nationality."

"I was born here. My parents are from the Philippines," I add reluctantly.

He nods politely and decides not to say anything more. I shrink. I can't think of anything else to say to him. I look at him from the corner of my eye, wondering why he even wants to know. Am I like a roadside freak attraction? Or do

I need to be explained, like some piece of modern art in a museum that you couldn't possibly understand without the little white label beside it? I bend into Paul's warm side. He turns to look at me, then at Henry, and smiles brightly.

"She's going to the Lener," he says.

"I'm not in yet," I say.

"You will be." He squeezes me a little. "What do you think, Claire? Show them how it's done?" he whispers in my ear. Henry's curious face looks over his shoulders, studies my face. "Of course, you don't have to. But I do think you're playing beautifully right now. You should show off a little. Just a little."

Despite Henry's eyes pinning me down, I lift my chin. "What should I play?"

"No idea. Surprise me."

I break away and go to wash my hands. I check my face: the flush on my cheeks is unruly. Someone smiles encouragingly as I walk unsteadily to the piano, and I smile back, though it does no good. Fear still presses slowly into my belly like a small fist. I track Paul, watching from the corner of the room. The small muscles in my upper arms begin to ache, and I will myself to unclench them when I flop onto the seat with a squeak of leather. It's the wrong height, and it seems absurd to have to get up, twist the knob of the seat to lower it, but I do. How stupid and slow I must look. After, I smooth my hair in case it needs smoothing.

Finally, I bend my head to the keys and my fingers follow. A Bach prelude, from *The Well-Tempered*, the F-sharp Minor from Book II—respectable, but also something I feel all the way inside my body. There is a place in my belly, a vacancy, that has not left since I lost my virginity. I touch it cautiously, and it feels larger when I do, so I try to feel other things. I hear Paul's murmur of recognition; he sounds pleased. In the corner of my eye, he bends to speak into the ear of the person next to him. Paul's voice becomes fainter and fainter, like one of those old songs from the eighties my mother likes, fading out instead of just ending.

My head is dull from the wine, but I can still feel a tight string of emotion, thin and clear like the thread of a spider, and I try to handle it delicately, to make it run through the piece. The fugue, when it begins, has a soft, nighttime feeling. Every line emerges as if from dark, calm water, and sinks back in, leaving its velvety surface looking untouched, though larger and larger waves roll in. The last phrase is like a wave coming to a slow, frothy demise in all its minute, close glory.

The conversation burbles and fizzes in my ears. Has the room changed color? Or is it me?

Paul looks pleased. Making his way to me, he kisses me on the cheek, then smiles at a nearby guest. He shifts his wineglass to one hand, and brushes my hair back with the other. The man smiles without teeth, peering up at Paul, and then at me, through narrow, humorous eyes.

"You were lovely."

I throw a swift glance at the lady with the odd hair—the kind of hair I could never get away with—and am satisfied at the darts she's shooting back at me. Ha. That'll show her.

I walk back to the drinks table, grasp the neck of a bottle, and watch the purple fluid curl in my glass, trying to look like I do this all the time. I am triumphant. I am the golden child.

"Well done," murmurs Andrew, lighting the candles on the cake. "You're a born performer."

"Do you really think it was okay?"

"I do," he says. "For someone who's had how many glasses of wine now?"

"I haven't had that much."

"Hey, it's okay by me. Paul's all European when it comes to that kind of thing."

I happily watch each candle take the light and estimate the keys on his cake. Fortyish. He doesn't look forty.

Guests pour in, as if they magically know it's time for cake. Their eyes brush more heavily over me now that I've played. We sing "Happy Birthday," and someone with a proper baritone catches my attention, until a soprano starts to detach itself from the rest of the body of voices. Paul looks odd among these people. I peer at the man who called me lovely. These are Paul's friends? I think of Paul's face during lessons, its brooding but pleasant, concentrated focus. Here his face seems stretched tight and colored in, and he keeps smiling, even as he blows his candles out.

Henry comes in and stands beside me. "That was quite moving!" he says. "Ang galing! Did I say that right?"

"Right enough, I guess," I tell him.

"Don't you know Tagalog?" Henry asks. I wince at his pronunciation—every white person says it as if it rhymes with *bog*. TAG-a-log. Like it's a children's game. It's tah-GAH-lohg. Emphasis on the second syllable, rhymes with *vogue*.

"My kindergarten teacher convinced my parents that I was mixing my words up in school, and that I should be spoken to in just one language. That I would be more likely to succeed if I did."

He looks uncomfortable, and I move my eyes away from him, to look at anything else. That guy makes me feel like I don't belong.

Paul hands me a slice of cake, and I hide in an empty corner of the kitchen. The room starts to drain of people, including Henry. A woman drops her clarinet voice low into my ear. "Beautifully played." Her smile is stiff. People are clasping Paul's hand, coats draped over their arms, saying good-bye.

"I never thought I'd be so old," Paul says, setting down his cake half-finished beside me and picking up his wineglass.

"You don't seem old."

"It's just an act," he says, bringing his glass to his lips and draining it. "It's necessary."

"Well, at least you've got friends."

"Of a sort. I see my students more often than any one friend."

I look around at the people who've stayed. A woman with boots up to her thighs leans against the wall, tucking a glass of wine to her chest, drawing in the man in front of her with eyes like tractor beams. Her hair is in soft brown waves, and she tosses them a little. He talks very fast. His laugh is strained. Another man roots around what's left of the crumb-strewn table.

"People love you," I tell him.

He smiles, not looking at me. "That's sweet."

An elderly couple comes up to wish him well on his trip. I continue to eat the cake, scraping the frosting off the paper plate, waiting for them to leave. My mouth tastes horrible—sweet and sour at the same time.

"How late is it? Don't you need to catch your train?" he asks.

"Eventually."

"You should, before it gets too late. You know, your playlist was the loveliest present. I can't wait to listen to it."

He walks me to the door. I reach up on tiptoe to kiss his cheek, but it lands on his lips. Light and dry. I risk a glance. His eyes are steady.

I reach for the doorknob as if nothing happened. "Bye, Claire." I don't look back.

The air is cold and damp. My hands are shaking. I find my phone in my bag, put my earbuds in, press play. The first tentative notes of a Chopin nocturne shoot through me like a star.

CHAPTER
—— *Twenty-Three* ——

The house is cold, and the light from the window is color-less. It feels empty without Paul. I've never noticed before how you can hear every bus go by, the click of heels, gusts of wind. But it's still Paul's house, filled with records and these glorious pianos, warm great beasts that look poised to fly.

I can't believe I'm allowed to be here by myself. It feels like a secret.

Paul's cat, Ludwig, is generally shy, Andrew told me, but he must be eager for company. His orange paws look too small to carry his massive weight. He's huge. Not fat, just big. When I reach down to pet him, his orange-striped head rises and knocks into my hand, and he rubs his head against my shin, as if he owns me. Dean is going to sniff me forever when I get home. I open a can of cat food, the sound of it drawing an insistent rumble from his wet throat.

It's cold. Mid-July in the city feels like November at home. I find some cheese left over from the party in the fridge and put the kettle on as if Paul were here. While I wait for it to boil, I notice that his house isn't quite perfect. There's a ring on the kitchen table, dust on the sills. Somehow, it makes me more comfortable.

I slosh water on the crooked blue-green roots of the purple orchid in the kitchen window—its complicated, mysterious face seductively peering up at me—and head down the hall to the bedroom to water the fern on his nightstand.

The room has dark polished wood floors, white pillows, a white coverlet, white curtains, pale-blue walls. An oil painting of a man at sea hangs above the bed. I slide a hand over the coverlet, then underneath it, just a little. I don't know why I feel like I shouldn't be doing this. It's not illegal. Nor is it really snooping. It's not like I'm looking for drugs or trying to find out if he has some weird fetish.

Beneath the coverlet is a nut-brown blanket, soft and nappy as a teddy bear, and I slide my arm all the way inside. It's so soft on my skin.

I pick up the coverlet and lie down.

The bed is cool. The sheets smell like soil. For a moment, my mind goes blank. The curtains move, a little bit inward, a little outward, like breathing. I didn't sleep well last night, and now all I want to do is sleep.

Did he mean to kiss me? Or was it an accident?

The teakettle shrieks and I jerk, thud hard on the braided rug with both feet, and run out of there. Ludwig's moony, judging eyes pierce me when I enter the kitchen, and I weaken beneath his gaze.

It's too quiet now, so I dip into Paul's record collection — Solomon, Cortot, loads and loads and loads of Beethoven. Some of the albums are very old, with sleeves that have gone pulpy at the openings. I choose one, lay it down, and set the needle bobbing on the surface like a gull on the sea. A delicate chaos unfurls.

I take a picture of the record shelves and post it on my Instagram, select a book from the shelf — Blake, well used and water-stained — and lie next to the speakers, ignoring the cat sitting there coolly, licking his paws. The house can wait.

I've never been allowed to touch the black Steinway — the brown piano is for students. I guess because he'd rather keep the black one nice. It's utterly gorgeous. It has the kind of gloss that makes you think you can press your hand straight into the lacquer.

I open it and play a scale. It takes more strength to play this piano, but then you get more from it. The deeper you reach into its bed, the richer the tone. Its loud is louder, its quiet is quieter, and there's a sharper, glass-like sound to it right when you hit the key that disintegrates so slowly.

I try the ballade, with its first white-hot, ragged climb up the scale, the first line pleading, the second line answering, only to mumble into a jagged waltz. Chords like bursts of sunlight free themselves from the murk of it, are eaten alive; the return to the first theme is a whisper of its former self. I stop before I launch into the coda.

Damn. It's fantastic. Easy to get lost in. You can really work here.

I peek inside Paul's bedside table. Quarters, some dollar bills, a lighter, condoms — Trojans — and KY jelly. A photograph facedown. *Anna, Consrv. steps, Toronto* it reads, in watery blue ink. His handwriting. The woman looks past me, one white arm draped over a green knee-length skirt. Behind her, Paul talks to someone behind the camera, his eyes keen, without regret, happy. His hair was fuller.

In Paul's medicine cabinet: Mylanta, Tylenol, a safety razor, the tube of lipstick. I put it on, then wipe it off.

The week swims by. I'm barely at home. Alone in Paul's house, I imagine him by my side, keeping me company, looking at my fingers on the keys, telling me how to phrase things, commenting on records as I go through them. He looks over my shoulder to read the book I'm reading on his sofa, paces around the kitchen as I make tea.

I used to do this with my dad, too, even before he died. I'd imagine elaborate fantasies of going camping, roasting marshmallows, canoeing. Footraces. My mother avoids the sunshine — she doesn't like being dark — but my dad was brown, walnut-skinned, and in my head we would sit in the sun.

For the Paul in my head, I pretend to be charming. He sits in the corner of the room with his arms folded and his legs crossed, watching over me as I work out a trill for a Bach fugue. "It sings more this way, doesn't it?" I say to imaginary Paul, demonstrating. "Better than this way, which is a bit more morbid."

"But we may want it to be morbid," imaginary Paul says.

I imagine him prepping me for the competition, looking me in the eyes as I'm just about to go on with the kind of look he had in his eyes when he kissed me. A look to send me off into the future. To carry me to the end, like the music he plays.

He's in Rome now, according to his schedule. An ancient city. Buildings ruined and washed and purified by age. My song will reach him. I woo him from a distance.

The acrobatic leaps of the left hand, the quick, lithe turning of fingers on fingers aren't working today. Playing the ballade is like talking to a con man. You can't pin it down—as soon as you've got one thing safe in your pocket, your other pocket's getting picked.

I'm about to quit for the day when there's a knock on the door. Through the keyhole stands a tiny blurry version of the woman in the photo. Anna from the conservatory steps, Toronto. Her hair is shorter now.

She looks as surprised to see me as I am to see her. Her facial features adjust.

"Oh. Hello."

"Hi."

"Is Paul around?"

"Nope. He's out of town. I'm house-sitting for him?"

"Oh. It sounded like him playing." I'm flattered. Maybe it doesn't sound as bad as I think.

She puts one leg behind the other. Both hands are shoved into the pockets of her green dress, as if she's cold, though it's warm today. "I was wondering if there might be a violin here. I left it a while back."

I look at her a little more closely. The fine lines at the corners of her eyes don't matter. She's beautiful with or without them. "Do you want to leave your number? I'll call Paul and ask." I think for a moment. "Tomorrow. It's too late now."

She relaxes at my offer. "Sure," she says. "Maybe that would be better."

I close the door and walk down the dim hallway and start thumbing through his record collection, choose Verdi, turn it up loud, and spread myself out in the middle of his bed. I don't feel like playing right now. Of course it's her violin.

I open the book he's left on the nightstand and read half a page before I start studying Anna's face in the photograph. Her silhouette must be Paul's type—it's the same as the sketch in the practice room. She reminds me of the faces in those French movies, *Red*, *White*, and *Blue*, that my mother likes.

I slip my hand beneath the pillow to feel the pressure of his cool sheets against my skin and picture them here. Anna's reading a magazine, right where I'm lying, and Paul's head is in her lap. She smells of citrus. Her left hand lightly rests on the back of his head. She wears a cotton dress that she sleeps in.

His hand slides over her dress, and then beneath, look-ing up to meet her eyes before he lifts her hem and ducks his head beneath. Her thighs separate as if what held them closed has been cut. She slides down. Her hand never leaves his. A sound escapes her. The magazine slides to the floor. She presses against him.

Afterward, her smile is wide. He cradles her, all the way around, and they breathe together like one being. They haven't said a word.

Anna comes back a few days later.

After my thinking about her having sex, it's hard to look at her. I hand her the case, avoiding her glance. "I hope it didn't bother him, that I needed it."

"I don't think so. He seemed fine."

"Yes, he's always fine," she says, almost to herself.

I had e-mailed Andrew after she left and was surprised how quickly I got a call back, right from Paul. It just hap-pened to be ten thirty in the evening. Air crackled over the line, and he sounded far away, as if he were in a jar. "Give it to her, if she wants it."

"You don't want her to wait until you're back?"

"Nope!" I could hear his breathing over the phone. "Probably better that she doesn't see me. She's a bit . . . well, melodramatic."

"She does play the violin."

"True. Avoid violinists, Claire."

"Too late," I said, thinking of Lee.

He laughed. And then we talked for thirty minutes. Thirty whole minutes.

She sits down on the porch and sets the case on her knee. It's furry on the edges where it's been scuffed on too many floors, and the closures are slightly loose. She unsnaps the clasps.

Inside, the lining is a glossy emerald green, or was once. It's gone mousy. But the violin gleams at the zeniths of its curves.

"Is it old?" I ask.

"Mm-hm." She runs her fingers over the strings. Her skin is delicately pink in the wrinkles of her knuckles.

"How old?" A small, wire-bound notebook sits in a small pocket, next to an old cake of rosin for the bow.

"Not so old. It was made in 1908."

"I wish I could hear it."

"I mainly just play for me." She smiles, closes the case, and turns to go. The back of her neck is white in the sun.

CHAPTER
—— *Twenty-Four* ——

On the day Paul comes back, August heat makes the city noises sharp and the car sounds slice through the walls. Anna's photo is back in its place, facedown in Paul's nightstand. I cleaned all morning, and I probably pulled at the corners of the bedclothes twenty times, trying to erase every wrinkle. It's so hot the doorknobs are warm. The just-washed floor steams.

I peel off my damp T-shirt, clean my underarms in the bathroom sink, put in my new contacts. Julia was right: they do make me look older. I sift through his record collection, trying to find the right thing to play. Arias from Maria Callas? Too much. Beethoven? Too angst-ridden. Chopin? Romantic but moody. His happiness never lasts. Something Apollonian, golden, steady. Mendelssohn's *Songs Without Words*, soft and bright and heroic. I put it on the turntable so it's ready, just in case.

In the heavy, cottony air, the silence feels heavy, too, as if the whole city is waiting. The silence at Paul's isn't quiet, though. A truck puffs like an old man. A siren shrieks in the distance. Every vase is filled with thoughts, warnings. Even the face of the woman in the sketch looks annoyed. It's as if everything in the apartment needs to be adjusted, moved an inch to one side or the other. Pictures need straightening. The dust behind the books in the bookcase needs cleaning.

I know why I feel this way. Obviously it's a chance I'm taking, but I think he's interested. He's hinted it to me in all kinds of ways. The kiss. The picture he took of me. Even the way he talked to me on the phone just the other day. He wanted me to stay.

You have to take risks. Almost every good piece of music is good because it takes risks. Nothing good happens without them, right? I wouldn't be here if I didn't take them.

I find the lipstick in the medicine cabinet and put it on. It looks a little heavy, but now I like the way it makes me look. Like a grown woman.

I settle myself on Paul's couch and try to read a book, but a sentence about mango trees won't sink in and I keep reading it over and over until finally I put the book aside. I can't stop thinking about what will happen, though I also think that if I keep thinking about it, nothing will happen. This needs to be natural if it's going to work.

My eyes fly open at a touch on my shoulder. Paul's face looms, smiling. "You've made yourself comfortable," he says.

"Was I asleep?" I smile, the widest smile I can possibly

give, and stretch my arms out, half in a yawn, half in hope that he'll bend over so I can drag him to me and kiss him, right then and there, but he turns, walks into the kitchen, and I stumble after him, groggy and rubbing my eyes.

He's shed his jacket, rolled up his sleeves. He reaches high in the cupboard for a bottle. Pernod. I hover close, stand so my cheek is barely an inch away from his arm.

"Did you miss me so particularly much?" There's a look of amusement in his eyes.

"Particularly much," I say, waiting, my face upturned. "Did you miss me?"

"A little." A mild apologetic smile lets me down easy, but still it's a letdown. "In ways."

"In ways?" I pout.

He laughs. "Well, I missed home. Travel makes me feel off. Not like myself. I miss feeling like myself." He takes a glass from a cupboard. "Want one?"

"Uh-huh."

He takes a second one down and fills them both with ice. "That smile just isn't wearing off, is it?"

"I could be more serious if you like."

Glugs of Pernod transmute to a creamy white. He thins it with water.

"I've always thought young people shouldn't be forbidden a drink," he says, giving mine to me. "It makes them alcoholics. Cheers."

I sip my drink and gag—it tastes of licorice. "The thing

about Pernod," he says, walking in front of me down the hallway, "is it makes your lips wonderfully numb. A little like at the dentist's office. And it spreads to your whole body."

He stands beside the concert black, testing the keys. "Out of tune" is his verdict. "But I suspect it's the heat." His eyes slip over the corner of the carpet where the violin once rested. His face goes slack. "So. She came?"

"Yeah."

"Women," he says, scratching his temple with two fingers, and then pointing up at the ceiling with them in a gesture of helplessness. He brushes past me.

"How about I put on some music?" I suggest. Set the mood.

"Nah. Don't feel like it." He drops onto the couch in the other room with a grunt and clasps his dewy glass against his chest. His face is petulant.

I curl up right next to him. My knee touches his thigh, just barely. He doesn't move away, to my rejoicing. "How did it go?" I ask. "Any groupies?" I give him a playful poke in the arm, hoping to cheer him up.

"Ha. Groupies. No, it was exhausting."

"The groupies were?"

"Ha. Everything was," he says, evading my question. "I played awfully."

I widen my eyes. "You couldn't play badly in your sleep."

"I have my days."

"Even in Vienna?"

"Especially there." A swift tilt of his glass into his mouth.

"It was very automatic. Very muscular. No emotion. And, you know, people come to see a show. To see you love things, or at least have a good time. So I faked it. The others were annoyed, but I passed it off okay."

"You should never fake it," I say, and immediately wish I could take it back.

"*Should* is a strong word. Sometimes you just have to get through things. Sometimes you need to get paid. You can't just not perform if you don't feel anything."

"I've never not felt anything," I say.

"Well, that changes when you get older." He sips his drink.

"I'd never not have anything to give," I say. "There's always something. There's something wrong if you don't."

He sits blinking, and I wonder if my words have any effect at all. "You know, people never talk like this with me. Most people, anyway."

"What about Anna?"

He swallows audibly. "Yeah," he says, drawing the word out.

I think of her face. Her skin is so clean. Like she washes it in milk. "She's beautiful." Jealousy wets my voice.

The wrinkles around his eyes deepen. I notice how dry his lips are. "Isn't she? She could start a war." He examines his glass, which is empty, and gets up. "If you ever fall in love, don't fuck around. It's not a game."

"I thought you said I should play with boys." I watch him pour another inch of Pernod onto the melting ice.

"You're young," he says.

My heart deflates. "I guess." He flops back on the couch. His swallow is audible, grandiose. I sit down right next to him. We touch. I take a tiny sip of my drink and try to look at him casually. Not staring. "Anyway, I do like people, you know. Love people."

He stares down at his drink, which he holds in both hands.

This isn't at all how things were supposed to go. We were going to play music, eat cookies, I'd dazzle him with what I'd learned while he was gone, and then he was going to nudge me playfully, and I'd nudge him right back. And then I was going to kiss him.

I put my drink down. "I should go," I say.

"Oh, you don't have to go. And leave me to my misery?" He nudges me with his thigh. "I haven't seen anyone I actually wanted to see in a month."

I nudge him back.

"I could finish your drink. I know you don't like it."

"Is it that obvious?"

"Wonderfully obvious." A little smile pulls at his lips. "Do you want to finish your nap?" he says. "I feel bad I interrupted."

"Well, I guess I haven't been sleeping well." A lie. "Can I nap here?"

"If you like. I'm probably going to take a shower in a bit. You'll have the couch to yourself."

"Well, I'm small. I don't need a lot of space."

I curl up on my end of the sofa, pulling my dress up high so the air hits my thighs. Tease him a little. I close my eyes. "It's too hot," I say.

I feel a cold glass on my leg and squeal. He laughs.

Okay, this is definitely going in the right direction. I close my eyes again. Ice rattles. A glass knocks the coffee table. The familiar, polite rhythmic padding of cat paws, and a rippling meow. The cat asks, demands, to be touched. He murmurs softly to him. Love words. Someday I might hear such things in my ear. I curl up tighter in envy and fear. I hold myself so tightly, my body begins to hurt as I hear him settle, his breathing slow.

I stretch out my leg, sticky with sweat, and nudge his thigh with my toe to see what he'll do. Nothing. He doesn't move. I stay where I am, keeping contact. He isn't as warm as I am. His skin is tepid. The cat curls up on top of my feet, all slinky and silky and seductive. I fight the urge to kick him off.

I concentrate on the sensations in my toes, where the pads of them rest on his thigh, it resists reassuringly. I won't sleep.

He said once, "Boys, they'll just flock right to you. All you have to do is stand there long enough, put yourself in their way, and don't move. They can't help themselves."

He's fallen asleep. His face is peaceful-looking, slightly bored. Without his glasses on, his eyelashes look darker and longer. Crosshatches are etched beneath his eyes. His hand cups his chin. His glass and mine are drained, except for watery milky puddles at their bottoms.

Don't be timid now.

I move closer, pushing the cat away, who resists and then gives in, jumping onto the carpet with a look of scorn. I lower myself down next to him slowly, so he doesn't wake up.

I'm not ready. No, I'm ready. I want to be ready, even if I'm not.

The skin of his lips is transparent and smooth, and shines a bit like rice paper. I pencil the ridge of his upper lip with my finger. It gives like a sponge.

He flicks his head to the side, as if shaking off a fly. For a second I think he's waking up, but he doesn't open his eyes. And what if he did wake up? I aim carefully. Our lips touch. I feel a thrill of daring. I've given him a secret blessing. His breath smells of coffee and bread and licorice from his drink.

My heart thumps. It hurts a little. This is too much. I'm scared. I curl up beside him, my cheek against his arm, and close my eyes.

Absorbing his warmth, I relax. When he inhales, I rise like I'm riding a swell of the sea, and I sink when he breathes out.

I kiss him again, more firmly this time, placing my lower lip between his—*what am I doing?*—I hear him inhale a deep breath, he's waking up. I jump back.

For a split second, I worry that I've made a mistake. Or done a really bad thing.

But he doesn't seem upset. He just blinks, a little amused,

as if he just told himself a joke. His eyes flick down over the curves of my body, then settle on my face, crystallizing as they focus.

He brings his right hand to my face, and brings me close again. Falling onto his chest, I giggle nervously, but he just keeps kissing me, these short, full kisses that curtain off the rest of the world.

He slips the straps of my dress off my shoulders.

A hand drifts lower, to my arm, to my rib cage, where my bra would be. Cooler air touches my belly. Tension spreads from any place he touches. I tighten, shrink. My stomach muscles have contracted so hard, it's like they've been punched. He opens his mouth, and I think we're about to stop. I wouldn't mind if we did. I want to talk to know how he feels, if he's been hoping, too, and then I could tell him how much I'd been hoping, ever since Lee, since he showed me Billie Holiday. How at last I felt loved.

But instead he draws me up along his body. I'm on my knees, straddling his rib cage, and can see the top of his head. He kisses my nipples, and when I put my hands on his shoulders, they're so unexpectedly soft that I feel like I'm the grown-up. He's the child.

His breath rides across my belly. His fingers follow, touch me between my legs. It cuts my breath. His lips trace the span of my hip bone where it protrudes. "You have the softest skin." He slides down between my legs, kisses the inside of my thigh, and then moves upward, touching the darkest place I have, defining it for me.

Thunder in my ears. My body burns like a wire. This is so easy. It's easy to be in love. It does just happen to you, the way they say. And he's so gentle, the way he touches me, nothing like Lee.

My thighs begin to shake uncontrollably and I draw him up—we're face-to-face—and he starts to pull his pants down, his pale-blue boxers. I lean over to kiss him, and he shifts his body, pushes gently on my arm.

I know what he's asking me to do. He smiles, and I brush my fear away like a stray hair and move lower on his body, kissing him on the way down. Trying to make it slow.

He smells of salt and the way bedrooms smell in the morning. His cock rests between his legs, a blind, soft-bodied sea creature. It's ugly. It has nothing to do with Paul, except that it is, in fact, Paul's. It's smaller than Lee's. I wasn't expecting that, for some reason.

I look up at him, and his face is inscrutable, harsh.

Blow jobs look easy enough on the Internet. I try an uncomplicated movement. Is it really that simple? It isn't like kissing at all. Pretty unromantic.

"You're really good at that," he says softly.

I'm surprised. I keep going. My hair shields me from his face. It gets wetter and wetter, and more uncomfortable. The hair on his thighs is dark and stubborn-looking. My hands feel slick. I try to make this an act of love, but my arms ache and my jaw is locked open.

I push my hair out of my way, risk a peek at his face. It's soft and greedy. Terror blooms in my belly when I see his eyes. Irises like fractured sea glass. I've never seen his face look so strange. It's like he's not here.

I must be reading things wrong.

I wish there were music.

Alarm bells are ringing in my head. *Isn't this what I wanted? This doesn't feel good anymore. This is weird. I feel weird.*

I think I want to stop —

I pause for a moment to get my breath, looking down at him — the line of muscle a cushion against his hip bone. I lift my eyes to see his face. I don't know what I'm going to say. I've never told him no. Never protested a word of guidance, never questioned him. "Paul —"

His hand pushes lightly on the back of my head and pushes me forward on him. I cough. A feeling of shame washes over me. I don't want to fight. If I did, what then? Would he be angry with me? Refuse to teach me? His hand stays where it is, directing me.

I can't not try to please him.

So I start again, ignoring the growing feeling of foreboding. It feels wrong, but I just keep going. It isn't at all what I thought it would be.

I feel like a machine. It's really repetitive, and I slow down, tired.

His breath starts to become ragged and chokes in his throat. Relief washes over me. I wait and wait, hoping it will be over soon. He taps my shoulder rapidly, a little more urgently every time — *what do I do now?* He comes, watching my face. I can't stand it and push away.

His breathing quiets. He looks so weak, covered in goose bumps. It's spattered him—his thigh, his pubic hair—I touch my cheek—it's on my cheek.

"Could you please find us a towel?" he asks, as polite as ever. More polite even, as if I've done something wrong.

I start to stand up, then crouch, picking my dress off the floor and putting it back on as fast as I can, which isn't fast at all. It's slow. My body just won't do what I want it to do.

In the bathroom, I splash water on my face over and over again. In my mind, we should still be lying together. The rest of the day, and most of the night, too. I pull a towel off the rack and press it to my face, then rinse my mouth, noting the scary look in my eyes. I go back out and hand him the towel. "Thank you," he says.

He systematically dabs at himself. I sit next to him.

"You okay?" he asks, looking at the silk painting on the wall. Lily pads as large as berets. Surprised carp. He pulls his pants up, buttons them quickly.

"Yeah."

"Good. I'm glad." He smiles, touches my shoulder. Always gentle. A touch that doesn't mean what I thought it would. It feels final.

"Did I do something wrong?" I ask. My voice isn't the same. It's low, rumbles wetly.

"No! Jesus. No." He shakes my knee.

"Okay." A whiny scrape of a word.

He kisses me on the cheek and holds me again, for longer. But not long enough. "Thank you. That was nice."

Tentatively I examine the surface of my shattered heart, feel for the cracks, the enormity of it. I feel abandoned. He holds me until the panic of being alone after everything subsides a little.

I fetch my things, going from room to room. My bag, my sweater, a book. Everything seems farther away than it used to be.

I stand in the hallway and look to where Paul sits on the couch. A deafening pulse of desire to sit back down beside him again thuds in my chest. He smiles, but it's not sincere. He doesn't get up. And because I don't want to give myself away, because I'm determined to be grown up, to keep it together, I smile, too, until the door clicks shut.

I go home and cry so hard, my nose swells shut and my throat goes thick and I feel like gagging and then I do gag, but there's nothing in my stomach to throw up. At least my mother isn't home to see this.

In the shower, his sweat smell rises with the steam, and when it's gone, I open the shower door. A gust of cooler air hits my face, and I feel something soft, like feathers woven between my ribs. Some tenderness. I remember he held me, the way you're supposed to after, and for a moment everything seems okay.

He didn't say he didn't love me. Maybe it's all in my head, the rejection, the wrongness of it. It could be that this was just a casual beginning. There could be something better later.

That feels hard to believe, though.

In bed, my thoughts shift, reorder themselves. The hair dusting his body, bulkier than I expected. The pressure of his hand on my shoulder. The thrilling selfishness of his mouth. A wave of desire comes over me, despite feeling so muddy and gray, and leaves in its wake a nervous, queasy ache in my solar plexus.

Sunset. The house shakes when the garage opens, and soon after, my mother knocks on my door and opens it. I feign sleep; I don't want to see her face. I don't want her to see mine. She shuts the door again.

The sun is shining, as if everything's just fine. Through the kitchen window, a clean lawn and shrubs like beach balls on sticks. A model backyard, perfect and anonymous. No birds. In fact, nothing in the world is acting as if anything is wrong. No tsunamis, devil winds, or apocalyptic horses. There's been no judgment, though I feel it on the inside anyway, that I've been marked, as if the sun can't penetrate my body, or that nothing good is mine or deserved.

I fix myself a bowl of cornflakes and a cup of coffee and sit down next to my mother at the kitchen table.

"Do you need to go back to bed, Claire?" my mother asks. "You look tired."

"I'm okay."

She turns a page of the newspaper. "I wish you didn't started drinking coffee. You'll never be able to stop."

"Didn't *start*," I correct her. "It's a thing I picked up from Julia. Anyway, it's not a habit."

"Okaay," my mother says. "Well, maybe you could walk the dog this morning? When I feed him, he looks at me like he's being insulted. He knows, you know, when you don't visit him. And can you check the earthquake supplies? They say another big one is coming."

The next few days are thin and bitter. The sky seems tired of summer. It's always blue, steadily, endlessly blue. At least in the city, you can hope for sun. There's something to want there.

Julia. I wish I could tell her. She'd know what to think. Maybe she'd think it was all fine. Even cool. Maybe she's already done it. I wouldn't be surprised, considering her looks and talent.

Too bad she's at camp.

I don't do much. I don't have the energy to. Forget my next lesson with Paul, which is less than a week away. Forget college essays, Instagram, earthquakes, and the dog. Someone has used the inside of my chest like a bit of scratch paper — rubbing along the walls to test out pencils. Shreds of the ballade churn in my mind like driftwood, surfacing, then sinking back down as if under their own weight. Beethoven washes it away. Opus 110. One of his very last sonatas. It somehow contains forgiveness. You can listen to it in place of love. You can listen to it in place of a father.

I can't bring myself to play. I tried. It felt like someone was pressing on that scratched place in my chest, and the sense of doom I've been feeling began to conglomerate into real, clear thoughts, and I started to know things I didn't want to know: *Something has ended; a door has shut. I've debased myself beyond what I can live down. I can't see myself playing music. Not with him.* With that thought, I start crying again.

Tash sends me a feeler, how-are-you text.

I'm cool. You?

Her response: *I'm fucking awesome! I know three chords now. Come over! We're doing Cat Power covers. Not like the covers from her covers album, but covers of her own stuff. Haha.*

I text her back. *Maybe another time.*

CHAPTER
—— *Twenty-Five* ——

Friday afternoon is lesson time, but I don't want to go.

The latest headlines ooze onto the screen. The ocean is warming. Wildfire season is all year long now, so it's not really even a season; it just merely is. Part of our existence. Maybe it's just as well that I don't play music. Frivolous waste of time. I should be saving the world. Planting trees.

Dean is pacing beside the sliding-glass door, but walking him would take too much energy.

The garage door grumbles and squeaks open, and I hear the engine fan and tires running over something in the garage.

"Shut that off, please," Mom says after a quick look at the screen. Duterte, the president of the Philippines, is on the television. "I'm done with people like that today."

"Like what?"

Her keys glance off the coffee table, fall to the floor.

"Macho men." She bends carefully, picks them up, and grabs the remote, as I've failed to do what she's asked. She gives the smile she gives when she's annoyed, and raises a skeptical eyebrow.

Then she squints at me and feels my hand, the back of my neck. She makes a noise. "Are you sick? I thought you'd be at your lesson."

"Not going."

"Why not?"

I turn my head into the couch cushion.

"Claire. Come on." I feel her settling into the other end of the couch, her thigh against my toes.

"He doesn't want me."

"What?"

"He doesn't like me."

"But why?" she asks, her voice climbing. I turn to look at her. Her face, paler and rounder than mine, becomes sadder and sadder. This is why I don't like to tell her things. Whatever I'm feeling, she feels. Her face is like a magnifying mirror. All of a sudden, I'm reminded of the money we've spent. I've failed. I've failed her.

"I'm awful."

She sucks in her breath. "Why do you say that?"

I can't explain. I pull myself up, go upstairs, and bury myself in the cool sheets of my bed, will myself to cry but tears won't come.

I hear her talking in the kitchen to one of her friends in

Tagalog. Her tone is high-pitched, a keen that swings down and rights itself as she tries to piece things together, and subsides. I hate making my mother sad. She hangs up the phone and opens a cupboard. The microwave hums and dings. A minute later, she's talking on the phone in the kitchen again, a little too loudly, speaking in English.

I can guess who she's talking to from the pleasing tone of her voice. I swear, she's practically cooing. With her friends, she acts like a normal person. With people she's intimidated by, she starts to act shy and small.

Now she's laughing uncomfortably. They're probably laughing over me. Paul has a way of making jokes — of poking fun and making me feel small and warm at the same time.

A snake in my belly turns. A thrill of anticipation.

Footsteps thud on the stairs and then she enters, without bothering to knock. "I talked to Paul. He was expecting you!" She jostles my knee until I turn to look at her. "All of this over missing the piano tuner? I swear, Claire. Why do you have to take everything so seriously? It's like something snaps in your brain."

"Is that what he said?" All at once I can't stay in bed under my mother's eyes. I get up, look at my bookcase. Touch my fingers to the spines. She doesn't know. What a relief.

"Claire." Her clothing brushes against my elbow. "I know it's getting harder for you. The competitions are getting harder. Are you afraid?"

"No."

Her sigh is sharp. "You aren't quitting." She stands by the doorway, her arms crossed.

If my dad were alive, he'd take her side. Obey your mother, he'd say. Don't make her worry. His one rule for me.

I shrug.

"You're going. If not Paul, then another teacher."

She stands there, waiting, but I give her nothing. I don't want to go to another teacher.

"Claire," she pushes.

"I'm not going."

"After everything, you just want to throw it away?"

"I'm not going!"

I hear her joints crack as she shifts her weight. "I don't know what to do with you. I can't believe it. All the money we spent. Do you know what it is to regret? You will regret this." There's a tone of disgust. She's had it with me.

Fine. It's so funny how she is. When this started, she didn't even want me to go. Now it's an act of disobedience if I don't.

Not completely to my surprise, Paul calls me in the morning. I guess subconsciously I knew that if I didn't go yesterday, it would get his attention.

"Claire." He says my name delicately.

He wants me back. "Hi. How are you," I say, putting the same amount of weight on every word. I jab the pause button on the YouTube video I've been watching of Paul. His face a frozen mask, dulcet, deep in music.

"I'm okay," he says in a clipped, light staccato. "But more importantly, how are you?"

"Fine."

"Liar," he says in a joking tone. "You think it's my fault."

I shake my head, then realize he can't see me. "No. That's not true."

"You think it's you, then."

"Isn't it?"

"Maybe it was a little bit of both." I can hear him smiling. "But nothing we both can't forgive. You were looking lovely and sleepy and gorgeous and—well, I'm human."

"Ha."

"I'm sorry," he says.

"Really?" I don't believe him. I want to believe him.

"I am if I hurt you." The Paul on the computer starts to blur. "Can I make it up to you? Maybe we can make this awkwardness go away. I think it would be better if we did. People could ask questions. That wouldn't be good for us."

"For you, mostly," I say, clearing my slimy throat. I know he cares, maybe too much, what things look like. Still. I miss him.

"True. But will you come? I'd like to hear you play. I'm sure you've gotten up to something interesting."

At least it doesn't sound like he'll be mean.

———

How many days have I lost? Nine? Ten? I have no more time to lose. I can't go back unprepared. I need to look cool, accomplished. Better than when he left on his trip.

Scales first to loosen my fingers, so slowly that each note starts to fade before the next is played, rising on the note before it, and then again. Coming down is like an answer, a meager meal, a matter-of-fact reply, a disappointment, a hole. Coming back up is the sun coming out from beneath a cloud, zipping a zipper, the ring of a cell phone alert, eating a Pac-Man ghost. He seemed pretty chipper on the phone. As if nothing was personal. He didn't mean to make me feel unloved.

I try to play as evenly as possible, each note exactly as loud as the last. I play to bury things.

Dean scratches at the sliding-glass door downstairs. There's no time for him. The scales quicken. Climbing up is a long inhale; climbing down is a slick slide, slick like his chest seeping sweat. Shame bears down on me, makes me small and pathetic and worthless, then lightens when I remember that he apologized. It saves me a little, just a little, from disgrace. It had been a mistake, but a flattering one. He's attracted to me. He couldn't help what he'd done.

I'll wear a mini; I know he likes those on me. Knee socks. Something flirty. He's usually nicer to me if I'm pretty.

Mom is sitting on the sofa, talking to someone on the phone. I shake her shoulder. "Do you have the check?"

She puts her hand on the mouthpiece. "For Paul?"

I nod.

A stitch in the side of her mouth loosens. She nods. "In my purse."

She musses my hair, and with a bright smile that somehow manages to make me even more nervous than happy, she uncovers the phone and starts talking again.

CHAPTER
—— *Twenty-Six* ——

When Friday comes, I'm so wound up that the last thing I expect is to see Julia. Her hair is longer now, and her arms feel strong and lean, like rope, when she hugs me. Julia. Christ.

Above her shoulder, Paul looks clean and cool, standing at the top of the porch steps. He's wearing new glasses. She says something; I answer yes. Yes, yes.

"Did you get invited?" she asks.

"Invited where?" I say automatically, my eyes drawn to his body.

"The Lener."

I'd forgotten all about it. "Haven't heard yet."

"Oh, I thought you just said you had. Phew! Well, that's good. Must mean I still have a chance."

"Wait. You applied?"

"Uh-huh. Gotta keep busy." She gives me a hug, then strolls away. I feel a quake of nerves. I couldn't possibly beat her.

"Hi, Claire." An apology in his lilting voice.

He leads me into the kitchen, chit-chatting all the way. I don't know what I'm saying. I'm panic-breathing as quietly as I can. There's something knowing in his tone, as if we're in on the same secret, and I feel dumb. He slides open drawers, pulls out forks and plates, and places a slice of cake—white, with strawberries—in front of me on the kitchen table. I know what he's going to say. How we need to just move on. How the past gets erased.

"I'm not happy, you know, about what happened." His words are stiff in his mouth. "But we can go on as before if we don't make a big deal about it."

I don't touch the cake. In my heart is an overtone, a high-frequency shudder that won't go away. If I look at him, I won't be able to pretend I'm not in love with him. I stare at the crumbs strewn on the table. "I know."

"I'm not a bad person."

"I know."

"You're really okay?" He takes my hand and the touch is a quick pain, like being nicked by a razor. I can't believe he still wants to touch me. He tilts his face, playfully, like a puppy. "I really do want you to be okay. It was just a total slipup for me. You know how it's been. With Anna and all."

Was I any good? I want to ask. "I'm fine. Really."

I have no idea if I'll be fine again.

"Good." He drops my hand and runs his hand through his hair. "Well, that put a bit of a wrinkle in things, didn't it?" He stretches his legs out beneath the kitchen table. His smile is more open now. "You don't mind if I put on some music, do you? And have myself a glass of wine? Though we really should get going soon."

"Get going?"

"You know. The piano." He twinkles his fingers.

"Oh."

He pours himself a glass of wine, then ducks into the other room, and I pick up the fork and consider the cake. Mahler lieder echoes in from the next room. A bright voice soars, defiantly declares its existence, descends to a minor key.

"There's so much to talk about." He spreads his fingers out on the table "Your repertoire. Have you begun to play anything new? Is there anything you'd like to play?"

"Well, there's the ballade. . . ."

He waves it off with a flat hand. "That will be stale by the fall." A mild rebuke. I stop midchew. He eyes the clock. "Well, you must have been doing your exercises, the Czerny and so forth?"

I purse my lips and shove them sideways. Exercises. Passionless exercises. "Debussy études and the Czerny."

We leave the cake and his glass of wine, and I show him quickly how the Czerny's been going.

"Well, the speed is really not baaad," he says when he's heard enough. "But the articulation could be better in the fourth and fifth fingers of your left hand. Their shape . . ." He gently lifts them to where they should be. The walls of my heart thin, turn vaporous. "How did this happen? Your technique is generally quite nice."

You were gone. "I'm slower when I play your way." More than a little.

He doesn't respond. He's already jumping to the next thing. "Perhaps Scarlatti? Or Ligeti. It would be impressive for auditions."

The Ligeti études are placed in front of me.

"So the first étude. A rule breaker."

We split it apart. He takes the right hand, I take the left. Chaos ensues. The right hand is all white keys, and the left hand is all black. His right hand plays longer lines that begin and end around and before my shorter ones, dance in circles around them, cascade around them.

I've missed this. I've missed his voice and the way it made the strings of the piano hum at times, and the force that moves my playing along. Like a gentle push from behind, like a father pushing a child on a swing.

"Faster." He shows me the tempo. It sounds like conjoined twins trying to break themselves apart.

An hour later, I'm rolling on the soles of my feet, bouncing, bouncing kind of like the way Julia bounces, down the hill. Not quite childlike, almost elegant.

So odd. It was good to see him. There's still pain, but I feel less humiliated. Less crushed.

It's such a relief to know that he didn't think I did anything wrong.

Still, it's hard to think about when he pushed me to

continue. Was he really like that? No, he's a feeling person. I know he is. He wouldn't have done that if he didn't like me, deep down.

Time could wash this away. He could relax around me again, confess things to me. Maybe—and I know this is an outside chance—but maybe, someday, we could go on dates. I know it's not possible now, but I'll be eighteen soon.

It feels better to have hope, somehow.

"Everything's all good and forgotten, then?" Mom asks when I get home.

"Yeah. Yeah, I guess."

"That's good," she says. "I'm glad. Don't give up on yourself, you know? You have so much promise." She looks distressed, as if she needs this, as if she has somehow absorbed my dream.

CHAPTER
—— *Twenty-Seven* ——

School starts and it's like unpausing a show in the middle of a scene. Things don't seem that different. The conversations are as loud and abrupt as television commercials. I missed the songs of the summer. Sure, people are wearing a new shade of green, toss new slang around, I'm given new old schoolbooks, the bindings soft, but none of it's important. The counselor wants to meet with me about my future, like all the other honors kids.

In physics, I head Tash-ward, brushing away my hesitation. I never did text her back to get together.

Her hair is longer than I've ever seen it. Straight-ironed shiny. Jeans, oxfords, schoolgirl purse. The only thing left of the old Tash is her orange nail polish.

"Hi," I say.

She raises her eyebrows and gives me a bitch face. "Really? Just hi? As if everything's fine?"

"Look, I'm sorry. I meant to meet up."

"I texted twice? Three times?"

"Look," I say, moving to sit next to her and trying to come up with the words to explain.

She takes her things and moves to another table.

I watch her dejectedly. Maybe it's just as well. How would I tell her what's really happened? How would I begin?

I look around the room. David Gray, in his Pixies T-shirt, sits next to his best friend, Maggie, who's looking open-mouthed at her e-reader. He looks over her shoulder, says something, lips aslant, and she shoves him away.

Their smiles seem so easy.

Sophia, tanned from swimming, glowing, looking the same and so boring, takes Tash's just-vacated seat. She does a double take at me and starts laughing.

"I can't believe I didn't recognize you. No glasses. And the dress. So cute!"

"I got it secondhand."

"On the Haight?"

"No. Near Paul's place."

"Who's Paul? Your boyfriend?" asks Sophia.

I almost, almost say yes. "No. My piano teacher. I house-sat for him over the summer."

Duncan leans over the aisle. Duncan in his baseball cap and flip-flops, whom I've known since we were ten. "Isn't that just *très très*."

"Well, it was mostly work. I'm starting to focus on auditions for school. I got into the Lener." I flick my hair over my shoulder. The e-mail came just a few days ago. I texted

Paul, received a *Well done!* back that made me feel momentarily better. He was being normal, which means everything is normal. I realize I need so much more reassurance from him now.

"Okay," he says. "We get it. You're way above us."

I glance desperately at Tash, who isn't looking at me, then check my phone, scroll through my texts, to reread Paul's last encouraging words.

In the auditorium, I drive my fingers into the piano's yellow-stained keys. Ligeti. With Ligeti, it doesn't matter that the piano's ugly. The chords are bashed in. One hand does one thing, the other hand another, as if under the influence of different tides, different moons. It's an aural blueprint for schizophrenia.

My left wrist aches, a tiny bit, deep inside toward the outer portion, but not enough to stop. Paul would find it the mark of an artist.

I move on with some relief to the ballade. At least it's something I'm confident about. Lately I haven't felt confident about anything. The rejection and loneliness seems to be burrowing deeper inside of me. Something like disgust, too. I haven't been able to shake these feelings.

Maybe the ballade will move him. Maybe he'll be so thrilled with it that I'll finally feel like things were just like they used to be.

Outside, Tash is sitting on a picnic bench with Chris Langhorn — a skater guy I don't know too well — and

Charles Tran, who's in the year behind us. Of course she's made new friends.

She waves when I wave at her, crossing the quad, but hardly enthusiastically. I start to approach, but when she frowns, I veer away.

"This heat wave is unnatural. It shouldn't be this warm in October." The ice in Paul's glass tinkles neatly. "I'd rather be at a bonfire at Ocean Beach, wouldn't you?"

"I've never been," I say, heading straight to the bathroom to wash my hands. I check my eye makeup, straighten my skirt. Carefully dab on the lipstick from the medicine cabinet.

"It's not the prettiest beach," he says as I open the door, "but it's like you're at the edge of the world." He's leaning against the wall, his body angled over his drink. "Very bland. So much wind. If you stand still for long enough, I'm sure the sand would just bury you." He seems indifferent. He's barely looked me in the eyes since I've come in, and his tone seems superficially cheerful. Nothing genuine. Nothing with feeling, the way he used to be. He hasn't even asked how I've been.

"Why do you go, then?"

His eyes linger over my lips, and a corner of his mouth twitches. A spark of warmth flies through me. "Well, it's very desolate, in a romantic sort of way. But I just meant I'd rather be at the beach. Any beach. Wouldn't you?"

I watch the way the light shifts in his eyes as he says this.

"You want to go? We could, you know." I can't resist saying it.

His face draws closed. A misstep. "Let's just play, okay?"

We begin Scarlatti's Sonata in D Minor. The trills leap and spin, leap and spin. He points out misreads. I correct them nimbly, as if I'm not thinking of everything that's gone on, but of course I am. I keep looking for a reason to touch him, even if it's just his elbow or the cuff of his shirt. If I touch him and he smiles, I could relax a little.

"Very nice," he says. I fold my hands together and sit up straight as if I've been to charm school. "There's a very nice physical, dance-like quality to this piece. Seductive."

Promising. He shows me a different way of shaping the melody, a lighter, more even trill, and I fall right to playing it note for note, a perfect echo. He adjusts my shoulder, and I jump, flub and lose it like an ice-skater who's fallen on her butt midleap.

I don't look up. We both know the source of my mistake.

"Sorry," I say.

"Don't be sorry," he says, his tone light as a paper cut. "It's fine." He sounds detached, polite. As if he's above me. He slides his chair just a tiny bit back, a little bit farther from me.

"What's next. Beethoven?"

"Ligeti." I can't believe he's forgotten.

"Oh, yes. *L'escalier* I think it was."

I correct him again, surprised: "No, the first étude.

Désordre." He's never wrong. How can he not remember what I'm studying? It's like he really doesn't care at all. The thought makes my loneliness, my feelings of rejection, hard to suppress.

"I hate this piece," I say, lifting my hands off the keys in the middle of a phrase. "It's too cold. Too . . ." I mutter some chords. "It sounds like metal breaking off a tractor."

"Well, maybe you can use your hatred of it to make it more intense," he says patiently.

"But I hate hating things!"

"Then don't play it."

"You chose it for me."

"I only suggested it." He leans away from me in his chair, arms crossed.

He gets up and sits beside me. The few bars he plays set me wrong. My body feels crooked, as if some vertebrae have come out of joint. He looks up at my surly expression. "Come on. Be professional."

I try again, spiritless.

"See?" he says. "You're getting it."

I don't believe him. It's obvious how bad it is. "Liar," I say, trying to say it teasingly by tacking on a smile.

"No, really," he says. His eyes glint with amusement. So there is a little bit of flirtation on his side.

"Well, can't we just take a break from it?" I ask, looking over my shoulder at him.

"Fine. There's no point in trying when you're so . . . I

don't know what you have against this piece. Maybe you lack the confidence." I sag. He takes off his glasses and rubs his eyes, as if he's tired of looking at me and the piano. Still, I'm relieved when he suggests we move on to the ballade.

Finally. My chance to move him, to feel close to him.

A film of sweat has been collecting beneath my thighs, and I lift my skirt and knees up from the bench, one at a time to air my skin. His eyes show interest. Good. I bend my head toward the keyboard, close my eyes, and breathe as he taught me to. A last point of stillness. I know it so well, I don't need my eyes to play. It's like the notes unmoor—each one in longing, brilliant and unclean. The trick is to leave things slightly imperfect. I conjure cities, destroy them in his name, knowing that he could love me for this. Hope is high inside me.

After the last note, silence.

"Well, that was certainly full of passion." His tone is critical.

I'm crushed.

He thrusts a hand to the keyboard, chops the piece up, singing along with himself as he goes. I should provide more structure, here. More restraint. There are too many problems, too many mistakes. His eyes look up to the ceiling, off to the side, as if he can grasp the notes from there, pull them down. I can't see a trace of longing or pain or playfulness in his face. He's going on like it's business as usual, and I can't understand how he can do it. Did anything of what happened mean anything to him?

I can't do anything but stare. Just stare. My belly, which has been clenching so hard out of nervousness, begins to weaken and tremble.

"Please don't look at me like that," he says.

"Like what? I'm looking at you the way I always have."

He sits up straighter and crosses his arms over his chest like a child, nervously looking past me at the score. "Have you given any thought to new pieces?" he asks, his face careful.

"No. There's nothing I feel like playing."

"Nothing at all?"

I lift a shoulder. "There's the Beethoven Sonata, opus 110."

"Not a good idea."

"Why not?"

He leans back in his chair. "I mean, we can go over it, but I think this isn't the right time in your development to do it justice, you know? You need things you can perform success- fully for your applications. The 110 — that's not really . . . That one just goes too deep."

The dark crevices between the white keys go fuzzy, the dark keys blur and spread. "I thought you said you wanted me to do more emotional things. And now you don't."

The seconds tick and tick. I can't look at him. Is he being mean on purpose? It's like he wants to push me away. Anger begins to boil like tar in my heart.

"Don't be this way, okay?" he says.

"I don't know why you're punishing me," I say.

He sighs and leans forward. "I'm not! Christ. Look, Claire—"

He touches my hand and I jump, start laughing. Start laughing because I can't sob.

"What's so funny?" he asks.

"I'm sorry," I say, covering my mouth and clenching myself still.

"Okay, then," he says. He places his palms flat on his thighs and gets up. "This is it for the day, I think."

I look at the clock. "I still have twenty minutes left."

"We can tack it on to the end of another lesson, when you're feeling better."

I bend down to grab my books, hearing him sigh above me. *Don't break down.* I tape a smile to my face. *Don't break down.* I blink fast so the tears scatter when he can't see and make for the door.

"Hey. I'm not trying to be mean," he says.

"Then why are you kicking me out?"

"We're just taking a breather. You seem . . ."

"Seem like what?" I turn, shrugging his hand off my shoulder. I don't want him to touch me. I don't want him to touch me again.

"Oh, Jesus Christ," he says, his face frozen in dismay when he sees my face all wet. As if I were some freak. An ugly girl with a swollen monkey nose. A thick mess of a face. "You just seem . . . not yourself. Fragile."

"How am I supposed to feel?"

"Claire . . ." A cajoling tone. As if I can be pacified. He

doesn't love me. He's done with me, somehow, and so there is nothing he can say to make me feel better.

He will never love me.

The thought thuds through me. I don't want to believe it. I grab my things and run out the door.

"Claire! Come and eat anak." She strikes my name like a clock, grips on to me the minute I get home.

I trudge over, feeling trapped. She's always there, waiting for me. So demanding.

Two lit squares on her glasses reflect the glowing screen of her laptop. A pile of bills sits beside it. She's always working, always struggling alone, when she isn't sleeping. She's just as lonely and unlovable as me.

"How did it—? What are you wearing! You look..." She tsks. "Do you really want people to see you that way?" She gives an awkward laugh.

I go up in flames. "Like what. Like a slut?"

Her eyes pop like I've knifed her in the gut. "I didn't say that. You said that."

"Well, that's what you wanted to say." I march over to the cupboard for a glass. *Oh, my God,* I think. *Have I really made that big a fool of myself?* I look down at my clothes.

"Did you go to lesson like you're supposed to? Or are you . . . ?"

"Am I what?"

"Do you have a boyfriend?"

There's a burn in my heart. I jerk the faucet off with

a shaking hand. "I wish you'd stop asking such nosy questions."

"I'm sorry?"

She looks hurt, but I don't care. "You're always asking me questions, and I'm sick and tired of it. What are you doing? What time are you coming home? Did you eat? Did you feed the dog? You better not this. You better not that. It's a constant interrogation, like you think I'm doing something bad all the time. Like you think I'm headed for some awful life!" Her face is frozen in horror, but I'm yelling now and I can't stop. My heart is broken. I'll never be right again. "Like I can't do anything good and even if I do, it won't be enough. Even if I win things, it isn't enough! You don't relax! You can't relax, and it's poison! You're poison." Her chair squeals as she pushes against the table and walks out. I'm crying. Sliding to the floor, the dirty linoleum on my bare thighs, with my glass full, clinging to it with both hands.

CHAPTER
—— *Twenty-Eight* ——

A still blue morning. Waterlogged eyes. They don't open all the way.

My throat is hoarse from having yelled at my mother. I should never have said those things. I feel so guilty, I can barely move.

I find her at the altar beneath the window in her bedroom, changing the candles by the collection of Marys and baby Jesuses.

"Mom?"

"What."

I know I can't make it right. It was too true. I plunge forward anyway. I have to get this feeling of dread off my chest. "I just wanted to say I'm sorry. Things just got bad at my lesson."

Her eyelids are so swollen, they've changed shape. "And so you take it out on me."

I made the wrong move. She's in no mood for apologies. "I said I was sorry."

"So what." She shoves a new red taper into a candlestick. It topples over. Her hands are shaking so much, it makes me nervous.

"I'm just trying to have a life. The life you want me to have," I say, trying to explain. "I know I get caught up in it."

"This isn't the life I want you to have!" She turns. "Running around the city all day. Dressing like that. I never know where you are, if you're coming home on time or what. You walk around acting like you're better than me. It's like you just deign to live here. Like you aren't family anymore! I have to beg for you to play the piano for our friends. I have to beg!"

"That's not fair! I'm just busy. And you wouldn't be so upset if you were busy, too."

She whips around. "That's what you think?"

I wince, beat down by her pain-sharp eyes.

"Yeah," I say, running on fear, but also hoping that I can finally say what I've been wanting to say to her for a long time. "Actually, I do. You should get out more." I spit out the words, but I'm unable to look above her chin. She picks up the vase of spent flowers. A jumble of crucifixes and medals hang from her neck. "Praying isn't living. It's just dealing. I mean, how come you never date? You should, if you want to move on from Dad."

"I'm not going to live according to your rules! Like you know anything about what I've been through."

"Well, how am I supposed to know? You don't ever talk to me about anything, so how can I feel sorry for you the way everyone else does?"

She slams the flowers back on the altar and they upend over the cloth, wet the pictures. A small porcelain statue of the Virgin topples sideways onto the glass table. A sickening sound like bones cracking. Her beatific face continues to smile, though her praying hands have broken.

"Do you know how terrible you're being? Really, I can't believe this." Her words go flying into the upper registers, in flames. Her face is terrible. I start to back out of the room. She's never this angry, never. "I don't tell you about my life because I don't want you to be depressed about it. It's embarrassing, okay? You don't understand how terrible it is to be poor. I don't want to put that burden on you. As if you don't have enough burdens."

I never thought that maybe she was ashamed of her past. That maybe it was worse than anything I could think up, sleeping in my own room, in my own bed, living my comfortable American life.

"Mom—"

"I have spent my life getting you everything you want. School. Lessons. College. And this is what you think of me? I don't deserve this. No one deserves this! Just get out, okay? I don't want to see you right now."

I hide in my room, completely ashamed. I don't know why, but I've never really thought about what my mother's life must have been like. That she was even a child. It's hard to imagine, partly because we don't have any pictures of her when she was young and partly because she doesn't talk about it, ever.

What I know of her childhood: she was the youngest girl in the family, which meant she had to cook every day and do the housekeeping. She went to school to be a nurse, because that was what her family wanted her to do. When she got to the United States, she only had forty dollars in her pocket, and she put her life together with two jobs.

Mom really doesn't have a life now. She doesn't date or go to the gym or have any fun, except for prayer meetings. As far as I know, she never has, and I've never understood why that was. Never tried hard enough to understand.

Julia texts. The walls are still reverberating with my fight with Mom.

Interlochen was a series of affairs, she tells me. The music was good. Food was bad. Boys—men, actually, she calls them men—were gorgeous.

Do you want to hang out? I ask. I can't stand being in the house right now.

I'm free.

"We can't stay here," she says when I get to her house. "It's a disaster inside." She shuts the door quickly behind her.

"But I have to go to the bathroom."

Julia half purses her lips in a sullen pout and thrusts her hand into her purse, retrieves the key, and unlocks the door.

"Just be quick, okay?" Her face is tight. It's like she doesn't want me inside, but I have to pee too badly to think much about it.

"Sorry."

Her house isn't a disaster at all. It's golden and beautiful, and so still, it reminds me of my house. I can't stop thinking about my mom.

I walk down a dark hallway, a soft beep interrupting the silence every ten seconds or so, like a smoke detector with its battery gone bad. Some kind of soft alarm.

I find the bathroom. There's the bedpan leaning against the tub, the spit basin on the bathroom counter, the bitter smell of liniment and tiger balm.

The alarm continues to beep. I realize it's a medical alarm of some kind; I recognize it from when my dad was sick. There was a special bed, equipment that looked like it measured sound frequencies, and other machines that buzzed and hummed.

I'm filled with the oppressive gloom I felt when I looked at my dad, his eyes steeped in guilt. He thought it was his fault, all the trouble. "Don't give your mother any grief," he told me. "Try to make her happy."

I haven't done so well by him.

I flush the toilet and turn on the faucet.

"Jules?" her mother calls in a thick, tired voice that somehow still has a trace of music in it.

I speed down the hallway and out the front door. "Your mom's asking for you."

She blinks, rolling her eyes. "I'll text Seth." She thumbs her phone.

"Are you sure? What if he's sleeping? She sounded . . ." She sounded forlorn. "You should go." She doesn't.

If my mom died, I'd be totally alone.

The curb is clotted with European cars in stately blues and greens, and Hondas and Toyotas in their muddier, warmer ones. The day is warm, as warm as at home, and for once, I don't need a jacket in the city and my arms are bare. We're propelled by the rhythm of our collective steps by gravity down the hill.

"Is everything okay?" I ask, speeding up to match her pace down the hill. I'd rather talk about her than about me right now. Everything is too tender, and I'm nervous to tell her anything about what's been going on with me.

Julia lifts a shoulder and tilts her head toward it. "Eh. Same old." She's applying for the National Merit Scholarship. She got into the Lener, too. No mention of her mother.

She has to be pretending. I keep looking at her shoes, her cheekbones. Even now, with her eyes irritated, as if she had allergies, she looks beautiful. She's browned by the summer, her freckles reminding me of cute drawings of lionesses — they mark where her whiskers would be.

I'm never going to be That Girl. The girl in the movies. The Every Girl. The girl everyone is in love with.

"Hang out with anyone? Any boys?" she asks casually, awkwardly.

"Well . . ." Three paces. Four. "I house-sat for Paul," I say, all nonchalant. It's the closest I can come to telling her. I wish I could just open my mouth and spit it out. Maybe it would make me feel better, but I can't.

"Oh, that's right. What's his bedroom like? I've always wanted to know."

"Why?"

"I don't know. He seems too poised. It makes me think he keeps, like, I don't know, whips and chains in there."

I laugh, feeling a ripple of joy in knowing something she doesn't. "It's sparse. Like the rest of the house."

"Any porn?" She looks at me slyly.

"Shh. People can hear you. And yes." I giggle. I don't mind telling her.

"Well, what do you expect? He's a guy. Did he have, like, magazines?"

"Yeah."

She guffaws. "He's so old. Musicians are just total perverts, aren't they?"

She's so laid-back about sex. She'd probably be open about Paul, if I told her what happened.

We go into a bookstore and part ways. I drift among the books, unwilling to get caught in the fantasy section, thus revealing to Julia what a dork I really am, so I linger in the nonfiction—titles about the oil crisis, climate change, super PACs, money, murderers. I pick up a book about the Philippine-American War—I never see books about the Philippines—flip to the back. I didn't even know there was a war. I tuck it under my arm.

"Have you ever read 'The Little Mermaid'?" A massive book, *The Complete Tales of Hans Christian Andersen*, fills her hands. "Devastating."

"I thought it was supposed to be all happily ever after."

"Nope. That's just the Disney version."

She pays for the book, and I pay for mine, and we walk back outside.

"Here," she says, handing me her bag. "You should read it."

"What?"

"It's a present."

"But why?"

"Just because." She gives me the sweetest look. I give her a hug. I don't deserve a friend like her.

"You made my day," I tell her.

We keep looking through the shop windows at collector lunch boxes, coffee mugs with woodland creatures on them, Japanese ceramics. Moved by Julia's gesture, I buy a necklace for Tash, silver with flower petals captured in a sphere of resin. A peace offering.

Couples and strollers and bicyclists swing past, squinting into the sun that glazes the tops of every surface. It feels like one of those forever days, the kind when I was younger, much younger, making sandcastles with whoever there was to play with at the playground. For the moment, home, my mother, doesn't matter. Everything is good. Life is beautiful.

I'm next to a friend. I hug the book, both books, to my chest until they're warm.

"I kissed Paul," I say. The words launch out of my mouth like they're on springs. "We did things."

Her eyes fly open. "No way! Is it a thing?"

I shake my head.

"No. I don't think so. I thought maybe it could be, but . . ." I shrug.

She doesn't answer. Her face says everything. "Well . . . he's very charming." After a moment, she takes a sharp breath. "Whoa. I can't believe he did that. That's seriously . . . whoa. That's disturbing," she mutters, half to herself, half to me. As if she's not sure what to say.

Her reaction is like a punch to the stomach. "It just sort of happened."

She blinks rapidly. "I guess I'm not surprised," she says, her features rearranging themselves back to her default expression.

"You're not?"

"No." We look up at a mannequin wearing a gown that flows down to a froth around its knees, surrounded by clear glass bubbles. "You're very sensual. Asian girls," she says, and shakes her head. "Men kind of slobber all over them."

I always forget that she thinks I'm hot. I hear jealousy in her voice. And something else. Like what happened was bad. Not silly high jinks or a minor transgression, but a terrible thing.

I leave her at two, after a coffee. Julia was so preoccupied for the rest of our hangout and so was I. The thought throbbed in me all day, after watching Julia register what happened: *Quit lessons. Leave Paul.*

I speed walk through a stretch of restaurants and laundromats, as if I can leave these thoughts behind.

I'm not supposed to feel this way about Paul. I'm not supposed to think of him as bad. There's something forbidden about it, the way you're not supposed to yell at men because they could hurt you; or be homeless, because you'll be invisible; or ugly or fat, because people will scorn you; or Muslim, because people will think you're a terrorist; or shy, because you'll have no friends.

A thought fills my belly: *None of those rules are real. Leave Paul.*

Well, maybe I can just fall out of love. It would hurt for a while, but if I just stay the course and keep taking lessons with him, I'll have gotten what I came for and get into a good college. If I can just hold out.

No. That's not possible. Do you really think you can get over him if you look at his beautiful, charming face every week? You have to leave Paul.

But I need his lessons. His musicality. Our lightning-quick hours. I need this chance for a better life.

No, you don't.

I don't see how else I can do it.

The voice grows quiet.

CHAPTER
— *Twenty-Nine* —

Our house is still a war zone. It's like invisible knives are dangling from the ceiling by their handles, waiting to be taken down, one by one. It takes forever for us to get over things because, like many Asian families, we fight, and then, instead of talking about whatever's bothering us, we hope silence will take care of it.

Back at school, looking down at the worn piano keys, I wait for the urge to play to glow like an ember deep in my belly, the way it always has, regardless of whatever's going on.

When it fails to emerge, I text Julia instead.

You aren't going to say anything, are you? About Paul?

No way. I'm not touching that.

Okay, thanks.

Actually, I wish you hadn't told me. I hate keeping secrets.

I'm sorry.

It's so horrible.

Another shock, to hear her say it so plainly. I don't text her back.

Nothing happens at the piano. No quickening force, no match struck in the dark of my body. Usually I don't have to will myself to play. Sometimes I find myself playing before I even realize I've begun.

Leave Paul. Leave Paul.

The thought continues to throb in me. Deep down in my body is a feeling of unworthiness.

I can't feel this way, can't fight with myself anymore. I just can't. I slip off the bench, and relief floods through me; I know it's the right choice as soon as I make it. I walk offstage, down the stairs, and then I crumple on the floor and cry.

At the end of the week, tiny blossoms rain down in sweeps of wind and gush down Paul's street, catching on windshield wipers and pavement cracks and between the strands of Julia's hair.

She says hello like nothing is wrong, but it's not true. In her eyes is something that wasn't there before, a caginess. I sense immediately that she doesn't want to talk to me, and I don't try. She walks quickly down the street, as if she's cold.

I sense Paul watching and catch his eye through the window. A thread of nervousness draws itself through my gut.

"Are you in a fight? You two?" He takes a sip from a glass of wine he's brought to the door with him.

"No. Why?"

"She's been acting strange. She doesn't know, does she?"

I can't stand lying—it makes me even more anxious. "Yes, I told her but—"

"Why for fuck's sake did you tell her?"

I jump at his tone. He leans against the wall, like a boy loitering outside the 7-Eleven, annoyed at the whole world. I wanted to say good-bye in person, but now I wish I'd stayed home. Sent him an e-mail. The parting would have been quicker, less painful.

A car roars by, and he reaches to shut the door behind us. "What did she say? Wait—what did *you* say?"

"That we did stuff."

It's quiet enough now that I can hear things tap on the window. Little dry flutterings, maybe the blooms from the tree. He cocks his head, surveying me like a bird looking at the ground. I've turned my body half away from him, like it would be harder for him to take aim from the side. I think about leaving. Why endure this? My nose has begun to run in the sudden warmth.

"Stuff? Nothing explicit?"

"No."

"What did she say? Was she upset?"

"She's not easy to shock."

"That's true. She's far more pragmatic than you are. She could . . . Well, it doesn't sound dire."

I look at him out of the corner of my eye, see the muscle behind his jaw popping. A jaw that looks carved by an artist. Did I really find him beautiful? I don't now. There's a priggish flare to the openings of his nostrils. His face looks swollen, spread. "No, she's not going to go off and slit her wrists or post it on Instagram or whatever. She doesn't care what you do."

He takes his glasses off, drops them on the hall table, and rubs his eyes. "You won't go and tell anyone else?"

"No. Jesus."

"Because it's not just my career on the line. It's yours, too. People won't think of you as an artist. And it's not like this is a common occurrence for me. I don't *usually* dally with students."

Dally. "I get that."

"It was special."

My heart feels its longing. And its disappointment. "Not special enough, I guess."

His face dulls. "What do you want? I know all kinds of people. At all kinds of schools."

"I don't want anything from you."

"Well. Think about it."

"You know I can't believe you're being like this. It's kinda . . . disgusting." I'm afraid to say the word, but it feels so true.

His eyes pop. "Of course I'm being this way! I do have to live."

There's a bitter taste in my mouth, like I've bitten into something black and sour—bad fruit. He looks so fearful. Weak. I feel sick. "I have to go, Paul. I'm done."

A deathly pause while I wait for his response. I've known all this week that he wasn't going to take this well. My heart is twisting itself into knots.

His lips squirm into a smile. "That's fine. Maybe it's just as well," he says, picking lint from his shirt. "You know it doesn't bode well for your career, running away from complications. You need to be able to handle things like this to work professionally in music. Writing it, playing it, composing it. They're all tough roads. It's possible you don't have it."

I absorb the blow. I feel like a fool, but I can't come up with any words.

He lifts a shoulder. "You know I'm sorry. I've said that before." He walks quickly down the hallway, leaving me in the foyer.

Back at home. Mom's gone off with her novena group to pray. The house feels rearranged, as if someone's come in and moved everything around an inch or two. On the piano, my score for the ballade. That ridiculous, overemotional, sentimental, disastrous piece of music. I seize it and rip it in two down the middle crease, and then into nice, long strips. Down the bits go, onto the floor.

Something snaps; I'm outside myself, toppling books, banging my hand on the piano. I yell something—I don't know what.

I hear a ping inside the piano and stop.

My hand prickles. Pinpricks of light pink blood well up through the scraped skin. My pinkie is curled into itself. The piano chimes out tunelessly, a few keys sunken like dents. My piano. My father's piano. I touch the sunken F key, near to middle C. The hammer doesn't lift. No sound.

I whisper an apology to him, as if he's perched somewhere along the avenues of the clouds above me.

Four months after my dad had passed, my mother asked, "Did you feel that?"

"Feel what?"

"I feel like someone just touched my shoulder." She looked around at the density of the air.

I've overheard her tell her friends that she thought Dad would come visit. "We're being watched. He's watching over us." And I would privately think there was something wrong with her.

Strange to feel this way now. The world has shifted. Nothing is steady. School. College. Music.

I should be nicer to my mom about being so sad.

Every word Paul said vibrates in me, grates on my bones. Sleep is good.

It feels like only a few hours later when my mattress shifts. I'm covered in sweat. The sound of my mother: her soft clothing brushing against itself.

"What happened downstairs?" I picture the wreckage: the busted piano, the torn music. She sharply inhales. "Oh, my God . . . what happened to your hands? How are you going to play?"

"I'm not going to." I bury my face in the pillow.

Silence like water. She takes one hand in hers and looks at the swollen purple fingernails. She holds my hand so gently. It's like our fight, the remnants of it, are completely gone.

"Don't be nice to me," I tell the pillow. I don't deserve it.

She leaves, then returns with a glass of juice. Holding it makes my hand ache, but it's cool, too.

"Can you move your fingers all the way straight?"

I show her. My right pinkie strains to come all the way flat. She makes a noise, as if it's her excoriations, shakes her head.

"I'm sorry we got into a fight, Mom."

She sighs. "I'm sorry, too."

She never apologizes. Her eyes are troubled, but mercifully, she doesn't say anything more, just gives me some Advil and a Ziploc of ice for my hand, then shuts the lights off again.

CHAPTER
— *Thirty* —

I spend the weekend in bed. I can tell Mom has questions, but she doesn't ask them. She gives me more Advil and some chicken soup spiked with ginger. Her face is heavy, like I'm dragging her down. She must know what it all looks like. The short skirts and heartache. There's a despair around her eyes.

"Do you need to see Dr. Holloway?" Her gynecologist.

I manage a yes. She blinks as if the word hit her in the face.

She sits down. The bed slants. "Is it Paul?"

"No. A boy." She nods slowly, the edges of her face crumpling. She's never said I shouldn't have sex before marriage, but I've always assumed, the way she just won't talk about it, that she would think it sinful.

I cinch myself into a ball, bracing myself for judgment. "Are you mad at me?"

She rubs my shoulder. "Are you going to be able to make it to school?" she says instead. It's a kindness that comes from nowhere. The way she asks me reminds me of how I am with her on days she can't get out of bed.

I'd like to know what's really left — what the true course, the map of my life really is, if I took away all the things that are unreliable. The children's books on my bookshelf, the fairy tales, every story, every book with a happy ending, every illusion, and put them all in a box, everything but things that stay. That are really here. The sun rising, the colors we see, the stirring of wind, the sound of a glass of water sliding on the table. Those would go on the map. Hunger and thirst go on the map. People don't. Anything that can't be relied on doesn't go.

Feelings about Paul emerge from their hiding places. How he pushed me back down. It passes through me like a ghost, locking me in fear at odd moments. On the bus merging into traffic. Selecting a dress in the morning. Streaming cooking shows with Mom, which has been occupying a lot of my time lately.

I don't play. It's like my body is soaked in his scent and his salt and his fluid, and my body holds his habits. He's written his name in my hands. And when I try, I feel like he's right there with me. It's too much. It's just too much. The way people leave their marks. They color everything.

A week later, Monday afternoon. My college planning appointment with the school counselor, Mr. Colicchio. His office is the size of two broom closets. His desk barely fits inside. Behind him is a poster. STAY COOL. STAY IN SCHOOL. A Hispanic girl with dimples holds her diploma and grins like she's in a fast-food ad.

"Claire! Have a seat." He gestures with a thick hand to the upholstered folding chair against the wall. The chair of opportunity.

Dingy and greasy, it looks like a million kids have sat in it. Fat kids and skinny kids and stupid kids and genius kids. Kids with disabilities. Kids with broken homes. Kids without any future at all.

In front of him, my name is printed in ballpoint pen in large, administrative capital letters on a manila folder. My record. I feel a sense of doom. All the things I could have done, if only I decided not to sleep. I never built a habitat for humanity or saved a whale.

"This will be quick. I just wanted to touch base with you, find out what your safeties are, your reaches. You know, make sure that everything is in order for your future! Super exciting! Do you know where you'd like to go?" He talks to me as if he loves kids. Bent forward, glasses on the tip of his nose, but smiling. He must live a completely different, happy life, one with a wife and family to visit at Christmas.

"Well, I'm hoping Cal. UC Santa Cruz. Cal State East Bay. Though honestly, I don't really know right now."

"Really?" he says, as if now I'm an unusual specimen.

"Yeah. I've been doing piano competitions. Placing pretty well. But that's probably not going to keep going, so." I shrug.

"Is that right?" he asks. "Well, that would mean Stanford, then, with their music department. Aren't you considering it?"

"I have, but don't I need more? Like, honors societies and marathons?"

"Well, I think you have a chance."

"I do?" I've frozen in my seat.

"Yes! Judging by your ACTs and your piano playing. I hear you playing, you know, at lunch. Just exquisite."

"What do you think of Oberlin?"

"Oh, definitely Oberlin. Fine school. Places like that are looking for you. They really are. Oh, come now. Don't cry. . . ."

When I leave his room, my whole body, which has been aching as if I haven't been getting any sleep, lightens. School. There's still a future ahead. It's like a gift. I text Mom. I can't wait to tell her.

When I get home, I dig for my keys and come up empty.

They're not in my backpack, not in my pockets. I turn around and look at the street and the parked cars on the curb as if someone's going to hocus-pocus a key for me. Dean's whine from the backyard pierces the stillness, and I enter through the side gate, check the back door, just in case. Also locked.

Dean's eyes have the rage of the jilted. When was his last walk? Early summer. I haven't let him in my room in weeks.

I sit down on the concrete beside him and appease him with an ear rub, call Mom.

"I can't leave work early. Can you wait at Tash's?"

I don't know if it's a good idea to just show up at her house, but she only lives a couple of blocks away.

At the gate's opening, Dean jabs his nose between my shin and the door in a bid for freedom, then shoots out like a bullet. He looks back, stubborn and defiant, to check my reaction.

"It's okay."

He waits for me to catch up.

I'm not too nervous about seeing Tash — one day at lunch I gave her the necklace and apologized, and things have been better since. But we haven't really hung out, partly because I know that if we spend any amount of time together, I'll tell her. And I've been so low lately. I haven't really wanted her to know how low I am. I've always wanted her to be impressed by me — to be the more successful one. I've always thought, and I know this is so stupid, but if I wasn't successful, she wouldn't like me anymore. And I don't know if she'd still like me if she knew about this. I haven't heard from Julia in a while, and I know it's because of what happened with Paul.

Tinny drums trickle down the street, growing louder as I get closer to her house. Must be her band.

The garage door is open, and Tom is spread out on a couch the color of dirty-yellow daisies, with a natural wood and ivory Fender on his lap. His pants look like they've been patched with dental floss—or a thick, cotton string—and brown flannel. Charles Tran picks his fingernails at a drum kit. Chris fiddles with a pedal.

Blue Christmas lights, unlit, hang from the ductwork along the ceiling. The shadow of the tree in the front yard leans against the washing machine. A Wodehouse paperback (Tash loves those silly books—they make her laugh) lies open, facedown, on the cement floor. It looks romantic. A little dirty, but beautiful.

"Dean!" Tash's face lights up with pleasure when he rushes up. She squats and puts her arms out and Dean curls his body into her. "Ugh. Stinky." She kisses his nose.

I feel a moment of relief, seeing her happy to see, if not me, then at least my dog. "I got locked out. Okay if I stay here until my mom gets home?" I feel my face go hot.

Charles looks at me, his curving fingers still held up to his face for examination. Tom looks suspicious, like I'm going to hurt Tash or something. I wonder what he's heard. I feel tears start to spring into my eyes.

But Tash just nods. "Sure, you can wait here. But we're practicing."

"That's great! What are you calling yourselves?"

She suppresses a grin. "Sunchaser."

"Cool."

I go inside and grab a glass of juice and come back to find them lurching through "Havalina" by the Pixies. They aren't even. Chris doesn't hear himself. Charles has a limp, uneven roll on the snare. Everyone uncertain. It's everything I didn't want, what I knew I'd be in for if I joined, but at least they're playing. At least they have the heart to try.

They creak along to the bridge. Guitar and bass meet on the same downstroke, and after half a beat Tom punches down on one of the guitar pedals in a chain at his feet. A burnt shimmer of distortion. I see the way Tash and Tom look at each other, talking without having to say anything out loud. She opens her mouth to sing into the microphone. A clear note.

They finish the song with a spurt of guitar. "I didn't know you could sing." I can barely say the words, I'm so glued down by jealousy. It occurs to me that maybe I didn't want to join, at least in part, because I didn't want to be out-shone.

She frowns; she knows I can't possibly think much of it. "Yeah, I was always too shy to sing in front of you." Her bass weighs down her thin neck. "Tom thinks I should sing more."

"You should."

"Yeah, stop hiding," Tom says from the corner.

"Is that the one you were talking about?" I nod to the keyboard in the corner.

"Yeah. Here." Tom flips a switch. I touch a key. He shows me the oscillating knob, how to tune it. It's like an alien cousin to the piano.

"Whee," I say, sending a note surfing away with the oscillator.

He laughs. He seems nice in a way Lee never was.

Why did I choose Lee? Why did being handsome and talented have to be more important than kindness?

Suddenly tired, I slump on the couch.

"You okay?" Tash has always been a quick study when it comes to my feelings.

I shake my head.

"You wanna talk about it?"

"No. I'm good."

"Okay. That's odd. You losing your keys. Since when do you forget anything?"

"I know. You guys should keep going. Ignore me."

"Are those your Snoopy socks?" I look down at my yellow socks. She smiles. "You still wear those?"

"Laundry day."

"Yeah, right."

I laugh, and she tosses me an old cotton blanket from a pile of folded laundry beside the washing machine. I know the smell of her laundry detergent.

I get the impression that they don't usually have people watch, and didn't know how much harder it would be when someone's eyes are on them, until now. When Tash butterfingers and sends her pick flying, she steals a quick look at me as she chases after it, and I try not to look like I notice. Chris picks it up for her, and she takes it with a sheepish look, nods her head in time, and joins back in again, fingers shaking doubly. I try to look like I enjoy it, feel guilty that

266

part of me doesn't. Not because it's bad—there are things here that sing—but because part of me wishes I were her, mistakes and all.

"What do you think?" she asks cautiously afterward.

I could say so many things that could make her quit. I know exactly what to say, and how to say it. I could even make it sound as if I were helping her, like Paul would.

"You have a good ear. You just need time to get your fingers to catch up."

"Could you teach us some stuff?"

"You don't need me." The truth of that is a relief. I'm not better than her. "You just need practice."

She gives me her rakish grin in response and rolls her pick along her knuckles.

See? I tell the imaginary Paul in my head. *It isn't that hard to be kind.*

Dean gets up, sniffs a wire and a microphone stand like they are the smallest wonders of the world.

The band wraps up practice. I stay on the couch, watching the shadows of the trees glitter and shine on the dryer.

Tash bounces on the cushion at the far end, and Dean crawls up onto my shins, leans against her, gives me his resting, effortless, deep-love look with his half-blind eyes.

"You seem more confident now," I tell her.

"I do?"

"Even your grades are better. I saw your last physics quiz."

She flushes. "Yeah. I felt left behind when you started taking music more seriously."

"You shouldn't have. I mean, I shouldn't have done that. I feel like a heel."

She rolls her eyes. "Haha. A callused one."

That's when I know it's going to be okay.

CHAPTER
—— *Thirty-One* ——

Lunch with Tash becomes routine again, but a different one. The boys make room for me on their picnic bench near the soccer field at lunchtime. I generally just stay on my phone and let their chatter roll off me. Television shows. One of them is learning to shoot skeet. He has a dog he's training to hunt.

One of Chris's friends, Noah, sometimes eats with us, too. One day, he tells us he's been having sex with a twenty-seven-year-old woman who lives in an apartment complex down the street. I sit up at this. "There must be something wrong with her," I say.

"Why would you think that?" he says. Noah's one of the prettier, cleaner boys in school. Sharp-chinned. The skin on the insides of his arms is baby smooth, like pale, moist clay. As far as he's concerned, he's been chosen.

"She's using you."

"In the best possible way." Awkward laughter.

"Does she shave?" asks Charles, goggle-eyed.

Noah rolls his eyes back, pretends to be basking.

I give him a scathing look. "That's disgusting."

Charles looks guilty, but Noah looks at me. "I never took you for a prude."

It's a lost cause. At least I know that for me, sex matters. Every single time. I don't get how people can be so casual about it.

Tash feeds me music, new artists, new songs. Today's new band doesn't leap out at me but sinks quietly into the background.

"It's okay."

"Just okay?"

"You know how it is. You have to be in a certain place sometimes to like things. Remember when you hated the Pixies? And then one day it just happened."

"Okay. Well, I'll just keep playing stuff for you," she says with a grin. "You'll come around eventually." She sticks her tongue out at me.

"I guess." The truth is, I don't know what I'm supposed to like anymore. I put my earbuds in tentatively, jolted by the musicians' proddings to be joyful or sad or horny alongside them. I'm nervous when my body responds as two voices meld.

I wash Dean over the weekend. He needs it so badly, along with a bunch of other stuff. Like his blanket, one of my dad's old ones, is too riddled with flea eggs to bother cleaning, so I throw it in the trash bin outside and poke around for a clean one. I find other things instead in the boxes stacked against the garage walls: my dad's old records, his record player, my mother's clothes from when she was thin and fashionable, bolero vests and peach-colored T-shirts with shoulder pads. I find the comforter I had when I was four, its stuffing pilled. Pink- and blue-haired cartoon kids among moons and stars. I fold it up and put it in the corner of the garage for Dean.

"Thank God," Mom says when she sees me with arms full of old towels, flea shampoo, and ear wash.

His big black marble-like eyes close slightly when I clean his ears. Then I put cotton balls in to keep them dry and bathe the rest of him. He's all quivery. His eyes, jelly-like a few minutes ago, shoot hate in his misery, but at least he stops shaking when he's foamy.

I dry him with the old towels. He smells minty and warm. Still like a dog, but better.

While he dries, shaking himself occasionally, I poke around Dad's records and CDs. There's stuff I remember — an album of the ballet for *Romeo and Juliet*, Dionne Warwick — but also stuff I've been curious about. There are Deutsche Grammophon recordings, Columbia recordings. Things I've seen at the library but never had time to check out. He's got the Kinks, too. Amazing. I love the Kinks.

I put a new flea collar on Dean and open the door for him, and he sniffs the floor briefly before making his way up the stairs and into my room, trodding on the sheet music and clothes.

It's a mess. Eye shadow cases scattered on the floor. Shirtsleeves wound around the legs of my bed. The protective case on my laptop cracked from when it slid off my bed.

I push Dad's new-old CDs onto an already crammed shelf. Throw away the copy of *Crime and Punishment*, which I'd bought only because Lee had read it. I thought it was boring. I know I'm not supposed to think that, but I don't care anymore.

Mom pokes her head in. "Why don't you turn the statue the other way?" She gestures to the Holy Family statue, made of porcelain, that I've turned to look beatifically out the window.

"Because it gives me the creeps."

"It watches over you." She turns the statue the other way, then stoops to pick up a CD. One that Paul had recommended to me. "Where does this go?"

"In the trash."

She puts it on a shelf in the closet. "This one?"

"Oh. That's overdue. From the library."

"You'd better go return that soon."

"Okay."

"Tomorrow." She sits down on my bed. "You haven't played in a while, huh?"

I go to pet Dean, who's lying in the corner, and sit against the wall. "The piano's messed up."

"How do you mean?"

"A few keys don't play anymore."

"We could get it repaired. Or we could buy a new piano."

"Well, I don't think it's worth repairing." I can't help it, but I feel a thrill of hope when she mentions buying one. "But that's nice of you."

She turns off the music—one of Tash's playlists; it has absolutely no association with Paul, but lets me feel things— and, with effort, lowers herself to sit beside Dean and me on the floor. Dean points his nose toward her, checking for something, then sneezes. "You know that competition you were working so hard for. It's only a month away."

"I know."

"Are you going to go?"

"I honestly don't know if I can."

"Yes, you can. Of course you can." She puts her hand on my arm. "You need to move forward. This isn't the time to wallow."

Sorting through stuff has left me in a mood. "Well, what about you? You don't move forward."

She looks caught. "I know."

"Maybe it's time to go to counseling." The idea that my mother should do that has been on my mind for so long that it's a relief to say it.

She laughs. "I have God. That's my counseling."

"Maybe that's not enough."

"I *am* happy." I give her a look. "Really! Most of the time, anyway. This is a good life. I have the life I want here. Do you know how rare it is? To have your own house? And not need a man. It's nice, not having to answer to anyone."

"But you could have more."

"This is how I want it. But you, on the other hand. You can't pretend that you can just throw this away and not regret it. You can do this." She gives me a kiss on the cheek. "I have faith in you."

Downstairs, I lift the lid on the piano seat and catch a whiff of another time. Savory, almost spicy, like a kitchen pantry. There are other old things hiding in here. Primers. Manuscript paper explaining the circle of fifths. My dad's old sheet music, their covers magenta, chartreuse—colors from another era. Albéniz. Granados. He liked the Spanish composers. I flip through his copy of the *Goldberg Variations*. His handwriting was similar to mine—light dashes, whisked fours. Immediately I start to mentally trace the movements of my fingers. Hear him play. Hear Paul play.

Everything beautiful has been tainted.

I close the bench.

The next day, I drag myself over to the conservatory to return the CD. I don't feel like playing, even if my mom wants me to, but I can at least return the CD.

Being there is like I've been swept out from under the bed back into the light again. The golden shine of the floors, the doors lining the atrium leading to salons and theaters, each one named after a person with money. There's a fluid bustle to the place—every sharp sound buffeted somewhere by sound panels and heavy doors. It's graceful. I feel greasy and crinkled up, trudging up the stairs. Flashes of memory. A different life.

"Claire!"

Goose bumps. I turn, and stop short. It's Andrew. I feel a sense of déjà vu. Everything I've been trying to forget seems realer than I want it to be. I miss Paul, I think, then wish I'd never met him. If I could erase it all from my brain, I would.

"You've lost some weight, haven't you? Are you on a diet?" he asks as he approaches. His smile is warm.

That's right. I've always liked Andrew. I shake my head.

"Well, you look svelte."

"Thanks."

"I was sorry to hear that you'd left Paul." His mouth pulls down, one side and then the other.

A small clasp in my chest pops open at the sound of his name said in such a measured tone. A tone for breakfasts and the weather report. A rivulet of longing threads hot along my breastbone.

"Me too."

"Well, I hope you have a new teacher that suits you better."

"She's fine." It's easier to lie than to explain that I'm not with a teacher at all. "Closer to home."

"Well, close is . . . good." He laughs. "She's up to preparing you for the Lener, I trust. I imagine you're still going?"

"Oh. I don't know if I'm going yet."

"But you got in?"

"Yes, but—"

"Oh, that's so exciting!" A crinkle forms between his eyebrows. "You know Paul will be there."

"He's going?"

"He usually does. It's just so beautiful there. December in the mountains. It's like a vacation to him. A tax write-off." Another clasp in my chest pops open. Sorrow floods me. "I worry sometimes. I know he can be . . . well, hard on his students. This isn't the first bitter end I've seen. Are you really okay?"

More clasps pop. I think I'm going to cry.

His lips set flat and grim. "That bastard. Well, you know, if ever you need a letter of recommendation or, really, anything, please e-mail me, okay? I'm an excellent forger." And he hugs me. Out of the blue.

Buried in his chest, I hear him say, "Don't let that sad, hollow man get you down."

Sobs and sobs. Even though we're in the hallway, he stays. I'm so surprised. But he stays until all the tears are gone.

He kisses my cheek good-bye. "I'm going to call you and make sure you're okay. No. Really. DM me." By the time he's out of sight—down the hallway, and around a corner—I feel different.

I was right to leave Paul. Sometimes I haven't been sure, and now I know. Andrew would know better than anyone.

I hear music flowing from a room I can't see, and I feel it in my body again, feel its beauty.

———

That afternoon, I watch Paul playing the *Hammerklavier* on YouTube. A smile stretched across Horowitz's face. Horowitz! Of all people. And Paul's playing unfazed.

I guess you can be talented and still be awful. I feel so pathetic that someone so awful can be so loved by almost everyone, but to me, he was terrible. And I don't know why. I feel as if it's my fault, but I'm sick of thinking about it. Mom is right: I have to move past this.

Out of curiosity, I put on an old recording of me to see what can be salvaged.

Damn, I'm fast. Clumsy sometimes, but there are colors I like.

I shout down to my mom from the second floor. "Hey, do you remember when you offered to get me a new piano?"

That evening, we go to Ranch 99 for fried fish. We pass the Filipino bakery, the church, the pho spot that Tash likes. I dream of the Sierras. A glass-paned auditorium nestled into a stark plain behind which mountains loom. The Lener. I'm going. It feels like something has snapped into place. It feels right.

We pass the Middle Eastern bakery, sari shops with their beautiful shining fabrics in hothouse colors. Another small, insignificant high school.

"What if I want to go to school away from home next year?" I ask my mom. "I need to know you'll be okay." *I need to know you won't hide away and never get out of bed,* I think.

"I'll be fine."

"Are you sure you don't need therapy?"

"I have church!"

"Yes, but you've always had church. And still, sometimes, you're not okay."

"I'm fine," she grumbles. "You need to stop worrying about me. You're the one who should be going, not me."

"You think I need it?" *More than you?* I want to say.

"Well, you won't talk to me. You need to talk to some-one."

I don't respond. It's too soon.

She stops harping as she starts hunting for a parking spot. The lot's always crowded.

The place smells of fish, even though the market is large and the seafood is all the way in the back of the store. There are tanks of different kinds, clams of different sizes, scallops and snails and mussels. Mom picks out a tilapia from a tank, and we watch the man behind the counter hack the scales off of it with a long knife. Scales and blood fleck the wall. He slips it into the wok.

I wonder what Julia would think of this place and its fish with their rainbow reflections, lying in crushed ice, blood filling their pearly eyes. She'd probably be grossed out and find it strange. Lee would think it was cool. Paul would probably find it exotic and try to say something witty about it. But it's normal for me. A normalness that I can't explain to any of them.

The oil chortles over the fish.

"You really want to go away for school?" Mom asks,

shifting her weight to her other foot. The wait is long.

"If I can."

"We're going, aren't we?" she says. "To the competition."

"Yeah. We're going."

"Good." And she looks at me with so much pride, it almost makes my chest hurt with happiness.

On the way back inside the house, I grab Dad's record player from its old, dusty box and a few records.

The player's lid is caked with dirt and it's sticky when I take a dampened cloth to it, so I bust out the Windex and soap and scrub it on the kitchen table until it's clean. It doesn't look so bad. I'm not too sure about the needle, but there's only one way to find out if it's okay.

I choose Dionne Warwick, set the needle. The speakers pop at the touch, and the kitchen fills with a solid presence, as if a woman sways in the corner, wearing a glittery gown from the seventies, smiling, her eyebrows lifted as she sings. I'm back in time.

Mom walks in and looks at the records I found. Elton John, the album cover yellowed, color missing in spots. The Beatles. The Guarneri String Quartet's complete Beethoven quartets. Paul had that one, too.

"Dad had a lot of good ones, didn't he?" she says.

"So much R&B."

"Yeah, he loved that."

Mom sings along. She sounds young when she sings, and it comes from the chest, like it does when she prays. She laughs. "Do you remember when we used to dance to this?"

For the moment, I think of my father sitting in the kitchen, taking up space, breathing, warm with sunlight. "He was always trying to get you to dance."

She hums along, placing the fish on a plate, spooning out rice for us. I snap a photo of the fish's eye and add it to my Instagram. "He was." She laughs. "He didn't want me ordering him around all the time."

"Really? So even he got your inspections."

"Ha. You're funny."

The record has a slight warp—the long rise of a hill, a hiccup of a smaller one, a silent inner rhythm of its own. "Did you know Dionne Warwick is related to Leontyne Price?" she asks.

She starts to wash the dishes, swaying to the beat. She dances by herself in the kitchen, just like I do in my room. She's like me; her grief comes in waves, and between the waves, there's just as much sun and goodness as there has always been.

After dinner, with a belly full of fish, I get on the computer to start looking for a new piano. I want one with depth. With strength in its voice.

CHAPTER
—— *Thirty-Two* ——

I've been dreaming of the tone of the piano I'd want for so long, I know immediately when we've found the right one when I try it, and we pay for it to be delivered as soon as possible.

The old piano weighs so much, it may as well be a cement block on one end of the room. I thought it couldn't be moved. I had forgotten it had wheels until the movers come and it glides like a shopping cart.

My mom and I stand to the side and watch them, these hulking men that smell like salt and metal. I blush, and then blush more because I realize I'm blushing.

"No, we're keeping the bench," my mom says when one tries to pick it up. She follows them down the front stairs, Dean watching.

The heart of the room is gone.

It uncovers a perfect narrow rectangle of dust overlaid with a net of long black hair. There's a bit of bright red fuzz, a hair clip, a couple of pencils—the wood has browned and softened—a penny. The *Appassionata* sonata, wrinkled, its corners bent, sags against the wall. I pick up the penny and put it in my pocket, then pick up the old plastic hair clip. It's from the fifth grade, bow-shaped, in a color of pink I've since stopped wearing.

I try it on in front of the mirror. It doesn't look that bad, or at least not as bad as I thought it did back then. I chucked it because I wasn't as pretty as I wished I could be.

A mover's groan signals me to come out. I toss the barrette in the trash. It's too childish now. They're lifting the new piano through the doorway—an upright, full-size brown Kawai we found used.

The movers count to time their maneuvers. I worry for their backs. They barely give a glance at the room or my mother arranging the chairs, shoving them into new places with her knees so they face both the altar and the piano.

The room just smells like lacquer and fresh wood now, and the piano throws filaments of light off its surface like a woman's hair, onto the chairs, the painted dishes and vases my mother likes, and the flowers. I get the sense that it isn't truly still, but waits intently, like a choirboy awaiting the wave of a baton.

It was a good deal. A woman had bought it on a whim, then realized she didn't have the time to learn.

"Well," she said, when she heard me play, "you should definitely have this piano."

I set my sheet music for the ballade on it, crisscrossed with Scotch tape and assaulted with notations and erasures.

I play straight—no flourishes, just the piece.

My fingers aren't as strong as they were, so it doesn't sound quite the same, though nothing does. Everything's been altered. The darkest parts of the piece are sharp, menacing, and its brightest colors, the ones that used to come so easily to me, are harder to form or are eluding me entirely.

I cut myself off midmeasure and put my forearms along the black keys, my head in my arms, and close my eyes. This may go nowhere. Maybe we shouldn't have bought this piano. It doesn't speak to me the way the other one did. It doesn't resonate with the afternoons when I could lay the soft inside skin of my father's wrist against my cheek and smell his salt and blood. It doesn't have his soul inside it. There's nothing reassuring here. Even though it's very pretty, it will take time for it to feel like an extension of me.

My mother touches my shoulder. "Anak."

I sit back up and try again.

One day, at lunchtime, I pull Tash aside to my hiding place under the bleachers and tell her what happened between me and Paul.

The words I have to force out feel heavy and sharp. Time slows down as I tell her. Everything starts to contract—my knees up to my chest, her eyes into worry and rage.

"That bastard," she finally says after I've finished.

"I know, right?" I say, tentatively glad to hear she's on my side. I don't know why, but I wasn't sure she would be.

"You could get him into trouble, you know."

"Why would I do that?" I shift to keep from getting stiff. "It was my fault, too."

"Not as much as it was his." She examines her sandwich, looking at it as if trying to figure out how to attack it. Like it's something to be assaulted. "You're underage!"

I stare at the grass. "You know, I did want to stop. I tried to say something."

She looks up from her sandwich. "You did?"

"Yes."

"And he made you keep going?"

"He . . . encouraged me."

"If you wanted to stop, he should have let you stop. That's rape."

I jump at the word as if I've been pricked with a pin. It can't be. Rape is what happens to other people, to people in stories or on TV. I curl up even tighter into my body, a feeling of worthlessness bursting over me like a dark wave.

Her fingers touch my arm, as softly as I've ever felt her. "Are you okay?"

I shake my head. It's such a familiar feeling lately, worthlessness. "Do you think that's what it was?" I ask. "I didn't actually say no."

"You're so much younger. He's your teacher, and he has this crazy amount of influence over you. When you met him, it was like he could do no wrong."

He definitely did take advantage of how I felt about him.

Why didn't he let me stop? It wasn't right. In fact, it was absolutely wrong.

She puts her arms around me, and I cry, thinking I'm going to fall apart, every part of my mind obliterated by the thought, the horror, of it. I've been feeling as if I'll never be happy again, that the world has lost its colors somehow, and now I know why.

For a while I wonder if I'll ever stop crying. And then I do. And there's the sunshine. There are the kids, far away, playing basketball.

CHAPTER
Thirty-Three

I finally go to the doctor — Dr. Holloway, the ob-gyn — with my mom. Even though Lee and I used a condom, I think I'll feel better after everything if I do things to take care of myself: eat well, drink well, be nice to myself, see the doctor.

My mother is quiet on the way there. "It's good to get birth control," she finally says out of the blue. "It's safer."

I hadn't mentioned it outright, partly because I've been so afraid of what she'd think, but when she asked if I wanted to see the doctor, I knew it would be a good idea to get some pills even if I don't know when I'd actually want to start taking them. "You wouldn't be mad if I got some?"

"No."

"But we're Catholic."

"Yes, but better be safe than sorry," she says. "Trust me, you don't want to have a kid until you're really ready."

"Am I so bad?"

She laughs. "It's hard. It's really hard." I laugh, too.

"Trust me, there's no way I'm having sex again anytime soon," I say.

I have to admit, she does look a bit relieved when I tell her that.

In the exam room, Dr. Holloway says, "I know it's an uncomfortable question, but we're required to ask. Have you ever been sexually assaulted?"

"No," I say immediately. I'm not ready to talk about it, especially to someone I barely know. To have her judge what happened. Besides, then what would happen? I think of the headlines in the papers about sexual assault, the harassment women endure, the names they're called. It would be a fight just to be believed.

She goes through her routine. When she asks if I want contraception, I say yes. I feel a little ashamed, asking for pills, but her face doesn't betray any judgment.

"What's your pharmacy?" she asks.

"The one downstairs."

"I'll order it. You can pick it up on your way out."

I have to wait for the pharmacist at a special window. She hands the pills to me in a brown bag and tells me when to start taking them, what to do if I miss a dose. Her face is similar to Dr. Holloway's—all business, no judgment. I suppose it would be weird for her to be like, "Congratulations! You're on the pill!" but on the other hand, I guess I wouldn't mind a little support.

It's all so loud and public, I know that people can hear. I feel a passing glance, an unfriendly one. I flush. When the pharmacist is finally done with me, I hurry back to my mother. Her face is concerned. But still, she doesn't say anything, she just puts her arm around me as we walk out, into the parking lot, the small paper bag still seeming conspicuous as she holds me tight.

One day, a warm, dry, nothing type of day, I receive an e-mail from Stanford. Early action. A yes. I've been accepted, but still have until May to decide. My mother gasps, then buries me in a hug. I never saw her so happy, so proud. "Wow, anak! Wow. I'm so proud of you! We have to celebrate. What do you want to eat?"

That's it. It's done. I don't have to practice. I don't have to even study. I just have to graduate, apply for scholarships. I can finally relax if I want to.

But I don't. I have an itch to play again. At school, at home, for my mom's prayer group. For the people walking by our house.

The thing about music is you can put everything into it. I can put happiness in for my mother. Sadness for my father. The shock of the word *rape*, like a knife in the belly.

I decide to learn the 110, the piece that Paul said I didn't have the depth to study.

I'm fueled by anger.

I practice it in the evening, when the television is off and my mother is settling into her prayers. It sounds like someone is struggling through the hardest part of living, and in the end, finds some sense of peace. I can sink right down into it, forget everything but the music, the sound converging with the sound of every other time the piece has been played, through centuries, all over the world. I feel like there's an audience with me, of everyone who has felt this song, mothers and teachers and lovers and fathers and pretty girls and smart girls and brokenhearted ones.

When I play it, I like being me, no matter what I look like or the color of my skin or what I'm wearing. I feel settled in myself just a little bit more, and then, when I play it again, a little bit more.

There are parts of the 110 I've been confused by, phrasings and notations that I'm not sure about—I don't always know what it should sound like, what would make the piece sound the most solid. So, two weeks before the competition, I head to the conservatory library.

Paul at one time would just tell me how to play. He'd already know the answers, have studied the manuscripts, and would tell me during a lesson. But I don't need him. I've got everything I need to find out exactly what I want the piece to sound like for myself. Sure, it's a little more work, but that's okay. This is what I'll be doing in college anyway.

Outside the school, I spot Lee unlocking his bike from a parking meter, a little way down from the school.

How long ago did we sleep together? Months? It feels like years. What happened between us seems so small.

He touches my elbow to stop me from moving past him.

I become super-self-conscious of everything. My drugstore nail polish. My blue backpack from Goodwill. My scuffed Target ballet flats. I forgot to put on lip gloss.

"How's it going?" he asks. He looks straight at me, and I look at his bicycle, a cream-colored one that belongs in a Wes Anderson movie. A brown, polished saddle. The tiny little leather pocket strapped just beneath the seat. Mint-green, smudged sneakers. The holes in his jeans are beautiful.

We talk about our summers, his vacation in Vietnam. Nothing special. Nothing important. My replies are mono-syllabic. I expect nothing from him. I'm just anxious to get upstairs.

"Are you okay?" he asks.

"Yeah, why?"

"I'm really sorry if you were upset about what happened. I wasn't looking for anything serious."

My eyes rise to meet his. He looks sincere. It's a shock. A real apology. "It's okay."

"You sure?"

"Yeah."

He brightens, walking his bicycle into the street. Suddenly I'm jolted with a touch of anger. He had hurt me. Before I know I'm doing it, I'm weaving through the parked bicycles.

"Lee." He looks over his shoulder. "Don't do it again though. Don't just act like nothing happened afterward. It means more to some people than it does to you."

He looks startled when I say that. "Okay," he says awkwardly.

"I mean, I'm a whole human being. Not just something

to do. Like lunch. Or a bus ride." The words rush out in a tumble.

I march up the stairs, feeling lighter. Maybe he thinks I'm crazy now, for saying so much. Maybe he thinks I'm hysterical. I don't know, and I don't care.

CHAPTER
— *Thirty-Four* —

We leave for Bishop early: me, Mom, and Tash.

"See, Mom? You're fine. It's just like driving at home," I say as we coast along a dead straight road.

"Piece of cake," she says.

We're getting close. On the far hills, the trees meld into a dusty green, except for one red tree that stands out. Autumn colored. I could sink my eyes into the hills and be completely entertained with every dip in the road, every new exit name, every new pose the hills strike. Little simple things. Traveling means you don't have to do anything else. You can just rest.

This isn't going to be like any of the competitions I've ever been to. For one thing, I have to play for twenty minutes straight—Bach, the ballade—just in the first round. So much can happen in twenty minutes. You can psych yourself out a hundred times in twenty minutes.

"If there's an apple stand," Tash says from the back seat, "you know, or, like, some giant bear made out of chewing gum–type attraction, can we stop?"

Mom leans back, one hand on the wheel, the other twirling her hair. She does seem relaxed. I wonder how much of it is to do with her new therapist. She went for the first time last week. I asked her what they did. She was very nonchalant about it.

"Oh, you know, talking-talking." She lifted her shoulder, embarrassed. "It's not bad actually," which meant it was good.

By the time we get there, it's cold and dry and our shadows are gigantic on the gravel path up to an imposing building—white, with a reddish-brown roof—owned by one of the competition sponsors and donated for the long weekend. Everyone competing stays here, and some of the social events happen in the conference rooms, which means that most likely, somewhere around here is Paul.

We pass through curved, whitewashed archways. The doors are heavy. Our shoes click on the polished floor. A man in a blue-gray suit at a folding table checks us in. He gives us programs, a timetable, a map, and keys. There's a reception that evening.

Our rooms are gray and cool, with misty-white curtains. Small windows look out onto a pool and dry gardens with narrow, poisonous, bright blooms. I flop onto the bed.

"It's bone-dry here," says Tash. "I need lip balm."

"Do you want to get something to eat?" my mother asks as I hang my dress bag in the small closet.

"Nooo."

"Just have some juice. Or a banana." She knows this

mood of mine. "If you don't eat, you don't sleep. If you don't sleep, you'll lose focus, and then . . ." She clucks.

We eat at long tables. The wooden floor is dusty and scratched. I'm reminded of old dour Dickensian private schools and monasteries on TV. The walls are lined with arched windowsills so deep you can sit in them and really think, if it were quiet.

But there's a palpable edge to the room — like everyone's in a bomb shelter, waiting for the all clear — faces wound tight. My eyes dart from one musician to the next — they stand out, glowing, in party dresses and baggy suits. Girls shake hands firmly, like they mean it, without a sense of humor, smile like child actors. One boy, his tie in bold diagonal stripes, sits back and grins an athlete's smile. He's used to winning. Across the room, one girl, one I've seen at other competitions, sits with her parents. I force a wave.

The parents are smaller. They have questions in their eyes, some of them. Others are hawkeyed, silently measuring everyone up. You can tell the teachers — they're older and seem to know everyone. Then there's the quieter, older crowd, the adult pianists, sitting in the corners of the room, huddled together. They hold their nervousness in a different way — like they're used to it.

We spot Julia, Seth, and Gabrielle in one corner of the room, sitting at a long table, and join them. Julia's wearing mirrored sunglasses like a cop.

"I wish I had those," I tell her, looking at a pair of faces, my own, distorted in the lenses.

"They don't give anything away." She doesn't take them off, but throws out her skinny arms for a hug. "You're here! Yay."

Seth is thinner, his voice flatter than I remember.

He shakes hands with my mother, who looks as if she doesn't know what to make of him. She smiles tightly. I wonder if her quietness is basic shyness or nervousness or both.

"How's it going, Gabrielle?" I ask her, figuring she's neutral territory.

She shrugs her boyish shoulders.

"Don't mind her," Julia says. "She's not in the mood. Neither am I, actually. Mom passed."

"When?"

"Two weeks ago."

I touch her arm, about to say something, but on the other side of my mom a man, close cropped, stubbly chinned, leans in. "Which one is yours?" he drawls out. She laughs, more uncomfortable than anything, I think. She needs rescuing.

"I'm Claire."

"Hello, Claire! And where are you three from?" Including Tash in the equation. I eye Julia.

"San Francisco."

"No. I mean, your nationality."

I point to my mother with my thumb. "She's from the Philippines." My mother laughs for no reason again.

"My family is Vietnamese," Tash says.

"Oh, so you're not all related?"

"No. What's your nationality?" I ask, hoping he'll take the bait.

His smile dies a little. "I'm from Boston," he says, his eyes cooling.

"Oh, so you must be Irish, right?"

He sews up his lips and moves away from us. Tash rolls her eyes. Julia isn't paying attention.

"Where are your manners?" my mom says, but I can see the tiniest smile around her lips.

Adults come by to gawk and gush, shiny-eyed. We shake hands and tell them our names—the usual rigmarole like at Paul's party. Yes, we must be so talented. It must have been terribly difficult to be accepted. Tell me, do you have lives? Friends? What's your favorite piece of music?

I nudge Tash. "That's Paul." Across the room with a tray of food, Paul in solid, warm, breathing form, talking with a woman that reminds me of Anna, but younger. How beautiful she is. The poor woman. She must be getting duped.

"That's him?"

I nod, feeling exposed somehow.

"He looks like he belongs on a nature show."

"Like *Wild Kingdom*?" asks Julia. "As the narrator or the subject studied?"

"Like, you know, some handsome commentator on the pelican or something."

Paul spots us and waves. I don't wave back. I just stare, at a loss as to what else to do.

"We should go say hello," says Seth, perking up. He gestures to my mom, who looks at my face.

"You go," says Julia.

"We have to go," says Seth. "He'll want to know about Danielle."

My stomach flips like a pancake on a griddle, and I look at the apple in my hand. "I don't think I can eat anymore."

Seth walks over to Paul, who smiles agreeably until Seth leans toward him. Paul's face droops in a warm expression of sympathy. In all the months I've imagined him, I'd forgotten how nice he can seem.

I wish I didn't hate him. I wish I could believe him, like everyone else does.

"Come on," says Tash, looking at my face. "Let's go."

"I'm coming, too," Julia says.

From the outside, the performance hall looks like a huge tangram of triangular tinted glass joined by steel frames. The scrubby plain rolls out like a carpet at its feet. Frost-gray shrubs. Lion-colored grasses. Shades of mauve and flinty green in the distance. So much sky.

I think this place could make you crazy.

"See?" Tash whispers, gesturing at some of the other girls gathered outside, dressed in wildflower colors—buttercup, scarlet, violet. "We should have bought you a dress with more color."

"I don't want to look like a cupcake."

Julia and Tash strike up a conversation about the *Lord*

of the Rings movies—because the arid landscape is Rohan-esque—then move on to the actual books, and then *The Silmarillion*, which they've both read.

"Ugh, *The Silmarillion*. Nerd book," I say.

"It *is* hard to read," says Julia.

"But I think it was necessary to make the whole trilogy seem more real," says Tash.

"Did you read the trilogy again after you read *Silmarillion*?" asks Julia, visibly impressed.

"'Course."

They look so different beside each other. Tash's skin is dusky, Julia's pale as dawn, and narrow, as if pulled carefully upon a frame. Tash's face is dish-round and can be read, whereas Julia's is a chessboard. You have to peer into it and guess.

Julia's eyes. They're frayed at the edges. And she's all bones now. It makes me worried.

"That's one to watch out for," says Julia, gesturing with a tilt of her head to a girl twenty feet away, a long braid down her back. "She studies with a Curtis professor."

"So?"

"There's only three finalists, and she's going to be one of them."

"How do you know?"

"It isn't rigged or anything, but, well. People know people." She tilts her head toward an Asian girl in a carnation-pink dress. "That's the niece of the conductor of the Montreal Symphony Orchestra. And that girl over there studies in New York with someone at Juilliard."

"Why are we even here?" I say.

"Sucks to be us, huh?" she says in a tone as dry as her father's.

At the performance hall the next day, the air conditioner is on full blast, but I'm still sweating. Hot armpits, cold arms. I don't like the way my tights cling. There's no air on my thighs.

After hearing the first few auditions, I know no one stinks here, that's for sure. One girl, I overheard in the dressing room, was accepted into Oberlin but decided to take a year off first. And another boy here—Michael Chan—played a Brahms intermezzo that made me forget everyone I'd heard so far today.

These people are headed for conservatory. Which means I could head for conservatory, too. A thought that floors me.

But what about Stanford? What about staying close? This place makes me wonder. Where should I go? How far? Every time I realize what's possible, it makes me reconsider my dreams. Maybe I'm not dreaming big enough.

There have been no bizarre interpretations, nothing mortifying. Julia played as if she couldn't wait to be done. Note-perfect, quick as a zipper. "Better out than in," she said, making me laugh, breaking through my fear. If I can just make it through this round, I'll be okay.

Every one of us looks tortured for a moment before we start—drawing into ourselves for the ability to play. As if it's deep within, not on the map, but somewhere that requires a special key, a password, the right barometric pressure. Some place so real, so true, we don't even notice what's in front of our eyes. It's amazing to think that every single one of us has that focus.

Fear brushes my heart as I hear my name called out. *Don't try too hard,* I tell myself. Don't try so hard that people think you're trying too hard. But at the same time, look like you're trying. No, don't look like anything. Be artless.

Don't be like Paul.

I toddle on my heels onto the stage, and my blood starts to sink into my feet. The audience feels like a million eyes trying to leave a mark. I bow with my hand over my heart, partly so that no one can look down my dress. None of that chintzy curtseying for me. A judge nods at me. Another, with too much lipstick on, smiles encouragingly. And one isn't looking at me at all but at something on the table.

Paul is far in the corner, looking attentive, like any other audience member.

I can almost hear him speaking to me, telling me what to do.

The bench smells of leather and squeaks under my weight. The keys are a puzzle — neutral as ever. Waiting.

I fall in. My mind goes speechless; there's nothing to think about, nothing to protect. I will myself to breathe. A pattern entwines with the air, folds in on itself, turns upside down, dancing with itself. It's over quickly and I leave it.

Then, three slow beats before I'm off again to begin the ballade. My fingers fly, nudge the piano to speak without words, laughing inwardly at the absurd amount of work I put in — those hours at Paul's house, trying to hear what he heard in the first bars of the ballade. The dark hours in the school auditorium. Studying on the train. I slip beneath the music, into the weaving of its universe. Its world is solid, warm against the desert and all the thoughts in the room. I can make it so with my breathing and my patience and all the heart I can pour into it. Phrase by phrase, I play what I think love can mean, let the sound fly through the room, to Paul, to my mother, to Tash, over the hall and through the roof, and into the world.

I bring my hands to rest on my thighs. Applause shatters the feeling of the thing, brings me back to earth.

Afterward, I'm in a daze, on the bed, immobile, in shock. I can't do any better than what I've done. I can't believe that it's happened. That it just came out of me that way.

It was like magic.

Hours later, Tash drags me down to the commissary to read the results.

We push through people too oblivious to move out of the way, through waves of relief and heavy silence and laughter clear and sharp like cut glass. Parents are lecturing and storming and comforting.

My mother grips my shoulder too tight as she reads my name over my shoulder. "Oh, wow. Wow. I'm so proud of you," she whispers close to my ear.

I'm one of seventeen remaining. My heart leaps, then

sinks in fear. Happiness isn't possible. Gloating would be just obnoxious. Inside, I feel the tiny prickle of my happiness, buried deep. I could place. There's a chance.

The crowd shifts, parts as we move away from the results board. And there, with a bland smile on his face, looking older and puffier than I remember, is Paul. "Congratulations."

For a moment, I don't know what to say. What did he expect? What did he fucking expect? "Thanks."

I walk past him, to a safe corner.

"They wrote about your dress." Tash shows me the competition commentary on her phone.

> Claire Alalay gave an erudite, glossy Prelude and Fugue in E Minor from Book I of The Well-Tempered Clavier, followed by a passionate yet polished interpretation of Chopin's Ballade in G Minor. Her performance displayed a serious, circumspect quality—a common trait amongst students of San Francisco-based Paul Avon—and a rigorous technique.
>
> Ms. Alalay wore a lacy floor-length black-and-cream dress with cap sleeves and pearl earrings.

"I'm not his student anymore. Do you think we can correct it?"

My mother looks doubtful. "I don't think it's worth it, anak."

"I want to."

"They didn't say the dress was nice. I wonder if maybe

you should have worn a brighter color."

"Aren't you happy for me?"

She looks at me, astounded. "Of course I am. I'm just saying . . ."

"You played wonderfully," says a woman. Older, a pearl pin on her black lapel, a pencil skirt.

"Thank you."

"Heidi Garner. Bard College. You'll be applying there, won't you?"

"Um, I honestly didn't think I had a chance."

She beams. "Well, here's my card. I'd like you to e-mail me — we could arrange an audition."

She walks off, and I can't stop smiling.

"Whoa," Tash says.

"Where's Bard?" Mom asks.

"East Coast somewhere," I say.

She frowns.

"They make you double major," I say. "It's a serious school."

She stops frowning. "Really? Wow. That sounds practical."

"Do you think we can go visit? We never go anywhere."

"Maybe," she says softly. "Maybe we could."

I put my arm around her and we walk upstairs.

After dinner, Tash and Mom go right to bed, thank God. The trip has caught up to them. Mom says I should stay for the after-dinner schmoozing, try to meet more recruiters.

"But Stanford . . ." And staying close to home, in case she needs me.

She smile-frowns. "Well, don't you want to have your pick?"

I find Julia on the steps with her sister. "Oh, good," she says when she catches sight of me.

They're on their way home.

Julia's playing was a little too cold, I think. Too quick. But on another day, Julia could have been chosen. There's no such thing as the best, really — just the best on a particular day, and the players fluctuate like the weather.

Her dad is going to let her audition for dance programs. "Finally. Mom never would have let me." She rubs her eye, a little too hard, and sniffs. Her nose has started to run in the cold. "That's okay, right?"

"Why wouldn't it be?"

She looks down shyly. "I want her to be proud of me."

"I thought you liked her being annoyed with you."

She laughs. "True."

We hug. "Good luck tomorrow," Julia says. "You deserve it."

A few hours later, I'm taking a stroll in the garden, which is deathly cold. The alien silhouettes of fierce plants are visible by the porch lights. Music falls from the windows. Another person playing to heaven, wishing for it, but I'm more focused on the desert, listening to its hollowness. Things don't seem to reverberate here. There's too much space.

I start at the sound of Paul's voice. "Are you trying to avoid me?"

I flare my eyes. He's so pushy. "Yes."

"Well, I just want to congratulate you again."

His smile is a tentative overture, one I don't trust. "Thanks."

I cross my arms tight and squint into the distance, hoping he'll take the hint and leave.

An awkward pause. "Have you ever seen so many stars?" he asks. "To think there was a time, before cars, before streetlights, when people could see these every night, and be filled with glory. I'm sure they helped inspire the great classical composers and lent the music hope. Wonder. Beauty. Of course, nowadays people seem too distracted by their cell phones to look at the stars. Or they google the Milky Way to see why it is what it is, instead of just sitting and letting themselves wonder."

"What do you want from me, Paul?"

"Nothing. I just . . . wanted to say hello."

"You just don't want to feel bad about me anymore." I cross my arms even tighter.

The gravel crunches beneath his shoes as he shifts his weight. "You seem fine."

I shrug, but inside I'm quaking with anger. He has no idea. "So, you're still mad at me," he continues.

"Of course I'm mad at you. You trashed me, and then you left me to figure out how to fix it." My voice is shaking.

"Well, that's how it works." He pushes his glasses up his

nose with a forefinger. "You go through trials, and if you can withstand the shit, you get the glory."

"It didn't have to be that way. You didn't have to . . . let me make out with you." In the vague light, I can see a slight smirk on his face, and my anger spirals out. "You know I couldn't say no to you. I wanted to please you so much. I really did. But then it all felt wrong." I have a hard time saying this. "You pushed when I wanted to stop. I'm only seventeen. You were my teacher. You raped me."

He looks like I punched him in the stomach. For once, he doesn't say a word. I'm shocked by the look on his face. That I could wound him. That he's human.

Then he looks at me like I'm a bug on the bottom of his shoe. "What an awful, awful thing to say. Do you really think that of me?"

"I wish I didn't have to." I know he thinks rapists are other people, criminals and the mentally ill, that it's a way to deliberately hurt or punish women. But what if it's simply trying to get what you want without having to ask for it? What if it's simply being sneaky—the way you might sneak into a movie or grab a twenty from your mom's purse without asking. You simply do the thing you want to because you can.

"It wasn't that serious. It wasn't even sex!"

"Whether you call it sex or not, you pressured me—"

"I'm sorry I hurt you, Claire, but that isn't how—that simply isn't the case." He starts to move. He wants to escape. I don't blame him. "I get it. You're young. You—you don't have the experience to know that that isn't what happened. I have done everything I could for you to succeed. I have nothing more to say. I — I can't continue this conversation. This is unbelievable. Simply unbelievable." He shakes his head. His expression is closed in denial.

The door creaks as it swings behind him and clicks shut.

I've said what I've needed to say. And even if he doesn't want to listen to me now, he'll remember what I've said. Maybe, someday, he'll be able to see what he's done.

Maybe not.

I wish the world didn't work this way. Fear and anger leave me like they've blown away on a breeze. Heartache takes their place.

I look at the stars, glittering so hard up there and sprinkled throughout the sky, like pebbles at the bottom of a clear stream.

I wonder if I'll ever feel like I should tell the police. I don't know yet. I need more time.

Maybe I'll go to therapy, too.

I go back inside, where it's warm, almost stuffy. A thin, bright thread of melody unwinds in my head. My own melody. I pull out my phone and sing into it. A little memo to myself.

Maybe I could be a composer. Or a music teacher. A gentle one.

I'm in the wings.

Here are the fears running through me now: I'm a nobody, a failure; I've never been loved in my life and I never will be; there isn't a place for me on earth that I'll ever fit into; I'll have to fight for everything, and even then, I still might not get it. I'm afraid I'll trip over my shoes and hit my nose on the stage. I'm afraid to look most people in the eye, except Tash and my mom. I'm afraid people will find out what happened. I'm afraid it will happen again.

I chase all the fears away as well as I can.

In the sea of faces, my mom sits looking up at the glass ceiling, at the sky in repose on the roof. Tash is beside her, really, actually, listening. Paul's eyes touch my body. He's far to the side, close to the stage, where you can see deep into the wings, leaning against the wall. I don't have time to be angry; I don't have the energy to waste. A few buildings away, in our room, is a laptop full of my dreams: an acceptance from Stanford, my application to Oberlin, an e-mail from the Bard recruiter. I've already won.

A great applause, a waiting quiet, and I'm pulled forward by the sound of my name. On my face is the biggest smile I've got. My breaths race ahead of me. I try to catch up with them, to slow them down, to make them mine, while at the same time bowing in a gesture of hope to be loved.

ACKNOWLEDGMENTS

Many thanks to my editor, Kate Fletcher, of keen mind and sound grammar, who polished this book to a brilliant sheen; and to my most trustworthy agent, Jennifer March Soloway, who helped me bring balance and light to the manuscript and was my Gandalf — a guide in the dark through numerous revisions and the wondering, waiting, and hoping. This book would not exist without Carol Eisenberg, who taught me Bach, Chopin, and the mysteries of music theory. Anna Boonyanit, who has lived in the world of competitive piano, was gracious enough to read and ensure that I captured its likeness. To be believed in is to be carried by others, and these wonderful people have done so and made my heart full: Pascuale Santiago, Vivek Rao, Peter Fish, Lisa Taggart, Molly Watson, Kate Chynoweth, Dale Conour, Paul Harding, Chinelo Okparanta, and Janis Cooke Newman. Chyna Honey, Jim Honey, and Tiffany Hunter, you are wonderful humans without whom I would not have fulfilled this dream. To the Muses (for lack of a better name), thank you for singing to me during the seven years of writing this book, and thank you to my mother, who gave me everything I needed to listen to them.